LEGACY OF POWER

J.A. GATES

For everyone who believed in me.

Selendria
Northern Forest
Northern Backbone Ranges
Twilfell Basin
Milliger Pass
Snowmelt
Resahil
Kamde Forest
Milliger River
Southern Backbone Ranges
Umethrion
Monkwich Lake
Nu Aethel
Amathnore
Vafanas
The Sword Ranges
Chelmsman Iles
Estathemar
Ifellean
Omel Ortheiad
Roquevale
Krodon's Fortress

It is not death that a man should fear, but he should fear never beginning to live.

Marcus Aurelius

1

In the shadows of the warlord's fortress, death was on the prowl. Hiding himself against the corner wall of the stairway, Jacek waited for the guard to approach down the steps. He only had his war axe and a dagger with him for this job, as he needed to move silently. More than enough to get the job done. He drew his dagger and held it close.

As soon as a foot appeared around the corner, Jacek rammed the knife up until he hit soft flesh. The blade sunk in under the chin up to the hilt. The guards' eyes widened in shock then went blank as death caught up. The only sound emanating from the man was a slight gurgle as the blade was released. Jacek caught the body and threw him over his shoulder as he moved on up the stairs to the top. The guard wasn't small, but Jacek's height and strength hoisted him easily off the ground. He dropped the guard quietly into a dark corner where it would be some time before he was discovered. This was precisely why he did these sorts of jobs at night. Darkness was an old friend.

He wiped his hand down his short dark beard, now peppered with gray. On the right in the hallway was the door to the office. He had a map in his head of the castle, courtesy of the guard he'd taken the night before and interrogated. The man hadn't wanted to give up any intelligence on his place of work, but then things had gotten messy and he got quite chatty.

Jacek turned the handle and stepped inside. A table with a chair sat near the window, illuminated by a stretch of moonlight emanating from the far side windows. Various writing paraphernalia sat strewn on the desk. He was drawn to a large piece of stone placed on the table, sitting on some cloth. Approaching it, he saw that the stone had some engravings. It looked like elvish. He had seen it occasionally on antique artifacts sold by special merchants.

The Elves had been dead for over three hundred years. This stone tablet must be very old. Why did the Warlord Krodon have this? Jacek had no idea what it said, or where it could have come from. Whatever his reasons, they couldn't be good. His father was a tyrant and Krodon was rumored to be worse.

He was here for a pendant. Paid 30 Olons by a merchant to retrieve it, it apparently had a lot of sentimental value. Massaging the lined and calloused fingers in his left hand to try to get the feeling back into it, he continued to search the room, leaving everything just as he found it. Nothing. The bed chamber was next.

Back out in the hallway, he faced another door. Jacek silently turned the handle and peered through a small crack. The large bedchamber, lit only by the moon's light through a window, looked still and silent.

He slipped through the door, padding on soft leather boots through the room. A large form lay sleeping on the huge bed in the center of the room. It would be so easy to just swipe a blade over the Warlord's throat right now and be done with it. He entertained the thought for a second. He would be doing a lot of people a huge favor. But he was not getting paid for that tonight. He could always charge many Olons at another time to do it.

He padded over to the dresser where a few trinkets lay. A couple of rings, a comb, leather gloves... there. A necklace with a white stone pendant hung from a hook on the backboard of the dresser. It had an Elven rune engraved in the middle. It fit the description the merchant had given him. He lifted the piece of jewelry up and hung it around his own neck for safekeeping, tucking it under his leather jerkin.

Just then he heard footsteps in the hallway, coming towards the bedroom door. It sounded like two men. Had someone found the body of the first guard already? If so, that put a wrinkle in his plan. He would have to improvise.

He moved quickly to another door to his left, slipping through before the main bedroom door was opened. He listened carefully, but no one called out after him. It seemed Krodon was not a light sleeper.

Light filtered up from two torches at the bottom, revealing a dark stairway leading down. At the bottom, another heavy door blocked the way. This was Krodon's personal passage to the dungeon. Jacek didn't want to know why it led from his bedroom.

Beyond the door, he found himself in a subterranean hallway constructed of stone. Most of the fortress was built from wood. This must be part of the original elvish tower that the fortress was built around. Torch sconces lit the length of the hallway, making the light flicker and dance in varying shadows like macabre marionettes.

Heavy wooden doors lined the hallway, each with little barred windows on them. At the end, a staircase led back up to the ground level. He sped up as he headed for it.

"Who's there?" A small voice whispered out of the darkness. He skidded to a stop in his tracks. It sounded young.

Female. Oddly accented. Whoever it was had good hearing. He hadn't made much noise at all.

The nature of the voice caught him off guard. Was that a child? He said nothing, waiting to see if she spoke again. It had sounded like it came from behind one of the barred doors.

"Please, I'm very thirsty. Will you bring me some water?" the little voice croaked.

That was definitely a child. Slightly horrified but wary, Jacek moved to the door it had come from. Peering in through the bars, he could only make out a small shape against the back wall. He tried the handle. Locked of course.

Checking up and down the hallway to make sure he was still alone, he pulled out his set of lock picks. In only a few seconds the tumbler clicked loudly into place, unlocking the door. Waiting to see if anyone had heard the noise, he relaxed when after a few seconds the silence continued. He opened the door and peered into the darkness. He scrunched his nose up as the stench of body excretions and mildew assaulted him.

"Who are you?" He kept his voice low. It came out raspy and sounded like stones over a washboard.

There was a hesitation, then the sound of an inhalation. But no words came back. Was she afraid of him? A slight pull in his chest reminded him he was still human, even if he did cut himself off from everyone else. While he was used to people fearing his reputation, he didn't like the thought of a child fearing him in person.

"I won't hurt you. I'm not a guard here. Are you a prisoner?"

Another hesitation, then a "yes." The word was barely breathed.

"What did you do?" Jacek kept an ear out for footsteps in the hallway. His instincts kept telling him he needed to move.

This was going to get him killed, he was almost sure of it. But for some reason his feet stayed still, waiting for the answer.

"Nothing."

Right. Probably a thief. Most likely out of necessity, but a thief nonetheless.

Not that Jacek was under any illusions about himself. He knew he was a thief and a murderer. However, it was a necessity of survival.

There was a clink of chains as the child moved slightly. Jacek clenched his jaw and stepped over to her in the shadows. She scuffled back against the stone wall; the chains dragging on the stone floor, making a lot of noise. He winced.

"It's alright," he said in a whisper, his palms up in front of him to show he was not planning on hurting her. Although it was probably hard to see in this light. "I'll unlock these shackles and then you can go. But then you're on your own."

There was no way he was taking her with him. If there was anything he had learned in his life, it was that helping people was dangerous. Despite that, he drew the line at leaving her locked up here. Still, he didn't want her connecting herself with him.

In the dim light he saw her nod, wide-eyed with fear. Kneeling at her side he picked up the lock gently to lessen the sounds of clinking chains as much as he could. His left hand already numb again, he fumbled with the metal shackle and the pick. His time was running out. He was bound to be discovered soon. A prickle of alarm started in the back of his head. He had to get out of here or this would be his last job. Ever.

Finally, the lock clicked open. The girl scuttled back against the brick wall pulling her feet out of the restraints and putting as much distance between them as she could.

"Right, go. I'm getting out of here. You do whatever you want, but you're not coming with me."

The girl stayed still and silent where she was.

Jacek turned and left the room, the prickly feeling growing in his skull. He sped off down the hall to the stairs.

Starting up, he heard footsteps coming down. Cursing his decision to waste time with the girl, he considered hiding and letting them past. But then they would find the kid. He would have to take them out.

Opting for the quick kill, he rushed up the steps on well-practiced silent feet. Two men were walking down, lightly armored in breastplates and carrying pikes. Before they could react, he barreled into them, taking one by the throat and pushing backwards into the wall while kicking out the feet of the other from under him. There was a clatter of metal as the man went down flailing.

He continued to squeeze the throat of the man in his right hand; the soldier trying to grapple for Jacek's face. But his long arms proved useful and he just tipped his head back to avoid the reaching fingers.

The other soldier regained his composure, quickly rolling away from the large assassin. His pike had fallen further down the stairs, but he pulled out a knife instead. "You're dead, shit-eater." The soldier bared his teeth at him.

Still holding the other man by the throat, Jacek pulled out his axe and swung at the incoming knife. The man's hand flew off in a spurt of blood. Jacek flinched his eyes closed as blood spattered on his face. He groaned inwardly, realizing he would have to bathe later.

The soldier screamed, clutching his wrist tightly with his other hand. Great, maybe that hadn't been the best idea. Now the whole castle was alerted.

Jacek grabbed the soldier he had been choking and wrapped his arm around the man's neck. Dropping his axe, he snapped the neck in an efficient, practiced move. He dropped the body to the floor and snatched up his axe again.

The screaming ended when Jacek's axe was embedded in the man's skull. He had to keep moving, so it was down to a messy job instead of a quiet one.

Movement behind him had him spinning around, his axe raised. But it was just the girl, her hand covering her mouth in shock at the sight of the dead men. She raised widened eyes to his face. He saw himself in those eyes. A monster, he knew. Well. There was nothing he could do about that.

In the better light, he finally got a glimpse of her. Clothed in a filthy, thin shift, the girl looked to be no older than twelve. Skinny and dirty, she had long gray hair halfway down her back. No, it was most likely dirty white hair.

The urgency still there, he turned and kept running up the stairs. He heard the girl stumble slightly behind him - most likely slipping on the blood - but her light footsteps still trailed behind him. He pinched his lips together. She had better not get in his way.

The stairs opened out to a wide hallway, lit by smoky yellow oil lamps. He paused to listen before turning into it and heading in the direction of the entrance he had come in through. There was a kitchen in the east wing that had a back door opening out into a small courtyard. If he could get there, he could slip out through the side gate he'd left unlocked. He hoped it was still unlocked.

Clattering armor gave away the presence of more of the warlord's men behind him down the hall. If they had bows, he was screwed. Risking a glance back, he saw five men running, swords drawn. Small reliefs. But the girl was there too, close behind. She looked too much like she was following him. He gave her a snarl, but she didn't respond.

Down more corridors and hallways he ran, following the map in his head of the layout. The kitchen wasn't far away now. Just a few more doorways.

Just then a door opened on the left up ahead and out

stepped a gaudily dressed man in burgundy with a sword in his hand and four more soldiers behind him, brandishing steel. Jacek and the girl came to an abrupt halt. The man exuded self importance. Maybe the next in command for the warlord? It wasn't Krodon himself, that was for sure. This man was much shorter and had long ruddy hair. He blocked the way to the kitchen beyond, a smirk plastered on his red face.

The little man put a hand on his chest and smiled condescendingly. "I am Traslek, Warlord Krodon's right-hand man. He entrusts me with the security of this castle."

"Security. Now that's a good idea." Jacek rumbled.

Traslek ran his gaze over Jacek, disdain clear in his eyes. "A tall man with a scar across your face like that and carrying that axe. Looks like we've got ourselves the infamous Red Hunter." His smirk belied a confidence that didn't fit his physicality.

Jacek resisted the urge to rub at the scar. It did have the side effect of making him more recognizable. Which had its pros and cons.

"Some people have called me that." Jacek eyed up the soldiers behind him. They both kept shifting their grips on their swords and restlessly moving their feet. Particularly after hearing his moniker spoken aloud.

He glanced over at the girl, standing off to his left. She looked frozen to the spot, barely breathing. Great. Baggage. He could just leave her here of course. He had no obligation to take her with him. There was a job to finish. But something nagged at him. Something he couldn't put his finger on. Something about her that was different. But he didn't have time to figure it out. Right now he had to deal with this prick and his nervous goons. He imagined burying his axe in the stupid fop's face.

The clanking of weapons further back down the hall

announced the first lot of soldiers were catching up. Time to get out of here. With his free hand he reached into a little pouch at his waist.

"You know what I call people like you?" he asked, trying to distract the warlords' lieutenant.

"What's that?" Traslek's mouth curved up at the corners in a confident smirk. His backup was nearly here.

"Prey."

Jacek threw a ceramic ball at Traslek's feet, making sure he held his breath as the ball smashed on the ground. Sickly smoke poured out of the bomb, clouding up into Traslek's and the soldiers' faces. They began to cough and wheeze, clutching at their throats and doubling over.

Jacek grabbed the girl's wrist and yanked her after him as he charged through one of the men to the side, slamming him against the next man where they fell in a heap on the floor.

The two cut through the kitchen, thankfully empty at this time of night, and made for the door at the back. Even with Jacek's long legs, somehow the girl managed to stay on her feet as she was dragged behind him. She still made no noise. If it wasn't for the fact he was holding her wrist, he wouldn't know she was there. It felt tiny in his giant hand.

The door to outside was a heavy wooden one. Unfortunately it opened inward, so Jacek couldn't just smash it open with his shoulder. He had to slow down to open it, letting go of the girl as he had his axe in the other hand. The door swung open to reveal the courtyard beyond, lightly covered in white.

Footsteps crunching on the freshly fallen snow, they rushed across in the dark to the gate in the east wall. Once through, Jacek smashed another ceramic ball on the castle side to block their escape.

He made for the copse of trees nearby where Bandur was waiting for him. The mutt was hard to see amongst the trees with his dark fur, but Jacek heard the telltale sound of crunching snow where he was moving around in excitement. Waning moonlight caught frosted breath from the dog under a tree ahead. His only friend was more loyal than any human could ever be.

Bandur ran to meet Jacek, bobbing his head under his master's hand. The mercenary put his axe away in its loop on his belt and kneeled down to greet his friend, who licked his face enthusiastically. Then a growl came from Bandur's throat as the girl approached.

"It's alright boy." He turned to look at the young girl, rubbing the back of his neck, vacillating. That thin shift wasn't going to do much for her out here. And she had no shoes. He let out a heavy breath. He couldn't leave her now. So what was he going to do with her? She was a liability, plain and simple.

She stepped into a band of moonlight, looking wary. It was then Jacek finally noticed what it was that had been niggling at him about her.

Between strands of dirty white hair on either side of her head, two distinct fleshy points stuck out. Jacek had never seen one before apart from rock paintings. No one had. They had been extinct for three hundred years.

But the girl was clearly an elf.

❧ 2 ☙

Early morning light was peeking up over the foothills in the distance by the time Jacek and Bandur, with the kid in tow, saw a farmhouse in the distance. They had run through a small forest for the best part of an hour, and even though the kid wasn't showing it, Jacek knew she must be frozen to the bone. He felt a little bad that he had nothing to give her. He wore only his leather hardened armor. She was a tough one, he'd give her that. His brain had been going as fast as his feet while they were running. How had this young elf come to be held prisoner in Krodon's fortress? If all the elves were truly dead, how was she still alive? Based on the stories told about them, he knew that elves aged differently to humans, but surely she wasn't over three hundred years old? She looked barely thirteen. And what was Krodon doing with her?

He wasn't sure taking her along with him was a good idea. Considering she was an elf, Krodon would surely send everything he had after them to get her back. Helping people wasn't his thing. And he wasn't the only one. Folk around here generally weren't kind hearted souls who looked out for their fellow man. In this life, if you didn't look out for yourself first you got killed. That mantra had kept him alive all these years. And yet, she could be the key to helping him with his little problem...

Looking back at the girl to make sure she was still following, he saw she was panting, but otherwise didn't look too worse for wear. Her hands were surprisingly free of the blue tinge of frost burns. His own gloves were too big for her. He had to get her some warm clothes somehow. He turned back to eye up the farmhouse.

It looked like a cattle farm, owing to the few skinny cows sidled up to the fence on the other side of the house. The farmer must do alright to keep them alive through the worst of winter. He stopped at the fence surrounding the property and scanned the area, his gloved hands resting on the wooden railing.

"Where are we?" the girl asked, coming to a stop a few feet away, her hands planted on her knees while she got her breath back. She had a strange accent but Jacek guessed the elves didn't speak the human tongue three hundred years ago.

"Nowhere particular. I just figure I might be able to get you some clothes from here. Maybe they have a daughter." He turned to her, pulling off a large black kerchief from around his wrist. During the run feeling had started to come back to his hand, and he flexed it a little experimentally.

"I'm not too cold." She looked worriedly at the house.

Jacek raised an eyebrow at her. Was it an elf thing? He had no idea what their physiology was. There were only folk stories.

"Well, you're making me feel cold just looking at you, so we'll get you something. But first..." He brandished the kerchief.

"What is that for?"

He gestured to her head. "Your ears. Got to cover them

up. Not sure if you noticed, but you're an endangered species around here. Money doesn't come easy, and I'm guessing that Warlord back there would probably pay a good reward for your return. Or at least pretend to pay it." Adding the last as an afterthought. Odds were, Krodon didn't pay for much these days. His company of men had grown over the last year. They had waded through the nearby town of Roguevale, taking what they wanted and leaving a lot of dead and disenfranchised in their wake.

"Oh." The girl hung her head. Jacek suddenly realized what his statement actually meant to her. Was she the last of her kind? Were her family all dead? Wordlessly, he passed her the kerchief, and she tied it around her small head, covering the telltale points on her ears.

She then pointed at him. "You have blood on you."

Of course, he'd forgotten. He wiped at his face, but it had largely dried now. He kneeled down and scooped up a handful of snow, rubbing it on his face. It came away with a crimson stain. After some vigorous rubbing, he looked back at the girl for inspection. She nodded.

Satisfied, he turned back to the farmhouse and vaulted over the fence. Bandur slipped under the lower rail while the girl climbed through the middle gap.

The house was made of wood and hardened mud, thatched tightly with river reeds. It was as good a structure as one could get in Selendria. The farmer must have some decent resources. A barn sat further back behind the house, while smaller sheds and shelters dotted around a tidy snow-covered yard. The cows shuffled further away as they approached the front door.

Jacek rapped on the door, hoping farm people really were early risers.

After a bit the latch clicked, and the door swung inward to reveal a man with a lined face and a surly disposition.

"What?" It was less of a question and more of a warning. Jacek noticed one hand was hidden behind the farmer's back and made a note to not act threatening in any way.

"Sorry to disturb your household, but I was wondering if I could buy some warm clothes off you." He waved in the girl's direction. "My girl's clothes got wet when she fell in a river. I have Olons." He jingled a small pouch in his right hand.

The farmer narrowed his eyes at Jacek, but when they fell on the girl his eyebrows softened. "My wife probably has something. I have a son a little older. Some of his old clothes might fit." He jerked his chin up and stepped back to let them in. "You better come in out of the cold."

Surprised, and a little suspicious, Jacek cautiously stepped over the lintel and into the warm house. Bandur and the girl followed close behind.

A fire crackled heartily in the large room that held a dining table, a small cooking area along with various fur rugs and comfortable chairs. It was a room that projected safety and comfort. Despite his caution, Jacek's shoulders lowered a little.

Beside the fire, a short, busty woman relaxed on a cushioned chair, material sitting in her lap in the process of being sewed up. She turned to them as they came in, some alarm on her face at first. Then her eyes fell on the girl and like her husband she relaxed. Jacek realized the kid could be an asset in his line of work.

"Fynora, these folk are looking for some warm clothes for the young girl. Do you have something of Cynric's that might fit?" The farmer let the hand that had been behind his back fall to his side. A knife was held in it. He was obviously relaxing around them. That was a mistake. Jacek had little respect for people who let their guard down so easily. Especially around him. This man had no idea who he was. If he had, he would never have let him in the door.

The plump woman dropped her sewing and got up. "Oh, my dear, you must be frozen! I'm sure Cynric has something he's grown out of that might be small enough for you. Come with me." She took the kid down a short hallway to a couple of rooms beyond.

"I'm Ottar," the farmer put his hand to his chest and looked expectantly at Jacek.

Jacek just stared at him. He didn't care what his name was.

Ottar raised one eyebrow, but didn't comment on the snub. "So, you're lost?" The farmer put the knife away in a scabbard on his belt.

Great, he wanted to chat. Jacek was not accustomed to people being at ease in his presence. Having said that, he'd never traveled with a young girl before. What was it about children that made people put their guard down? He had certainly been a threat at her age. Was it the small stature? The look of innocence? Or was she projecting some elven magic that affected people's attitude to her? If she was, it hadn't worked on Krodon. He had to admit though, he certainly had not thought of her as a threat when he first saw her. He still didn't think she was, but he had a lot of experience to base that judgment on.

"We were. We've found the trail now." He didn't need to add any further details. It was bad enough he had to ask for clothing from them.

"Where are you from?"

Jacek shuffled his feet, wondering how long it would take for the woman to find the clothes.

"East."

The farmer nodded. "Would you like food as well?"

"No." He could go for a long while without food, and he had some bits of dried meat with him.

"Your daughter looks hungry."

Jacek shot the man a hard look. He didn't appreciate the judgment in his tone. He was not a father, nor would he ever be one. However, he had a point. The girl probably hadn't had much to eat in Krodon's dungeon. She did look very thin. He cursed himself for not thinking of it earlier.

"Fine. I'll buy some food along with the clothing." He pulled out three tungsten Olons from his pouch and handed them over. That would pay for a couple of meals and clothing in a small town.

The farmer took the coins and crossed over to the food area. Grabbing a pot filled with stew, he went to the fire and hung it over the flames from a hook on a metal pole mounted in the fireplace. Jacek took up a position by the door with Bandur sitting next to him, the dog's nose twitching at the cooking stew.

Finally, Fynora and the girl reemerged. The kid was clothed in a thick fur coat with a fur-lined hood. Cured leather pants tucked into soft fur-lined boots. She held a pair of leather gloves in one hand. Thankfully, the black kerchief was still tied around her forehead. She looked bulkier now, not so skinny, but Jacek knew she still needed to put on weight underneath all that. He gave her a satisfied nod. She nodded back shyly.

"I'm just putting some food on to heat for the young one." Ottar explained to his wife.

"Of course dear." Fynora gave Jacek a wary look and crossed to the fire to join her husband. She lowered her voice, but Jacek could still just hear her. "Has Cynric come back in yet from the barn?"

"Not yet. He's got a fair bit of work to do. I don't expect him for another hour."

"Very well." Fynora turned to Jacek. "Will you stay for a while?" She wrung her hands. Jacek got the feeling she didn't particularly want them to stay too long. He was used to seeing that look in people.

"We'll be going soon." He hesitated. He still didn't know the girls' name. Time for that later. "My girl can eat quickly and then we'll be on our way."

The young elf watched closely as the bubbling pot was lifted from the fire by Ottar and carried to the table. Fynora brought a wooden bowl over and spooned some thick stew into it. She unwrapped a loaf of hard bread, broke a chunk off and placed it next to the bowl. She nodded at the girl, who came over to the table and sat, eagerly dipping into the food with the bread. Fynora watched her closely.

Bandur gave a little whine. Jacek looked down, and the mutt gazed back up at him. Great, so much for a strong front. He pulled out some dried meat from his pouch and gave it to the dog. He took it gratefully; the meat disappearing in a single swallow. It would have to do for now. Bandur could hunt later.

Ottar and Fynora stood awkwardly in silence while the kid ate, until Fynora finally went back to sit in front of the fire. Jacek kept his hands rested on his weapons at his belt while staring at Ottar. He didn't spend much time in the presence of others, and he wanted to make sure the farmer wasn't going to turn on them and attack as soon as his guard was down. His guard was never down.

Once the girl was finished and the bowl wiped clean with the bread, Ottar cleared the table away.

"Thank you." The girl said to him. "It was very nice."

"That is a strange accent you have there." Ottar didn't miss a beat. He looked up at Jacek. "Your father doesn't seem to share it."

Time to go. "She was raised by her mother in the north." Jacek put an arm out as if to pull the girl in. She stepped toward him, but didn't come close. He opened the door and the cold burst into the room. Bandur led the way out, with the girl following behind Jacek. She was silent again. Probably for the best.

Jacek turned back to the couple in the doorway. Saying thank you was not part of his vocabulary. But he gave a nod anyway, acknowledging their help. Not everyone would have done that. Not many at all actually. He did not want to be beholden to anyone, and since he paid for it he wasn't, but he was grateful anyway.

❧

"Where are we going now?" The girl asked, her newly booted feet crunching in the snow behind Jacek.

"To a safe place where we can hide out for a bit and figure out what to do." He turned back to her. "And you can give me some answers." He raised an eyebrow at her.

The girl lowered her eyes. What was she hiding? Jacek hoped he could get some clear information out of her. Mostly about what her abilities were. Then he could figure out if she would be useful to him or not.

They walked in silence for another hour before starting to climb some foothills. The hills were densely coated in scrub and seasonal trees, now bare in the long winter. Jacek navigated his way through a nearly hidden but familiar trail, careful not to leave any sign they had gone through there. Bandur ranged out around them looking for game for his breakfast. The dog knew the area well, and would meet them at the hideout if they got separated.

At what looked like a dead end to the trail, a rock wall loomed up in front of them. Large bushes lay at the base. Jacek pushed his way through them to step around a large boulder. He looked back at the girl and beckoned with his hand for her to follow. She looked unsure, holding back. He waved her in again. Tentatively she moved forward to follow him.

He led her into a short tunnel behind the boulder, boring deep into the rock. After a few steps it opened out into a large cave. A small spring trickled into a pool at the back, offering drinking and cleaning water. In the center of the cave a fire-pit sat cold and still, a rack for cooking sitting over it. Jacek's few belongings lay in ordered piles around the edges of the rocky room. This was his home.

"You live here?" The girls' eyes roamed the cave, her brows knitted in puzzlement.

"I suppose you could say that. I'm not here that much. I travel a lot." Jacek kneeled at the fire and arranged pieces of wood from a pile beside it.

"You got a name?" he asked.

"Aleni." The girl moved over to the pool at the back of the cave and scooped up some water to drink.

She turned back to him. "And you? You haven't told me your name. The man in the fortress called you the Red Hunter. I'm guessing that is not your given name."

"My name is Jacek." He carried on with lighting the fire, pulling out flint from his pouch and scraping it against his axe blade to create a spark. He soon had a flame going, catching on the wood and bits of dry scrub.

After washing her face in the pool, Aleni joined him on the opposite side of the fire, wrapping her arms around her knees tightly. It was clear she still did not feel safe. She glanced over at the glow of light coming from the entrance to the cave. Was she thinking of escape?

"How did you come to be in Krodon's dungeon?" He placed a pot of water on the rack over the fire to boil some tea.

Aleni lowered her eyes, staring at the flames licking at the wood, slowly starting to catch. "I was placed in a magical stasis when my people were at war with the humans who came through the portals. It was the only sure way to keep me safe. We had no idea how long the war would go on for. My parents got called away at the last minute to an unexpected situation nearby, but they were supposed to join me." She stared into the fire for a silent moment. "I went to sleep expecting to be woken up when the war was over. But no one came back. When I woke, humans were staring at me, not my parents." She looked up at him now, the fear and sadness evident in striking blue eyes.

He raised his eyebrows at her. "That was over three hundred years ago."

She shrugged. "It is not long for an elf. Besides, the magic sustained me for that time."

"So who found you? Krodon?" he said.

She shook her head. "Some explorer found the chamber I slept in. Somehow he broke the seal on the magic that held me there and I awoke. He must have some understanding of elven magic. He was in the employ of Krodon, and took me to him." She was silent after that, lost in the memory somewhere.

"Your command of the common tongue is very good." Jacek commented. "I'm guessing you grew up speaking Elvish."

She nodded. "It was very easy to learn your language. I watched and listened to the explorer first, then Krodon and his men. It was not difficult."

"Right. Of course." If she was a typical example of intelligence in an Elf, he struggled to believe the humans had bested them in war.

"Is it true all my people are dead? Krodon said they were, but I didn't want to believe him." Her eyes were wide, hopeful.

He shook his head slowly. "Sorry kid. All the Elves are

gone." He watched her carefully. She turned her face away to the side. Jacek saw a single tear pool in one eye, eventually spilling over to run down her cheek. He was silent for a while, letting her grieve in privacy. He focused on building the fire up more.

Aleni sniffed, turning back to the fire after wiping her eyes. "So the humans obviously took over?"

He glanced at her, then turned his attention to studying the fire. "After the war, the uh, humans dumped all their criminals here. They needed room on the home world. Then they closed the portals for good. What you see now is a result of that crude society. The exiles made the best of a bad situation. Selendria does not exactly have hospitable weather."

"It was never this cold back when my people were around. Selendria had a warm and temperate climate."

"I've only ever known it to be cold. There are only a couple of months in the year when it's slightly warmer. We try to grow most of our food during those months. It's why food is scarce for everyone."

Aleni looked distressed, her eyebrows furrowed. "It sounds like it's not the same world I went to sleep in." Her shoulders slumped. Jacek looked away. She had lost everything. Her parents, her people, her world. Everything she knew was gone. Even her safety.

He cleared his throat, not wanting to dwell on that for too long. He moved over to where he had his food supplies piled up against a wall and retrieved some dried meat and cheese for himself. He offered some to the girl, but she shook her head. From a small pouch he produced some dried leaves and threw them into the pot over the fire where the water was now boiling.

"What are you going to do with me?" The quiet words broke the spell of the silence and Jacek stilled himself for a second before replying.

He did have an idea, but wasn't sure whether she would like it. The Wasting Sickness had started a month ago with numbness in his feet and hands that came and went. He had visited a herbalist who had diagnosed it, giving him a medicinal tea to drink regularly that would help. It was no cure, but it stopped his muscles from locking up. Eventually, it would deteriorate to the point where he would no longer be able to walk or hold a sword. Death would be the final stage. Jacek would do anything in his power to prevent that from happening. With her elven heritage, she might know of some magical cure. He had intended to leave her behind, but that was before he realized what she was.

"To be honest, I don't know. I'm looking for ancient elven artifacts. Magical ones. Maybe you could help me with that." She didn't need to know why he wanted them. Maybe there would be a cure from a magical artifact. It was his only hope.

Aleni's eyebrows shot up. "Possibly. The best place to look would be Y'ha Taesi."

Jacek's eyes blanked over at the unfamiliar name. He didn't even think he could pronounce it let alone find it. "I'll get right on that." He took a bite of cheese. "Might need you to point the way though," he added through his mouthful.

She smiled for the first time since he had met her. "I was born there. It is under a mountain in the north. Y'ha Taesi was the seat of all Elven power in Selendria."

Jacek shook his head in confusion. "I know of no such place. You're talking about a city of some kind?"

"Of course."

"It must be well hidden, because no one has found it that I've heard of. You sure you can take me there?"

"Provided the actual land itself hasn't changed, yes."

"As far as I know, it hasn't. Although if Krodon had his way, he'd probably want to control that too."

Aleni's eyebrows creased together. Her voice was quieter. "Can you tell me about him? Who is he?"

Jacek sighed and poked at the fire. "He's the son of the northern Warlord Tarkan." He spoke with a modulated tone, trying to keep the annoyance out of his words. "After building up a sizable following, Tarkan seized power a couple of decades ago. There was little resistance. No one else came close to having his level of manpower. His men roam the north, controlling everything from crops to merchants. Then Krodon came down to the south with a chip on his shoulder and something to prove. He holds power over the port at Ifellean and the town of Roguevale, and will most likely move onto Omel Ortheiad next."

"Sounds scary."

Jacek was silent.

Bandur came padding in from outside, a thin rabbit hanging from his mouth. Aleni screwed her nose up at the dead animal. Jacek patted his dog as he came to sit near them by the fire. Bandur dropped the rabbit in front of Jacek and began to chew down on it.

"We'll head off tonight under the cover of darkness. No doubt Krodon has men out looking for us. If we stay still and hidden during the day it'll be harder to find us." Pouring some tea from the kettle into a wooden cup, he passed it to Aleni. "Drink this. It'll keep you warm while you sleep."

She took it from him and started sipping.

He got up and retrieved a couple of thick woolen blankets from a pile off to the side. Dumping them on top of a large thick fur pelt lying near the fire, he motioned to them. "I can't offer you a fancy bed, but you should be able to make do with these."

Aleni stared at the bedding blankly. Her voice barely a whisper, she said, "I don't want a comfy bed ever again."

Jacek had no idea what that was about, so he wordlessly

turned to his own bedding set up to the left and made himself comfortable in a position on his side with his back to the fire and the kid. After a few seconds he heard Aleni lay out the blankets for herself, followed by a small whine from Bandur. He turned back to see what was wrong, but instead found the dog with his head in the girls' hands, his ears being massaged. Frowning, Jacek clicked his fingers to call Bandur. The dog looked at him, but didn't move.

"What have you done to my dog?" An annoyed tone filtered through, but he regretted it straight away.

"He's beautiful." Aleni said simply, continuing to rub the mutt's tawny head and ears.

"That's not an answer."

She shrugged. "I haven't done anything except show him love. He's free to do what he wants, isn't he?"

Grunting a reluctant assent, Jacek turned back over. She had a point, but something about it unsettled him. The tightness in his chest told him he was a little more than unsettled.

He listened to her whisper very quietly in Bandur's ear until her breathing steadied in the deep lull of sleep.

Would she get too attached to Bandur? More importantly, would Bandur get too attached to her? He had no plans for keeping her around beyond finding these Elvish artifacts and activating them. After that, he didn't care what she did, as long as it had nothing to do with him.

3

The sun had just risen over the horizon of the ocean, catching each wave and white-top in its embrace like a cold mother to her wayward son. The icy wind blew in off the waters, hitting the cliff and rushing up to kiss the edge of Krodon's fortress. An open window on the top floor began to bang in the rush of air, prompting the warlord to get up from his comfortable seat and close it. He swirled the drink in his hand, staring down into the golden liquid, a lump of ice rolling in the bottom. His chest felt tight and his stomach hard as he thought of the night's events. Someone had been taken from him. Someone that could cost him his future. The future he had dreamed of since he was young and living in his father's shadow.

Taking a sip of the alcoholic drink, he savored the burn as it went down. He crossed back to the fireplace, suddenly slamming the glass down on the mantel, spilling the drink over his hand. The glass cracked, but didn't shatter. He clenched his hand around the glass and threw it with all his strength at the far wall. It shattered into tiny pieces, spilling the remaining liquid on the floor.

Panting slightly, trying to loosen the tightness in his chest, he gripped the wood of the mantel hard.

The door to the sitting room opened quietly and his lieutenant, Traslek stepped inside. He must have heard the smash, for his gaze immediately found the bits of broken glass on the floor. He tracked back to meet Krodon's eyes.

"Tell me you found her." Krodon said, trying to contain himself again.

Traslek cleared his throat. "I could. But I would be lying. I'm sorry, the search party haven't caught up with them yet. The search continues."

Krodon squeezed his fists tightly and turned back to the fire crackling in the hearth.

"I know what she means to you." Traslek said quietly.

Krodon slowed his breathing, staring into the flames. "She means more than you know. She is the answer to the sickness that pervades Selendria. My father means to subjugate the land, by pillaging and raping it even further. That ridiculous war is the cause of all of this. Our ancestors were greedy." He straightened, running his hand through his long dark hair. "What they didn't realize, and neither do you was that the elves were an important part of nature here. I don't believe Selendria was always like this. This incessant cold. From my readings translated by the explorer Tidhelm, I believe this land was once warm and vibrant with life."

He turned back to Traslek, who had his hands at ease behind his back, standing comfortably.

Traslek's eyebrows narrowed. "Really? You think the snow wasn't here with the elves?"

His tone softened. "Traslek, my friend. You've known me a long time. You know I care about this land. More than my father ever did."

Traslek nodded. "I do, my Lord."

He pointed off into the distance. "That girl, she is the

promise of spring again. She will heal this land, mark my word. Through her, we will fix what has been done wrong."

"And what of the recruitment, my Lord?"

"That will continue. The people need my leadership. They are mindless sheep who need corralling. When I am in control, their lives will be better than they ever imagined. They probably can't imagine anything right now, they are so mired in the mud. I will bring Selendria into a new age. And to do that I need men. Men who are completely loyal to me, willing to do whatever it takes to achieve our goals."

He was calmer now. His heart had slowed to a normal beat and his chest had loosened. Talking of his dream always brought calm for him.

"What about your father, my Lord?" Traslek asked.

He briefly clenched his fists, loosening them slowly. "What of him?" He spat out.

Traslek shifted his feet slightly. "Well, he won't like to hear of what you're starting here. He might see it as a threat to his power."

Krodon crossed to Traslek and looked his friend straight in the eyes, searching for defiance. If there was even a hint...

"Let me deal with my father. I won't let him get in my way." Seeing no sign of Traslek looking to defy him, he stepped back. He reassured himself that he knew his friend, loyal since childhood. It wasn't him he needed to worry about.

"Send out more search parties. Get them to spread out, all the way to Ifellean. Those two will be along there somewhere. But just in case, send some men to Omel Ortheiad as well. It's a mud hole of a town, but I've heard stories that the Red Hunter was born there. Maybe he'll run back to friends."

"Of course, my Lord." Traslek grinned. "But I don't think you need to worry about that. The Red Hunter doesn't have friends."

Shaken awake, Aleni sat up with a start, confused at first as to where she was. Then she saw the stranger from the night before who had let her out of that awful cell. Jacek. He kneeled next to her on one knee. He must have woken her. The memories came flooding back. The flight from the fortress by the sea. Through the woods and to the farmhouse where they found clothes for her. She rubbed the thick leather pants she was wearing, the material feeling strange on her skin.

Something cold and wet nudged her hand. The dog, Bandur. He lay next to her on the floor of the cave, looking up at her with baleful eyes. The corners of her mouth twitched up at the sight of the animal. He radiated trust and loyalty to her. She was pleased one of the first gifts to emerge as she came of age was the ability to sense the emotions of animals. She had always loved animals, so it gave her a thrill to be able to bond with them in a way most others couldn't. Her mother had explained it was the beginning of a journey to find herself and figure out who she could be.

Her heart hung heavy at the thought of her mother. She missed her so much. Aleni struggled to accept she would never see her beautiful face again. Or her father. It was hard to believe all that had happened while she slept. It had seemed like no time at all to her. She pushed the memories away as she got to her feet. It wouldn't help to indulge them now. Looking up at the cave entrance, she realized with a start it was getting dark again. Had she slept all day? She must have been more exhausted than she thought.

"Roll those blankets up. We'll need them for the journey." Jacek's voice was deep and gravelly. Not unpleasant, but not particularly kind either. His manner had been abrupt last night, but he seemed curious about her. She did not know yet what to make of this man and whether his curiosity was a good or bad thing.

As he stood, he loomed over her, as tall as a five-year-old lashrimmon tree. Powerful arms strained at the leather binding them, ending in hands as big as bear paws. She shivered at the memory of what those hands had done back at the fortress. She had never seen so much blood in all her life.

The scar that ran diagonally from one side of Jacek's face to the other told of the dangerous life he had lived. Elves did not get scars; they healed fully. Staring at Jacek's was like a portent of doom. Would following him get her killed?

She started to roll up her blankets tightly. They had indeed kept her warm while she slept. Although she wondered how much of that warmth had been due to Bandur snuggling close. She was glad of the dog's company. He brought a measure of comfort that made her burdens easier to bear.

Which was more than she could say for Jacek. What did he really have planned for her? Somehow she sensed he was not telling her everything. Did he even really want to find artifacts? Or was it all a ruse? Should she trust this strange violent man? No one she had met since waking up had been trustworthy. Why should he be any different? He was violent, mysterious, and he wasn't telling her everything. She'd said she'd help him find magical artifacts, but maybe she'd be better off on her own. But he still seemed kinder than Krodon. And he knew this land better than her. She might have to bide her time.

Silently, they got everything they needed for the trip. Jacek found two packs to carry their gear. Into her small one went the bedding, some food, a canteen, and a pot. Into his went the same along with some rope, other cooking paraphernalia and medical supplies. Jacek, loaded up with a large sword on his back, his axe at his hip and a bow strapped to his pack, led her out of the cave and out into the crisp air. Her breath immediately fogged up into a cloud. It still fascinated her, and she huffed out a few times just to watch it.

Sensing eyes on her, she looked up to see Jacek staring at her, his face impassive.

"What? I've never had a winter growing up. Well, not one this cold anyway."

He just shook his head slightly and walked away down the slope, pushing through the brush.

The sun had set a while ago, and it was now growing dark. The trees waved their spindly fingers in the air, leaves long gone. Aleni wondered how long it had been since the trees had been green. All around them, broken branches lay on the white ground, a testament to the harsh weather.

The night air was quiet, broken only by the occasional hoot of an owl and the crunch of their boots in the fine snow. The cold bit at Aleni's fingers, but her skin remained pink and healthy under her gloves. They moved through a white forest of trees - the ground reflecting the milky peeling bark of the trunks.

Jacek, with his long legs, set a grueling pace and Aleni was forced to run at intervals to catch up. He did not seem to notice, or if he did, he didn't care. He was always alert, watching everywhere for signs of something. Aleni did not know what.

"What are you looking for?" She finally asked as they walked past yet another dead tree, the branches broken and hanging off the trunk. Much of this wilderness was dead and dying. Aleni had noticed several bogs of smelly, stagnant water along the way. Once upon a time these little ponds were probably lively and clean, full of fish and other water dwelling creatures.

Jacek eyed her for a moment before replying. "Signs that people have come through here before us."

"So we can avoid them?"

"So we can follow in their footsteps. Less likely they'll come back the same way. Search parties will try to cover as much ground as possible. Back tracking would not be wise."

Aleni nodded. That seemed right enough. She would keep that in mind for the future. She didn't know how long she would be with him, so she had to learn as much about surviving on her own as she could. Survival had not been part of her education growing up.

A noise off to the south alerted her then to movement coming their way. Something big and heavy crunching through the snow. Horses. A few seconds later, Jacek put out a hand to signal her to stop. He listened for a few seconds and then motioned her down behind a thick bush. She complied silently, although the foliage was prickly and unpleasant smelling.

"Do you think we'll find them today?" One man asked. His voice sounded young and uncertain.

"Nah, I don't think we'll ever find them," the other replied. He sounded much older, his voice rough and gravelly.

"What? But we've got a lot of men out looking for them. They can't possibly evade us for long."

Two men on horseback appeared through the trees, their horses moving at a walk. The older one had touches of gray at his temples, his hair tied back with a strip of leather at his neck. His lined face had the appearance of rumpled clothing. Dirty clothing. The younger one looked barely old enough to be a soldier. Definitely not old enough to grow hair on his chin. His head was shaved short, blond stubble starting to grow back. His red and black leather jerkin - Krodon's colors - was reinforced with a metal breastplate across the front.

"This is the Red Hunter we're talking about." The older man replied. "And as much as I respect our boss, this is a foolish errand, a waste of our time."

"He's that good?" The young man asked.

"Have you lived under a rock your whole life, lad?" His tone rose with incredulity. "The Red Hunter is a legend. The most feared and respected assassin in the land. He once killed the giant of Beremor. He would take out whole squads of men in the Arena in Amathnore, just for sport. And money. Tarkan himself says his days are numbered."

"Warlord Krodon's father?"

"Aye. I don't think Tarkan likes the idea of an assassin out there who could easily take his head off in his sleep if enough money was put on it. The Hunter infiltrated our very own fortress, got caught by Traslek and the fortress guard and still got out alive. With the girl in tow. If he doesn't want to be found, we're not going to find him. Mark my words, boy."

Aleni looked over at Jacek. *The Red Hunter*. So he was an assassin. And motivated by money. She shivered, but not from the cold. He seemed to enjoy bloodshed, this man. Was this really the person she should be traveling with? She was grateful he had freed her, but she had no illusions it was out of some sort of kindness. He had ulterior motives. The man was a loner. He wasn't looking for a friend. Bandur was his only companion. She was only safe as long as he needed her. And there was no telling how he would treat her along the way. There was certainly nothing soft or caring about him.

The men rode by in front of their hiding spot. Without warning, Jacek moved silently out from behind the bush. She watched as he approached the two men on horseback from behind, holding her breath.

He went for the older one first. Grabbing the man's arm and pulling him off the horse, he plunged his dagger into the soldier's neck, killing him quickly and efficiently. The younger soldier, startled at the sudden action, took a couple of precious seconds to react. He reached for his sword in its scabbard at his hip, only just managing to draw it before Jacek was on him too. The boy swung down at him wildly. Jacek dodged back to avoid it and drew his small axe. The young man whirled his horse, trying to get a better angle on The Red Hunter.

Jacek moved around to the opposite side of the horse to the man's sword arm. His opponent tried to chop down at him again, but it was clumsy and Jacek easily blocked it by catching the blade in the crook of his axe. He deftly curled his wrist and hooked the sword out of the boy's hand with the axe. The sword fell to the snow at their feet.

The young man had only a moment to register this before Jacek's dagger shot up and buried itself in his ribs. He gasped, his back straightening and going rigid. His breaths came in short pants, then turned into gurgles as blood dripped from his mouth.

Jacek pulled him from the horses' back and dumped him on the ground. The young man gave a grunt as he hit the snow. The white powder sprayed with red as Jacek drew his blade across the man's throat and ended him.

Aleni let out her breath finally, gulping in air at the finality of it. It had all happened in less than a minute.

"Kid." Jacek called out in her direction.

She slowly rose to her feet and stepped out from behind the bush. She stared at the still form of the dead man, his eyes wide open in horror. Blood leaked out of the gaping slash in his throat, staining the pure white of the surrounding snow.

Jacek patted down the man's clothes.

"What are you doing?"

"Checking for anything useful. Coin, anything of value." He pulled out a small coin satchel and jingled it. He then moved over to the other soldier and did the same with him.

"That's horrible!" She rushed over to him. "You've violated

these men enough, leave them be!" She reached down to stop him, not thinking.

His hand whipped out and grabbed her wrist tightly, holding it in place. All-mother, he was fast. She struggled against him, panic rising in her chest. He stared at her, his eyes narrowed, but he said nothing. She finally stopped struggling and looked away from those piercing eyes.

He pushed her arm away, letting her go finally and went back to searching the body. Tears pricking at her eyes, Aleni straightened and walked away from him, going to the horses. She reached out both hands to let the animals smell her first. The first one, a gray gelding, nudged her with his soft nose and gave a small nicker in greeting. She sensed his racing mind at the commotion that had just happened. Sending the horse calming thoughts slowed her own darting mind and she blinked the tears away. She had to be strong here. Showing weakness to this man would not be wise.

Aleni watched as Jacek carried the bodies into the bushes and covered up the bloody snow. Soon there was no indication they had ever been there.

"What will we do with the horses?" Aleni asked.

"We take them. We'll move faster on horseback." He moved to the side of one of the horses, a large bay stallion with a black mane and tail. He adjusted the blanket over its back and ran his hand down over the rump and down one leg to lift it and check its hooves. Satisfied, he proceeded to do the same for the other three legs.

"Can you ride?" He asked, checking over the gray next.

Aleni nodded. It was one of the earliest skills elven children learned. She looked around for a boulder she could stand on to mount up. But Jacek moved around to stand on the right side of the gelding, crouched and cupped his hands. Aleni stared at him, not really wanting to get close to him.

But he raised his eyebrows at her expectantly. She had no idea if refusing him would make him angry.

Holding her breath, she stepped closer and lifted her boot to place it in his hands. With a boost from him, she vaulted onto the animal's blanketed back. Jacek straightened, wiping his hands off on his trousers without comment. He launched himself up onto the other horse from the ground. Much easier with those long legs, Aleni thought wryly. She hated that she was even the slightest bit dependent on anyone, let alone him.

Grabbing the reins and clicking his tongue at his mount, Jacek led the way down the worn track through the trees at a trot. Aleni followed a few paces behind.

Silently, they trotted through the forest at a much quicker pace than before. Several times they had to hide in thickets to wait for patrols to pass nearby. When dawn finally came, Jacek found a safe spot for them to camp during the day to rest. He made a small, smokeless fire to heat water on for tea. They ate a simple meal of dried meat, hard cheese and bread.

Aleni drank the warming tea he gave her again and lay down in her blankets on a fur pelt to rest. She tried to stay awake, watching Jacek, who kept a lookout. He didn't appear to sleep much. Every muscle in her body did not want to relax around him, and she felt very vulnerable sleeping out in the open. Being so tense, she didn't think she could fall asleep, but it wasn't long before her tired body dragged her consciousness down into the depths.

After another night of riding carefully through the forested area, Aleni was starting to get even more suspicious of Jacek. He hadn't said much to her apart from necessary communication, but there was a strange heady feeling she woke up with each night they set out. It took longer than usual to get her wits about her. It wasn't until that night she realized what it was.

They had made camp again at dawn, Jacek heating the tea once more on a small fire. She had noticed he never drank the tea. When he handed it to her, she smelled it carefully. It didn't smell familiar, like any herb she knew of.

Was he *drugging* her?

The thought sent shock waves through her like a thunderbolt. She had thought she was just very tired each day after a night of traveling. But she slept all day each day. That was a long time to sleep.

And there were no dreams.

She had had bad dreams while in the dungeon. Being out among nature, maybe that was enough to put the nightmares to sleep?

Pretending to sip at the hot drink, she watched Jacek warily. He actually looked tired for once. Lines had grown under his eyes, and he had fumbled picking up a couple of pieces of wood. That must be what happened when humans got tired. She never thought she'd see him being clumsy. Everything he had done up until now had been measured and precise.

Perhaps he hadn't been getting much sleep during the day. She had no idea, she'd been sleeping.

As soon as his back was turned fetching more firewood, Aleni dumped the contents of the cup out onto the ground behind her, making sure to cover the spot up with more snow in case he saw steam rising behind her.

When he returned to the fire, Aleni placed the empty cup down next to him. He glanced at it and grunted an acknowledgment.

"Thank you. I'll go to bed now."

He nodded, but didn't say anything. She pulled the blankets over herself and lay down on her fur mat, tucking her knees up close to stay warm. She tucked her head under the blankets and slowed her breathing.

What was she going to do? She didn't even have any real plan. She just didn't feel safe with him. Perhaps she could make out for Y'ha Taesi herself. See if any elves still lived. Surely, not all had been killed. If she could just figure out where she was currently.

4

Jacek rubbed his left hand with his thumb, trying to get blood to flow back into it. The blasted Wasting Sickness was regularly affecting his limbs now, particularly his hands. After the girl went to sleep, he dumped out the tea and put more snow in the pot to melt. He was going to have to get more of the bitter hedge leaves for the tea for the kid. It had kept her asleep each day so he could rest and not worry about her running away.

He did feel bad for drugging her, but it was for her own good. She wouldn't get far on her own, even if she was an elf. He had no idea how to make her trust him. He'd never had to inspire loyalty in anyone. Living a solitary life had its cons. Watching her now, the small form under the blankets rising and falling gently as she breathed, evoked pity in him. He had no idea what it would be like to be so small and vulnerable. Even as a child himself, ever since his parents had died, he had relied on his size to survive. Street kids he had briefly run with had used him as the bruiser. He was never the lookout. That job was for kids like Ham. A pang of loss hit his chest at the memory of his childhood friend. The only friend he'd ever had. It had been over thirty years but the pain still stung.

Pushing the feelings away, he noticed the pot was boiling again. He added a measured amount of medicinal herbs and stirred it, leaving it to simmer for a bit. When it was ready, he poured it into his own cup. The steam coming off it smelled foul, but he knew he had to take it. It did help with the numbness, and he hadn't had a leg cramp for a week now.

As he sipped the medicine, a great fatigue came over him. He had only been getting a few hours of sleep a day. And now it seemed it was catching up with him. He had wondered how long he could keep it up. Before he had gotten sick, he could easily keep up that pace for days, even weeks if need be. It was also true he was getting older too.

Well, if he slept now, he could be up before Aleni needed to be woken at nightfall. He told Bandur to be on guard. The dog would wake him at the slightest disturbance. He lowered his exhausted body down into his furs and fell into a deep slumber.

It was like swimming under water, but in a thick muddy substance. Moving his arms got him nowhere, and his body suspended in the muck like a dead sheep in a bog. His muscles constricted to the point where his lungs would not draw breath. He was drowning; he knew it. The mud filled his mouth and poured down his throat. He couldn't breathe...

With a gasp and a jolt, he awoke. Heaving in great big breaths of icy cold air, he lay for a few seconds, trying to get his bearings. Thank the gods it had been just a dream. However, the fear it evoked was real. He feared that was how he would die from this disease. His lungs seizing up and unable to draw breath. Focusing on his work was the only thing keeping the terror at bay. The trees above him, naked in the almost unending winter, poked their branches out into the air like broken fingers. He stared at them for some time before his breathing slowed and normalized. Then he noticed the shadows the trees made. Gods, what time was it?

Late afternoon by his reckoning. He had slept too long. His treacherous body had let him down even in sleep.

He rolled to his feet, a maneuver that was getting harder and harder to do as the years went by, regardless of his health. His eyes found the girls' bed. Or where it should have been.

She was gone. Along with the fur pelt and blankets.

He gave a sharp intake of breath and searched around for any sign of her, his movements hurried. The gray gelding was gone too. She had finally run away. How did she wake up from the tea? Had she even taken it? Maybe she had started to suspect.

Shit.

He had no way of knowing how long ago she left. He packed up his gear quickly, there wasn't much, and soon his horse was loaded up.

Whistling for Bandur, he launched himself onto the horses blanketed back. He waited, turning his horse around in a circle to look in all directions. Bandur didn't appear. Shit, had he gone with her? So much for all the years of companionship. It seemed even dogs could betray someone.

Carefully scanning the area for signs of her flight, he soon picked up hoof prints leading off to the north. A smaller set of prints trotted alongside. Damn dog, following the elf without him. If he moved quickly, he could catch her before dark. It would be harder to track her then. He set off at a brisk pace, wondering what he would do with her when he found her.

 ❧ 5 ❧

The gray gelding cantered along the trail. Aleni was trying to get as much distance from their camp as possible. She knew it was dangerous riding during the day. The patrol could spot her a lot easier. But she had to risk it to get away from Jacek. She just couldn't trust him. Not now she knew he was drugging her.

It hadn't snowed for a couple of days and while the sun overhead wasn't terribly warm, the snow on the ground was no match for it. Bits of grass popped up in places, hinting at a world still alive underneath. More than once, a white bundle of fur crossed their path ahead, which sent Bandur off on a frantic chase. She was glad for his company, but worried he would run back to Jacek at some point, then leading him to her. Biting her lip, she wondered if she should tie Bandur up to leave him behind for Jacek to find. It was his dog after all. But then Jacek could still use him to track her by smell. No, it was better the dog stay with her. Besides, Bandur had made his choice to follow her, and who was she to argue with him?

She urged the horse faster. Looking back over her shoulder, she half expected the giant man to loom up behind her,

43

his axe raised to cleave her in half. Shaking her head of the fantastical image, she focused back on the path ahead.

Suddenly the horse shied up. Only through years of riding did she manage to keep her seat. She placed a calming hand on the horse's smoky gray neck, sending serene thoughts to him. What had upset him? She swung her head around, trying to see what the horse had sensed. But there was nothing to see.

When the horse had stilled, she closed her eyes and listened. Yes, there was movement nearby. Lost in her thoughts, she hadn't been paying attention. Silently berating herself for the lapse, she reminded herself she was on her own now. None of father's guards to look after her here.

Several bodies stalked through the trees, not far away, coming in her direction. Bandur started to bark furiously.

Spurring her mount to action, she galloped off down the trail, eager to lose whoever it was. She hoped the dog would follow closely. The horse screamed and stumbled when an arrow flew into its flank. But it managed to right itself and carry on. Aleni stared back at the ugly arrow, spots of blood flying back behind them.

As she rode out of the trees and onto a hillock covered plain, another arrow struck the horse in the side nearer its chest. The horses scream ripped through her head. She found herself flying through the air, the ground coming up to meet her suddenly. At the last second, she tucked her head in and managed to roll. She came to a stop on a patch of grass where the snow had almost totally melted.

Hearing running feet in the snow and grass, she realized she had little time to waste. Getting to her feet, she looked for her horse. The huge animal lay back on the path, kicking his legs out frantically, his eyes wide in panic. Seeing blood bubbling out of the horse's mouth, the arrow had probably pierced a lung. The poor animal would die a slow death. She shuddered as its terror hit her senses.

Bandur's barking brought her attention to something past the tree line. Something he clearly didn't like. Not Jacek then.

Panting slightly, Aleni stood frozen to the spot. The soldiers would catch her, then take her back to that awful cell where she would be a prisoner for the rest of her life. How could she get out of this? She tried to think, but her mind wouldn't move from the thought of captivity.

Hearing the stretch of bow strings and Bandur's growl, she realized she had closed her eyes. Reluctantly, she opened them. Arrows pointed at her from all directions. But it wasn't soldiers holding them.

Surrounding her were humanoid creatures with gray skin slick with sweat. They had hairless heads and menace glowed in their yellow slitted eyes. Smaller than Jacek and only slightly taller than her, they seemed to make up for the lack of height in bulging muscled arms and strong clawed hands. They looked like they could hold the bows taut all day if they had to.

There were five of them in total, completely surrounding her. They had huge spiked metal maces and sheathed daggers hanging from their belts. Her mother had told her about creatures such as these. She had never seen one before, but from their description she guessed them to be goblins.

Covered in ancient fierce-looking armor that spiked out in places, it reminded her these beings had survived the war that had taken the Elves by hiding away in their mountain tunnels. They were long experienced in warfare and survival. They had featured in her mother's stories about heroic Elvish feats in fights against the goblins. Individually they could be bested by an adult warrior Elf but in a pack like this they were a formidable foe. She was most certainly not an adult. Or a warrior.

One of them started to talk in their tongue. It was barely comprehensible as language, spat out through sharp pointed teeth with a black tongue slithering between them. She flinched back as spittle hit her in the face.

Hands with sharp claws grabbed her by the arm and pushed her to the ground onto her back. The pack spread out, obviously enthused about watching the upcoming show. The rasp of metal preceded the brandishing of a wicked-looking dagger with a hugely serrated edge. The point of which was shoved in her face, nearly slicing into her skin. The goblin continued his diatribe, the words forceful and menacing, grating on her ears. She had no idea what he wanted. For all she knew, he was saying a prayer to his god, blessing his food before he tucked into it.

Bandur kept barking, but he didn't attack, staying a safe distance away. Aleni sensed he didn't like their smell. Neither did she. A rancid, rotting smell like meat gone bad in the sun assaulted her senses. She closed her eyes, waiting for the moment she was sliced open from head to toe.

The unmistakable sound of an arrow thwacking into bone and flesh cut the goblin's words off. Her eyes flew open to see the creature with an arrow stuck into his forehead. All was quiet for an entire second, including Bandur, before the goblin crashed to the ground with a clank of armor.

Aleni twisted her head back at the direction the arrow had come from. Jacek stood back at the tree line, another arrow already nocked and drawn back. Despite her misgivings, she relaxed her head back in relief at the sight of him. Still, he was one man against five fierce creatures. Wait, make that four. He had just killed the leader of the pack.

The remaining goblins screeched and snarled in Jacek's direction, drawing their massive maces. Three started charging at him, while the last moved over to Aleni and pulled her up by the arm, pressing his dagger to her throat.

Bandur started barking again, adding to the chaos, though he continued to keep his distance from the goblins.

Another arrow flew from Jacek's bow, taking one of the charging goblins in the neck. It fell backwards and lay on the ground, gurgling.

The last two covered the ground between them in terrifying time. Jacek dropped his bow and drew his two-handed great sword from his back. Aleni's heart soared at seeing his display of strength. Surely the goblins couldn't last against him?

The first goblin swung his large spiked mace with ease at Jacek's head. The assassin ducked and rolled between the two, coming up on his feet again and slashed out at the second goblin from behind. The creature was fast, turning and dodging the strike easily, lashing out with his own mace at Jacek's neck.

The big mercenary blocked the blow with his sword, the metal weapons connecting with a clash and then a rasp as they slid down against each other. The other goblin weighed in with his own strikes, Jacek trading blows with both of them, pushing one back before the other stepped in.

Aleni watched it all with her breath held. The dagger at her throat loosened slightly as the goblin holding her watched the fight with glee. He actually jiggled up and down, obviously expecting his pack mates to win. He might not be wrong. Aleni wondered how good Jacek was. Could he really take on two goblins in hand to hand combat at the same time? He wasn't a young man.

Aleni suddenly realized the goblin holding her wasn't paying attention. Could she make a run for it? But goblins were fast. She wouldn't get far. She looked down at the huge knife in his hand. It was almost the size of a short sword for her. Maybe she could...

Seizing the moment, Aleni grabbed his hand and twisted

her body, pushing the knife back into the goblin's chest. It sunk in a few inches before the creature realized what was happening. Black blood oozed out of the wound, but the goblin just let out a screech and pulled it out. She let go and stepped back.

The goblin swung at her with the knife. She jumped back, light on her feet. He swung at her head and she ducked down. She had never been taught how to fight, but she had watched some Elf warriors training a few times to remember the basic concepts. She hoped it would be enough to keep her alive.

The goblin soon got tired of swinging at her and apparently decided to just charge at her. She had no time to try to get out of the way. He was too fast and too close. His muscular body crashed into her and took her to the ground, landing heavily on top of her. Her breath whooshed out of her and for a moment she was stunned, her only thought trying to breathe again.

When oxygen had reached her brain again, she finally registered the goblin kneeled over her, his dagger raised in both hands, ready to plunge it down into her body.

Time slowed as she saw her fate closing in. She felt the cold air being sucked into her lungs at half speed, her breath loud in her head. The rancid goblin smell invaded her nostrils. Suddenly facing death, she realized she welcomed it. Welcomed it as an end to the pains this era brought. She was alone here. Her family were all dead, her freedom limited. She would be chased forever.

It was a nice thought, knowing she would be free of all that in a moment. But then if she died her people would be forgotten. Their knowledge and history lost forever. And the humans would have won. She had a chance to make this right. She had a legacy to live for. She did not want to die.

All this flashed through her mind in an instant.

One second the goblin kneeled over her, sneering down at

her. The next, his head flew off his shoulders and bounced to the ground beside her.

It took a few moments for her mind to register what had happened. It took even longer for its body to register it. It hovered there for a bit, then started to topple towards her. Jacek appeared behind it and grabbed the back of its armor to stop it falling on her. He lifted the body easily and threw it to the side, blood spurting from the neck. It sprawled awkwardly next to the head, which stared in wide-mouthed horror back at her.

Jacek looked down on her, his sword pointed down at the ground dripping black blood. Aleni stared at the blood in horrified fascination.

"You alright?" Jacek asked.

She met his eyes briefly and nodded, gulping down more air. He had a new cut on his chin and she noted swollen knuckles on his right hand as he held it out to help her up. Without thinking she took it and was pulled to her feet. Uncomfortably, she realized he had rescued her from her own stupidity.

"Thanks for..." she glanced at the headless goblin lying off to the side, not really sure what to say. Thanks for being so violent? It was the very thing she was afraid of in him.

"Would have avoided them if you hadn't run." He gave her a pointed look. She squirmed. He was probably right. Then remembering his actions she squared her shoulders and glared back at him.

"Wouldn't have run if you hadn't drugged me."

He was silent for a long while. She wondered if maybe he wasn't going to say anything at all and looked up at him.

He broke the silence eventually. "I would never hurt a kid. I just had to make sure you slept through the day, to keep you safe. And..." He looked away. "I needed you to stick around to help me. I won't do it anymore. And if you want to leave.... well, I won't stop you."

There was something in his voice that held true for her. Somehow, she knew he wasn't lying. There was a gravitas to his face that spoke volumes. His eyes were honest. The realization unlocked her muscles and released the tension in her. Maybe she could relax around him. Give him a chance to prove himself. He already had, to a degree, with the goblins. She would be dead if it wasn't for him.

She nodded silently and looked down at her hands, chastened by his manner.

A noise drew their attention to Aleni's horse, still struggling on the ground back on the path. Her gut twisted as she realized she'd forgotten him in all the chaos. She rushed over to the horse and kneeled beside him, trying to calm him. Bandur padded over quietly and stood behind her, nuzzling her shoulder.

"Can you help him?" Aleni asked, twisting her neck to look up at Jacek, squinting against the sunlight. The horse was grunting, his breath wheezing loudly.

He was shaking his head slowly. "I can, but not in the way you probably hope. I can put him out of his misery."

Stricken, Aleni stared at him in shock. He was right, of course, but it didn't soften the blow. She had grown to like the animal, but she also didn't want him to suffer. Now that she was close to him again, she could sense his distress and fear. Thank goodness she couldn't actually feel his pain.

"Do it then." She said quietly.

Jacek drew his large sword from his back and hovered over the horse, holding the point just over the horses' chest. Aleni squeezed her eyes shut but kept her hands on the animals' belly. There was a grunt and a jerk and the horse gave a gurgle of breath and a slight whinny. Her awareness of his mind faded out.

Aleni breathed slowly and carefully, trying to stay calm. A single tear tracked down her cheek. Opening her eyes, she saw the stain of blood pooling on the ground as it bled out.

She watched silently as Jacek wiped his sword on the grass to clean it. He stood up and sheathed the weapon, the metal grating on the edge as it slid home. Looking up at the late afternoon sky he sighed.

"If you still want to stay with me, we'll need to move on and find somewhere to camp and rest until dark. We have to get off this trail. Especially with this horse here. It'll make them stop and search the area more thoroughly. Grab your things from the horse and we'll ride together."

He looked at her, waiting for an answer.

She was probably safer with him than with anyone else. Safer than on her own, that was for sure. She nodded at him and started untying her bag from the horse.

Bandur came to Jacek's side then, and he crouched down in front of the dog. "What am I going to do with you? Have you chosen a new partner?" He shook his head slowly. The dog cocked his head at him. "However, I can never stay mad at you. As our new companion has said before, you're free to do what you want. So," he stood, joints clicking, "you're forgiven." He patted the dog's head.

Aleni gave a small smile at the dog while the assassin left to retrieve his horse back in the trees. He rode back out and joined Aleni on the trail. Reaching down, he put out his arm for her to grab. She gripped it and he swung her up onto the blanket behind him.

$\mathfrak{R}$ 6 $\mathfrak{R}$

After traveling for an hour down the trail, Jacek spotted a sheltered clearing down in a small gully, out of view from potential soldiers. After resting and eating, they set off again once it was dark. They made good time through the night, keeping the horse at a trot to conserve its energy. The bay stallion was fit, with long legs and well-toned muscles. He was a good find in Jacek's opinion. Bandur ran along beside them, but eventually tired before the horse did. Jacek pulled him up onto the horse after that, sitting the dog in front of him.

Jacek guided the horse toward a quiet bay on the northern coast. The sheltered cove was used by captains who wanted to avoid the harbor at Ifellean. The harbor was controlled by Krodon's men, who took a heavy tax on all shipments coming in from Amathnore. Taxing merchants was the easiest way to raise money for his growing troops, especially since he had the men to enforce it. He claimed it was a 'protection' tax. So Sunstorm cove became a haven for a few shipping merchants 'in the know' to avoid Krodon's men.

As dawn broke through the horizon, they crested a hill

and the rocky coastline appeared, stretching out in both directions for as far as the eye could see. Jacek pulled the horse up so they could look down over the view and let Bandur down to the ground. The dog trotted around happily exploring the new sights and smells.

Water lapped at the jagged outer edges of the cove below and seabirds soared overhead, circling. A large ship was moored farther out in the bay with its sails lowered. Jacek never tired of viewing the ocean. To him it symbolized free-dom. It was one of the few things not frozen in Selendria, and the sea life that lived in it thrived.

"Oh wow." Aleni breathed. "It's beautiful."

Jacek nodded quietly to himself. It had been a long time since he had sat and appreciated something of beauty with another person. It was surprisingly refreshing. A strange thing happened inside him, lifting his heart and loosening his muscles. He relaxed as they watched the sun rise over the ocean, creating a corridor of light in their direction. Each wave caught the light and danced with it. It was a show of grandeur and majesty that eased the soul.

He looked over his shoulder at the girl behind him. Her eyes were closed and a small smile danced on her lips. She was having her own moment. Pleasure washed through him at the sight. She deserved peace, even if it was just a moment in time.

Eventually, Jacek prodded the horse forward, taking them down a winding path that switchbacked down to the shore-line where a group of men surrounded a campfire on the sand. Dismounting and stretching stiffly at the bottom, they walked toward the camp. A man broke away from the group at the fireside and walked towards them. He was an older man with a shaved head and a gray beard. His thick furs covered a rounded belly that had grown slightly since Jacek had last seen him. "That's Deems," Jacek said quietly to

Aleni. "He's the captain of the Gallant." He motioned to the ship out in the bay.

"Is that the Red Hunter himself? I don't believe it!" The old sailor approached, grinning at him.

There was no need to answer Deems, so Jacek just nodded in return, watching him and the men behind him at the fire carefully. One could never be too careful around others, particularly now that he had Aleni with him. It would be a new dynamic for him to juggle.

"And you have a companion with you this time?" Deems turned to Aleni and smiled again. "Hello there, dearie. How on earth did you get to be traveling with this ogre?" He pointed a thumb at Jacek, who decided to let that pass.

Aleni was silent. She stared at the captain with those icy blue eyes that made her stand out. Jacek had never seen a human with such eyes.

"I'm escorting her to the north." Jacek said. "A job." He kept his tone bland, brooking no further discussion.

Deems opened his mouth in an 'o' of understanding and nodded. "Well, come join us." He put out a hand to gesture to the fire.

Together, Jacek and Aleni walked over to the fire, leading the horse. Jacek tethered the animal to a large piece of driftwood. He spotted a bucket of fresh water nearby and grabbed it for the animal to drink from. Hopefully the sailors would have some oats to feed it. Aleni patted the horses head, murmuring quietly to him. Jacek gave some of the water to Bandur who then ran toward the beach, jumping in the waves. The dog was about five years old, but there were times he still acted like a puppy. Jacek was glad to see it.

"I take it you're looking for passage to Amathnore?" Deems asked once they joined him by the fire. Amathnore was the only port on the northern coast, so it was an obvious guess.

Jacek nodded. "We can't risk sailing out of Ifellean right now."

Deems nodded in understanding. "Aye, right there with you. Well, I can offer you a place on the ship for twenty Olons." He raised his eyebrows at Jacek.

"Ten, and you can have the horse."

Deems narrowed his eyes and looked towards the horse. "Doesn't look like much. Bit skinny."

"He's strong. Just carried both of us all night, the dog too at times."

"Fifteen," Deems countered.

"Twelve."

"Deal." They shook on it and Jacek pulled out the coins from a purse and handed them over.

"You're in luck." Deems said. He nodded to where five men were loading crates into a longboat. "We're loading up now with a fresh haul. We sail at noon."

Close to ten men sat around the fire, talking together while they drank and ate. Two stared at Aleni, who was watching another sailor feed the stallion. Jacek gave the men a hard look, not wanting them to look too closely at her, even though her ears were covered up. They got the message and turned away.

"Will you break fast with us?" Deems asked. He pointed to a pot of gruel over the fire, bubbling away. It was a welcome sight from the basic trail rations they had been eating.

After a gesture from Jacek, Aleni took a bowl from the cook who was ladling gruel into servings for everyone. She sat in a spare spot on the edge of the circle and ate. Jacek joined her with his own bowl of warmth. He soon felt heartened as the hot food hit his stomach. He hadn't realized how hungry he was.

"How long will it take to get to Amathnore?" Aleni asked

between mouthfuls. Obviously, she was as hungry as he was. Her pronunciation of the city name was odd to Jacek's ears. Her accent thickened whenever she spoke an Elven word. He would have to make sure she didn't talk too much to the sailors in case they started asking questions about where she was from.

"A couple of days. Three at the most."

"Oh."

"Is something wrong?"

"It's just that I don't like sailing. Makes me feel ill."

He narrowed his eyes at her. This surprised him. He had always had an image of elves having a strong stomach and iron constitution. The stories and myths about them had obviously been guesswork intended to entertain. "If we keep busy, it will help."

"Doing what?"

Jacek stared out at the bay, eyeing up the ship. "We can help out around the ship. We'll be expected to anyway. You can run errands for Deems."

"I like him." She mused. "He's nice."

"He's a rare one."

"Why are people so unfriendly and unkind?"

"We are all descended from criminals. Thieves and murderers. After the Cleansing," he suddenly remembered who he was talking to, "uh, the war, our ancestors sent the criminals through the portals to Selendria and exiled them here. The society that grew out of those exiles has not been a particularly friendly one. It came with a built-in mistrust of others." He thought of his parents then, attempting to teach people to care for strangers. They were different than most. He had often wondered what his great great grandparents had done to get exiled through the portals. They must have tried to change themselves for the better and taught their children different. "But even so, some have tried over the years to model a more friendly approach, but by and large people prefer to stick to their own clans and families. Unless there is good pay involved, like with Krodon or Tarkan's men."

"So, a crew like this?"

"This crew will have been built out of a single clan. They will all be related in some way."

"Must be a close-knit crew then."

Jacek merely shrugged. The last time he was close-knit with others, he was nine years old. It didn't end well.

They waited by the fire through the morning until everything was loaded on the Gallant. Then a longboat came back for the rest of the crew, along with Jacek, Aleni and Bandur. A couple of men stayed behind on the beach along with the horse. They kept a camp there for any other ships coming in or deliveries being made. The sailors helped Aleni aboard but stood back when Jacek glared at them for offering to help him. Once on board the Gallant, the crew set to and pulled up the anchor. The sun was high in the sky by the time they set sail. Jacek stared back at the beach, thankful they had made a clean getaway from Krodon's men.

$%$ 7 $%$

The Gallant was a three-masted ship with blue trim. She had a tendency to leak in some places. However, she was fast out on the open water, and Deems had often expressed full faith in her abilities. Jacek had ridden on her before and had yet to be disappointed in her performance.

As the crew set the ship moving, the first mate showed them a small cabin with a set of bunk beds. Two portholes close together looked out to the ocean and let in some natural light. The bare planks of the floor warped in a couple of places, creaking when Jacek put his weight on them. However, it was nice to be out of the biting wind, so he decided to catch up on some sleep while he could. He was required up on deck after dinner that evening for a shift on the rigging.

He put a blanket down on the floor for Bandur, who immediately made himself a nest and curled up on it, falling asleep in moments.

The bunk wasn't particularly comfortable, but it was a place to lie down at least. His legs were aching from his illness. Hopefully, some rest would help. He settled himself and closed his eyes, a rough blanket thrown over for warmth.

Aleni had scuttled up the ladder to the top bunk. He listened to her taking her boots off and wrapping herself up in the blanket that was on the bed. Before long, she was silent, and he was able to relax.

When next he opened his eyes, the light through the porthole told him several hours had gone by. It took him a second to realize something had woken him. The ship creaked and groaned as it moved through the water. But there was something else. A noise from the top bunk. The kid. She was mumbling and whimpering in her sleep. He rolled off the bed and came silently to his feet.

The bunk wasn't terribly high, so he was able to see level with her. She was twitching and shaking her head, her eyes still closed in restless sleep.

Should he wake her? He wasn't sure it was his business. He knew what it was like to sleep poorly, with ghosts haunting his dreams, but she might not want him to know. It might make her feel more vulnerable than she already probably felt.

She cried out again, and he reached out to touch her shoulder but stopped himself just before he did. She was so tiny, taking up less than half of the bunk bed. Her cries evoked something deep inside him. Something he long thought dead. He had survived this far because he stopped caring about others. He had worked hard to undo what his parents had tried to instill in him.

Now all that hard work might be undone.

He turned away. It was none of his business. He couldn't get involved. She was probably just mourning her parents. From his own experience, he knew she was better off dealing with that on her own.

He reached into his pouch for his medicine. Opening the

little bag, he saw there was only enough for one more dose left. He would need to restock in Amathnore.

He left the cabin and went to the galley to find hot water. The cook gave him a cup with some boiling water in it, which he added the herbs to and waited for it to steep. While he waited, he went up on deck, taking his cup with him. The wind was up. The Gallant plowed through the water like an otter. Jacek moved over to the railing to look out to sea.

Three dolphins swam nearby, diving in and out of the waves like children running alongside a visiting cart. Watching them made him think of the girl. What was he thinking, having the kid along with him? Even if it was to find a cure for his illness, was it really worth it? Could he find a magical artifact another way?

The problem with the elven artifacts, was there was a lot of fake ones out there being sold to hopeful people. It was hard to tell which ones were real. Some could be real, but possibly needed to be activated. Some people said an elf was needed to activate them. There had been no way to know for sure.

Until now. Maybe he should try to find one in Amathnore. Maybe a merchant there actually dealt in real ones. The kid might be able to identify one.

That was a lot of maybes. But would it be worth it to at least have a look? If they did find one, and it cured him, he could be rid of her sooner. Less chance of him losing his edge. She was a liability, that was for sure.

He drank his medicine slowly, letting the hot tea warm his insides. His legs still ached, but that would pass soon.

"So, what's with the kid?" Deems had approached quietly, but Jacek had heard his footsteps. The man wasn't anywhere near as stealthy as he thought he was. But then, Jacek had spent most of his life honing skills like that. He was alive because of it.

"Don't make me repeat myself, Deems."

Deems put his hands up in surrender. "All right, all right. You can keep your secrets. But she's a strange one. Very pale. Weird accent."

Jacek raised an eyebrow at the captain.

"I'm not going to get anything out of you, am I?" Deems sighed. "Surely, after all these years, I thought maybe you might start thinking of me as a friend?"

"Don't push your luck. You have a boat. I often need to travel over the sea. We have a business arrangement. That's it." Jacek kept his gaze locked on the horizon. He suspected Deems didn't actually want to be friends, but wanted to suck up to him because of his reputation.

"Maybe we could go into a different kind of business arrangement. I need better security on the Gallant. Particularly when going into port. Sometimes there are enterprising souls who think they can help themselves to my cargo while most of the crew are taking their leave. You could help with that. I would pay you well."

"Not interested." Gods, he would get bored quickly doing that. He did a job and then moved on. That was his way. Don't get involved, don't get attached. Besides it was a waste of his skills.

"Come on, Jacek," he chided. "You're getting older now, surely you want to slow down at some point. Take it easier. You can still earn coin, but you don't have to work as hard." The older captain sounded like he was talking from experience. But Jacek wasn't biting.

"Leave me be, Deems."

"Oh well, you know where to find me if you change your mind." Deems moved his gaze out to the incoming dark clouds in the distance. "Looks like we might be in for some rain tonight. Maybe even a storm. Might get a bit rough. You may want to warn your girl." He gave Jacek a pointed look and walked away.

Jacek eyed the clouds himself. Great. The kid was already nervous about being on the ship. A storm would just nail that home some more. The last thing he needed was a hysterical child on his hands.

☙❧

The courtyard in Krodon's fortress rang with the clash of steel and the stamping of hooves. The Warlord watched as horses were bridled and blanketed, readying for the next lot of soldiers to go out searching. The soldiers talked in hushed tones. Probably because he was walking the area. He knew the men were a little afraid of him. He liked it that way.

A practice area was in use, with his Master-at-Arms training a group of men in sword play. They were making the most of the day while it wasn't snowing. He wandered over to observe, his hands clasped behind his back.

Two men battled it out in the muddy space. Their breath heaved out in frosted clouds as they clashed swords. The master barked out instructions as they circled each other. They wore thick leather armor and fought with dulled blades, but there was still an element of danger. One man was tall and gangly, looking like he needed a good feed of horse meat to fill him out. The other was a little shorter, but not much bigger in muscle. They both looked like a stiff wind would take them out.

The taller one held his sword loosely and swung without much skill or accuracy. Were these the kind of men he was recruiting? The Master had better make a miracle with them or his secret campaign would stop dead in its tracks. His father wouldn't fear him, he'd laugh at him.

"Grip your sword tighter." Krodon said to the tall fighter.

All heads turned toward him. The tall one in the ring saw him and lowered his gaze respectfully. "Or your opponent will knock it out of your hand at the first strike."

The tall fighter nodded and gripped his sword. His opponent bent his knees again, readying to strike. The two clashed again. This time the tall one held his sword better, but was beaten easily by not blocking on the second hit.

Screw this, Krodon had to step in and show them. He approached the shorter man, who offered Krodon his sword. He took it and the soldier scurried out of the ring.

Krodon gripped the dulled sword and flexed his muscles under his furs. He knew the thick pelts that sat on his shoulders made him look slightly bigger than his six-foot frame, so he didn't bother shrugging them off for the demonstration. It didn't hurt for his men to think he was bigger than he really was.

"Now, do you know the basic five strikes of the blade?"

The soldier looked at the master-at-arms, who had his arms folded in slight defiance of the guest instructor. Krodon would talk to him later. The soldier eventually shook his head.

"Diagonal down strikes like this," he demonstrated swiping the sword down in the shape of an X. "Then like this," he cut backwards vertically across in front of him and back again in the opposite direction. "Then straight in for a stab." He demonstrated again. "Right, your turn." He loved showing his superiority in front of the men.

The tall soldier mimicked the moves in the air in front of him.

"Now try to hit me."

The man looked dubious, and glanced over at the master again, who gestured he should do as asked. So, he swung towards Krodon in a diagonal downward stroke. Krodon countered it and pushed back, knocking his sword back away from his body. He then stepped in and slashed across the man's stomach. If the swords had sharp edges, it would have disemboweled the soldier.

As it was, the strength of the blow doubled the man over, clutching his belly. Krodon brought his knee up, connecting with the man's head. The tall soldier crumpled to the ground, out cold.

The master stepped into the ring to check on his man. But Krodon wasn't finished yet. He had to teach these men a lesson. They should have no mercy for their enemy. Fear had to be used to control the masses.

He kicked the prone man in the head again. Blood gushed out of a cut around his eye. "You cannot let up! An unconscious enemy can eventually get back up and come after you when you least expect it." He dropped the sword and crouched down over the soldier. Grabbing his head in both hands, he twisted it violently. A crack was heard. Several soldiers around the ring looked shocked and took a step back.

Krodon stood back up and addressed the men. "A dead enemy is a good enemy. Never forget that." He looked at the master-at-arms again. "You need to teach these men quicker. We have a lot of work ahead of us if we are to succeed in our goals."

The master nodded silently, then glanced down at his now-dead man.

"Somebody get rid of this body." Krodon ordered. Stepping out of the ring, he didn't bother looking back at the men as he walked away. They would fear him now if they didn't already. He paid them enough to stay loyal, but they would fear his power as well.

Just then, the general murmur of men in the courtyard was broken by the running splatter of small feet in the mud.

"Papa!" A small, pale, dark-haired child ran towards him, her arms outstretched.

Krodon couldn't help a smile as he scooped her up in his muscular arms. His little Arlette. Nine years old and already getting taller. She was the light of his life. The only thing in this world he didn't want to lose.

"What are you doing out here?" Krodon asked, tapping her little cold nose. She was bundled up in furs, but her head remained bare. "It's terribly cold!"

"I wanted to find you. Will you play with me?" Her brown eyes held the hope of a little girl who had been shut up inside for a long time.

"Hmm, possibly." He looked slyly at her. "What's in it for me?"

The little girl put her finger to her lips, thinking hard. "Ten kisses," she said.

"Twenty." He countered.

"Um, alright." She smiled at him, her whole face lighting up. Then she started to cough.

Krodon frowned. "Let's get you inside. This cold air is not good for you." He held her close and walked quickly back inside the fortress. He took her up the stairs, still coughing, and into her suite of rooms.

A fire burned warmly in the hearth, heating the bed chamber cheerfully. A large comfortable bed was surrounded by various wooden toys and building blocks. A partially built castle sat on the floor, made out of wooden blocks of varying shapes and sizes. It looked remarkably like his own fortress which had been built around an ancient stone tower the elves had left behind. A similar tower erupted out of the middle of this one on the floor.

Drapes were drawn over the large windows in the western wall, keeping the warmth in and the daylight out. Oil lamps scattered around the edges of the room set everything in a low light. Krodon lay his daughter in her bed on her side, rubbing her back to calm the spasms of the coughing. Eventually she settled.

"Will you tell me a story, papa?" Arlette snuggled closer to him.

"What sort of story do you want?"

"Tell me about the elves again! I like hearing about them."

He sighed. He had told her a hundred times, but she loved hearing it, anyway. The things he did for this little girl. He didn't feel this way towards anyone else, even her mother, who was one of many women he kept for his bed. Somehow, when Arlette had been born, he felt something. Something he had only ever felt for his mother. She had always been kind, spending time with him in his studies and playing with him as a child. Like he did now with Arlette. Until his narcissistic father had killed her in a violent rage in front of him.

Krodon would never forgive him for that.

"Well, the elves lived for thousands of years in a beautiful land called Selendria."

"That's this world!" She piped in.

He grinned. She always added this in, as though she liked the idea that there might be elves out there somewhere. "Yes, it is. But it looked different back then. There was green grass everywhere, green trees, flowers, and lakes that weren't frozen. It's hard for us to imagine. But according to the writings of the elves, it was a lush, alive land."

"What happened Papa?"

"Well, about three hundred years ago, humans came through a *magical* portal from another world. They wanted to take Selendria for themselves. They were running out of room on their own world and needed somewhere else to live." He pulled the covers up to her chest.

"But the elves weren't going to give up their world easily. So they fought. The humans had superior numbers, but the elves were strong and had magic. They healed quickly so they could rejoin the battle quicker than the humans. The humans had powerful and strange weapons, but the elves held out."

"So where did they go, papa?" She knew the answer, of course, but her question was all part of the story.

"The humans were relentless. They got more weapons and used them against the elves. Eventually, the elves all died. The humans killed them all. No one knows how the humans won, but they did."

Arlette was silent. She always was at this point of the story.

"After the elves died, Selendria started to change. It got colder and colder. The humans hadn't taken the time to study Selendria. To realize that the elves were part of the land. That they kept it in balance. Selendria was dying."

"So they decided not to live here." Arlette said.

"That's right. They still had too many people on their world, so they sent their prisoners here instead. Then they didn't have to look after them anymore. It was the perfect solution. For them."

"And that's why it's always cold here. Cos there's no more elves around."

"But not for long. Your papa will change all that. I will change the land back to what it once was. For you." He patted her cheek. "Then you can go outside without coughing all the time." Her lungs had weakened several years ago, and the herbal healers all said the cold made it worse. She needed warmth and sunshine. Two things that didn't happen often in Selendria anymore.

He would do everything in his power to bring them back. For Arlette.

$\maltese$ 8 $\maltese$

Aleni awoke with a gasp, her body shuddering with a fear that was already fading. Suffice to say, her sleep had not been restful. There was something to be said for Jacek's 'warming tea'. At least she had slept peacefully with it.

The ship was rocking a lot more than it had when she fell asleep and it sounded like it was raining hard outside. She peered out of the porthole next to the bunk. It was dark, but her elven vision made seeing in the night easy. The waves outside looked choppy, and some were getting very high. A new fear started to build inside her. Why couldn't there be a massive bridge crossing the straight between the two mainlands?

The water level outside the porthole moved up and down with the tossing of the ship on the water, causing her stomach to turn.

Despite the rocking, she managed to slip off the top bunk and on to the floor of the cabin without hurting herself. Her bare feet slapped on the wooden planks, instantly wet. Puddles of water had formed, due to a constant dripping from the deck above in one corner.

Jacek was gone. Bandur slept on his bunk, ostensibly to get out of the puddles on the floor. Perhaps she should go find Jacek. Stepping out into the corridor, she looked both ways, but there was no one in sight. Rain pattered on the deck above, dripping down into the narrow corridor in a few places. At the end of the hallway a steep set of steps led up onto the main deck above.

Chaos reigned up above. Or so it seemed to her untrained eyes. The boards were slick with rainwater, while men ran in all directions trying to grab rigging and keep them contained. Several men were up on the higher booms, reefing the sails with rope to shorten them for the incoming storm. The smell of brine and seaweed hit her, reminding her of the trip over the water she had taken all those years ago with her parents that had brought her to this side of the world. It seemed like an eternity ago.

"If you don't get those storm sails down right now, I'm going to turn your guts into rigging when it's over!" Deems yelled up at one man over the crash of rain on the deck, snapping Aleni back to the here and now.

"That's if we're still alive when it's over!" The sailor yelled back. He saw Aleni and gave her a friendly wave. She smiled and returned it. Jacek had made these men out to be untrustworthy brigands who would stab them in the back as soon as it was turned, but maybe some of them were alright after all.

She suspected Jacek had some trust issues.

Deems turned around to spot her at the top of the stairs. "Ah, young miss! Things might get a bit rough up here for a while, you may want to go back down below."

Aleni looked around at the rain and tossing sea. It didn't seem too bad at this point and since she was already soaked through, she was willing to ride it out for now. "I'll stay, thanks. Where is Jacek?"

Deems pointed toward the front of the Gallant. "He's up on the foredeck, helping to tie more stays in."

Aleni followed his pointing finger and moved up to the bow of the ship, being careful not to slip on the wet decking. She soon spotted him helping two other sailors tie a massive line around a point on the side of the ship. He was using his size and muscle to hold the line taught while they tied it.

Not wanting to distract him, she held back, close to the mast, just watching. She held on to a metal stay in the mast as the ship tossed around. A wave rose high, crashing against the side of the ship, splashing water all over Jacek. He didn't waver. He was like an anchor in the water, unmoving. The sailors finally finished tying the stay down to stabilize the mast for the coming winds. It was obvious the storm was only just getting started. Clouds overhead rumbled with thunder while the rain continued to fall. Aleni was drenched through already.

Stumbling slightly with the deck lurching underneath her, Aleni finally stepped up to Jacek. The big mercenary spotted her and his brows crinkled. Water dripped from his sodden hair onto his face. His facial scar created a track for the water to cling to as it collected in his beard.

"You shouldn't be up here. It's not safe."

"And when did you become my keeper?"

He opened his mouth to answer, but must have thought better of it. He clamped it shut again, but didn't look pleased.

"I'm traveling with you, not being your charge."

His eyes bore into hers. "We both know you're not always capable of keeping yourself safe."

His words cut, a pang of guilt shooting through her at the memory of the goblins. It had been a bit stupid. She sighed internally. When would she be considered a grown up? Elves didn't hit adult maturity until their early twenties. She had a long way to go until then.

"Can I help at least?" She asked.

"I'm not going to suggest anything that will get you killed - which cancels out any job above deck right now. I need you to help me find those artifacts. So, no. Go back to the cabin." He turned away to help with another line.

Great, her value summed up by her ability to look. So inspiring. Despite all the chaos, she didn't want to go back below. She would rather face whatever happened from up here, where she could see it coming.

Just then something crashed to the deck next to her. She jumped, her heart leaping in her chest at the near miss. Staring down at the item, she identified it as one of the rigging blocks. Craning her head up to see where it came from, she spotted a young sailor with blond hair sitting up on a high beam looking down at her, a wince frozen on his face. The same one who had waved to her earlier.

Aleni glanced over at Jacek. He was still busy with the lines and hadn't heard it over the noise of the rain, thunder and groaning of the ship. Shrugging to herself, she picked up the block and hooked it over one arm. A rope net hung not far off the ground, which she eyed up briefly before jumping onto it and starting to climb.

She had never climbed rigging on a ship before, but it came naturally to her. She almost flew up the net, reaching the first beam in no time. It was only slightly more difficult than climbing a tree back in the forest she had grown up in. The only difficulty was the wind battering at her.

Very soon, she found herself straddling the beam next to the young man, holding out the block to him. His eyes were wide in surprise at her. Or was that awe? Perhaps she shouldn't have made that look so easy.

"Have you been on a ship before?" He had to lean in and raise his voice to be heard. "I haven't ever seen anyone climb like that before. You must have spent a lot of time up in the rigging!"

She felt heat rise to her face, despite the cold rain dripping down it. She needed to deflect some attention away. "Ah yes... my father has a ship that I grew up on. Learned to climb before I could walk," she lied. Handing the block over, she tried to look bored.

"You - you have a strange accent." The young man said, cocking an eyebrow. He stared at her face like he'd never seen a female before. Aleni looked away from the intensity, not sure what to make of him. She patted at her headscarf to make sure it was still in place covering her ears.

"Uh, I'm from the far north." That, at least, was true.

The older boy nodded as though that answered everything. He turned back to his work re-rigging the lines.

The rain started coming down heavier, the thunder more frequent. The ship groaned at the strain on her masts. Shouts and calls floated up from the crew below. The wind drove into Aleni's face, bringing sheets of cold water with it. Realizing she was no longer needed, she started to climb back down.

A large wave hit the Gallant, making the ship shudder. Aleni lost her grip on the netting and fell, a shriek escaping her lips before she managed to grab the rope again. It slipped through her hand briefly before she hit a knot and held on. Rough hemp fibers ripped into her skin, burning her hand. Pain shot up her arm. She cried out again, the wind swallowing it up and whisking it away.

With one arm holding on, her body swung around. Along with the violent rocking of the ship, it was difficult to swing herself back to grip the netting properly. She had to wait until the ship rocked back the other way to use the momentum to her advantage. Finally, with a lurch, the ship dipped, and she grabbed the netting with her other hand and held on.

As fast as she could with her hands scraped raw, she shimmied down the net to the deck below. As soon as her feet hit the planks, she felt a hand on her arm. Whirling around, she found Jacek staring at her, his brow furrowed. Was that worry on his face?

"What were you doing up there?" His voice, while a bit louder to carry over the sounds of the storm, sounded modulated.

"Helping out one of the crew." It was probably best to be a little vague.

"Don't go up there again. Not in this weather. Get below where it's safe."

"Why do you keep telling me what to do?!" Arms straight, fists locked, she yelled back at him, spitting out water at the same time as it drove into her face. She felt a certain indignation at being treated like a child again. It was her life - she could risk it any way she wanted, couldn't she?

"Because you keep doing stupid things!" He said, leaning in closer to her face. Water spat out of his mouth with each word.

"Well, it's my life to do what I please!" Gritting her teeth, she turned back towards the entry to the next deck. Sea water flew up the side of the ship just then and crested over onto the deck at the same time as the ship listed heavily to the side. Aleni was thrown to the deck, sliding down towards the lowered railing.

Jacek leaped after her, grabbing her leg before she went too much farther. He held out his hand, and she reached for it and gripped it tightly. Using a nearby barrel that was tied to the deck for purchase, he pulled her back up, away from the railing and up against the barrel. Together they huddled there, holding on while the storm raged around them. It was too dangerous to move anywhere without purpose for now.

Around the deck, the crew stumbled to their various jobs.

Captain Deems barked out orders over the blasting thunder and driving rain. The helmsman strained at the wheel, trying to keep it steady and the ship in one piece. Occasionally, the whole deck would light up as lightning cleaved across the sky, leaving a still impression on the backs of their eyes.

Deems was standing up on the aft deck, holding onto the railing and gesticulating wildly at his men, obviously trying to keep them all under control in the turmoil. Violent movement high above his head caught Aleni's eye, and she spotted a cross beam attached to the mast behind him. It had broken off and now swung wildly in the wind, only hanging on by a few ropes from higher up.

She tried to yell out, but her cries were ripped away in the howling wind.

Jacek placed a hand on her shoulder, a question in his eyes. She pointed to the wavering beam. He followed her hand and his eyes widened.

Suddenly Aleni heard a snap from up above Deems. He didn't seem to register it, but her elven hearing picked it up.

The beam fell.

Without thinking, Aleni reached out her hand as if to stop it, even though she was a quarter of the length of the ship away.

The boom halted in mid-air.

Shock ran through her body, along with a slight electric current that felt... powerful. Somehow, she knew she was doing this. She controlled that beam. Never before had she done anything like this, but in the back of her mind she knew this was a natural part of her. It felt right. She had often seen her parents manipulate objects with their mind, and her mother had told her one day she would do it too when she was old enough.

This was it. Inexplicable joy bubbled up from her stomach at the thought that she was coming into her birthright.

Strength flowed through her from deep within, a well of power moving out through her hands. It felt wonderful. How much could she lift with it?

The boom wobbled, reminding her the middle of a storm with a boatload of strangers was not the time nor place to explore her new power.

Slowly, she guided the boom down gently on the deck behind Deems where there were currently no men, who still hadn't noticed what was going on. Thankfully, it was still very dark. The hand on her shoulder tightened, reminding her that Jacek was right there beside her. Had he seen?

She turned back to him. His widened eyes told her he had seen it all. Now what would he do with her? Would he find a way to use her to make himself rich? Wasn't that what he wanted the magical artifacts for? Her heart quailed at the thought of being at another man's mercy. The dungeon...

"Come on, we need to get below deck," he yelled.

Helping her up, together they made for the hatch leading below. Water poured down the steps after them, making huge puddles in the corridor to their cabin. Aleni got the door open and clambered up to the dry top bunk, away from the cold water pooling on the floor.

Jacek grabbed a cloth hanging from a hook by the door and tossed it to Aleni to dry herself. His head disappeared from view as he sat on the bottom bunk.

Aleni, still reeling from the discovery of her newfound powers, ripped off her headscarf which was soaked through. Her hair hung heavy and sopping as she rung it out over the side of the bunk before trying to dry it with the cloth.

What now? She knew she had just become even more valuable, and it terrified her. She had probably already been the most powerful being in Selendria, just for the mere fact of what she was. She was the last of a powerful race of noble beings, now just a footnote in Selendria's history. She had some power, but it was new to her, still untested. If people found out about her and came after her, she could try to fight them off, but she was only one person. One girl.

Her only hope lay in this brute of a mercenary. Someone who had proven already he wasn't to be trusted. Sure, he hadn't hurt her, but he had drugged her against her will. And he hadn't been slow to dish out violence to others on their trail. He was clearly a violent and solitary man. There was no way he was going to keep her around once he got what he wanted. There was no room in his life for her, or anyone else. Would he then sell her to the highest bidder?

"What are you going to do with me?" Aleni finally asked. She had to know.

"What?" His voice grated the single syllable like a stone over a washboard.

"You saw what happened, didn't you?"

There was silence for a bit before his voice carried up from below. "I saw. Didn't know you could do that."

"Neither did I." She stared down at her hands, seeing for the first time, the rawness of her palms from the rope burn. It was starting to heal already. One of the perks of being an elf.

He stood, turning to face her. "You've never done that before?"

She shook her head. "Most adult elves can do it, but it doesn't manifest itself until puberty." She felt heat rise up in her face at the mention of it. The last thing she wanted was to be talking to him about her becoming a woman.

"Oh. Right." He cleared his throat and glanced away for a moment before training his gaze back on her. "Why did you ask what I'm going to do with you? I thought we'd made an arrangement already?"

She stared at him, trying to read his face. Was he faking it? "Well, now you've seen what I can do, will you use me for monetary gain? Sell me to someone? Use me to gain power over people?"

His mouth dropped open a little and his eyebrows shot up. "Why would I do that? Do you seriously think I would *sell* you?"

A little embarrassed, she said, "I don't really know you. And from what you've told me of this society, it's not a huge stretch of the imagination, you have to admit."

He opened and closed his mouth a couple of times before he answered. "Well, maybe others might, but I'm not out to make lots of money." He gestured with his hand out to the side. "As you've seen, I live a simple life. That's all I need."

"Then what do you need the magic artifacts for?" Her voice unintentionally rose, fear gathering as they got to the crux of things.

He stayed silent, gazing at the edge of the bunk, not meeting her eyes.

"Well?" She asked.

"It's none of your business. If you help me find them, I'll keep you safe. I'll help you stay hidden from people who might want to use you or sell you. Obviously Krodon knows what you are. Surely his men do too."

"Some. He kept me mostly hidden from them. Only a few actually had any contact with me."

He nodded. "That's good then. He won't be spreading the word around about who you are. We have that in our favor."

Somehow, his use of the word 'our' dispelled some of her fear. Maybe she wasn't so alone. Maybe she had a chance with Jacek. She would have to be wary, but he seemed genuine. His eyes didn't show any sign of subterfuge. His stance was relaxed and resigned.

"Thank you," she said.

He ducked his head, obviously not used to gratitude.

Well, he would need to get used to it. Jacek simply nodded and sat back down on the bunk below.

Bandur, still curled up on the bed next to Jacek, let out a doggy snuff, as though he knew they had made peace.

Maybe she wasn't alone after all.

এ 9 ই

The icy wind blew in off the ocean to tug and pull at Krodon's dark hair. He rarely tied it back, liking the look of the long scraggly locks. It made him look more threatening. The men of the lower classes tended to keep their hair short to make it less likely to get some sort of louse growing in it. Even some women shaved their heads. To have long hair represented wealth and power. Krodon's was just below his shoulders. Arlette loved to run her hands through it. When she was little, she had grabbed and pulled at it. Feeling the tug of the wind in his hair, he smiled at the memory.

Standing on the top of the central tower, he ran his hands over the rough stone. Since the Red Hunter had invaded his fortress, he'd realized it wasn't just the girl that had gone. A pendant from his bedroom was also missing. He wasn't entirely sure if the Red Hunter had taken it, but it was a bit too much of a coincidence. Did that mean the Hunter had been in his bedroom while he slept? Krodon was lucky to be alive. He clenched his fists at the frustration of not having caught him. Every day the man was free was an insult.

A cleared throat behind him heralded the approach of Traslek, interrupting his thoughts.

"My Lord, I have news." He raised his voice over the whistling wind.

Krodon lifted his head slightly to show he was listening.

"The Red Hunter and the girl were spotted by one of your men going to a smuggler's cove further up the coast. There they boarded a ship."

Krodon grunted. "I knew I should have dealt with that place earlier. Where are they headed now?"

"Probably Amathnore. If not there, then somewhere near it. There aren't many other places they can make landfall along the northern coastline."

"Unless they're headed for the eastern coast of the mainland."

"True. But Amathnore makes sense. It's the only actual port. They'll probably need to restock supplies."

Krodon turned to face his lieutenant. "What do you think he wants with the girl? Why risk coming here to break her out in the first place?"

Traslek shrugged. "What I want to know is how he knew she was here."

"Do you think we have a leak, Traslek?" Krodon gave him a piercing gaze.

"Oh no, of course not. I can vouch for all our men." Traslek moved his feet ever so slightly. What was he hiding?

"What are you not telling me?" Krodon growled.

The lieutenant's face stayed tightly controlled, but Krodon sensed he was holding back.

"Tell me, or you'll find yourself hanging over the side of that wall." Krodon pointed to the battlement on his right. Friend or not, if he needed answers, he would get them any way he could.

Letting out a breath, Traslek looked down at the ground

before speaking. "One of the guards went missing the night before The Red Hunter broke in. We haven't found him yet. I suspect he's either run away because he got paid off by the Hunter, or he's dead."

"So, he could be the leak?"

"It's possible, but not confirmed."

"What about the explorer? Tidhelm. He found the girl in the first place."

"And you compensated him handsomely for the find. He's out there now searching for any others." Traslek thumbed over his shoulder to the wilderness below.

"Do you have men watching him?" Krodon asked.

"I had to pull them back to help look for the girl."

"Send them back to keep an eye on him. I don't want him talking to anyone else. If I didn't need him to keep searching for ancient finds, I would kill him. He can stay alive for now."

"What about the search? Shall I send men to Amathnore?"

Krodon turned back to the sea, his gaze catching on his warship moored in the bay below. The majestic vessel's red pennants flew straight out in the wind. His father had given him the ship, mostly in an effort to get him out of Amathnore and away from him.

"I think it's time for me to pay a visit to my father."

◈

The port city of Amathnore was an ancient one. Aleni remembered it as a great city of architectural marvels and culture. Many artisans and city planners had spent a century building it to reflect the glory of her people. But as the Gallant limped into port, Aleni almost didn't recognize it.

Where previously the main harbor building was constructed of stone, it now stood as an ugly wooden structure that was entirely human. Squat and square, it reflected desperation and a lack of skill. She remembered a tower that had stood near the middle of the city, rising above all other buildings like a beacon. It had been where the ruling elite had sat and presided over Amathnore. There was no sign of it any more. It hit her anew that her entire people and their legacy was gone. Her heart ached at the loss. How could all this have happened? Her parents had been so unconcerned about the war with the humans. They were so sure they had enough magic and strength to prevail. It was only at the behest of their chief mage that they had put her into the magic stasis just in case it all went wrong. But they had been so sure.

How wrong they had been.

Feeling a wetness on her cheeks, she swiped at the tears. Just in time for Jacek to step up to the railing beside her, his pack on his back.

"You alright?" His guttural voice was unusually gentle.

She nodded. "It's just not how I remembered it." She gestured to the city getting closer by the minute as the Gallant steered slowly towards the pier.

Jacek nodded. "From what I understand it was found as mostly a pile of stone rubble. This was the city closest to the portals the exiles got sent through. So this was where the bulk of them stayed. They cleared out the stone and built anew. Some buildings were able to be saved, and they still stand today, but most of Amathnore is built of wood."

"So I'm guessing the forests nearby are a lot smaller than they used to be?" Aleni didn't mean it to sound so accusatory.

He shrugged. "Probably. I don't know, I wasn't alive three hundred years ago." He looked down at her with amusement in his eyes. "You were, though. You realize that makes you way older than me."

The thought hadn't occurred to her. She obviously hadn't aged in the stasis chamber, but technically she was over three hundred years old. If only that meant she had matured along with it. Then maybe she wouldn't be so vulnerable.

The Gallant finally docked at the pier, a couple of sailors jumping to the plankings to tie off the lines. Jacek passed Aleni her bag.

"Make sure to keep your head and ears covered as we go through the city. Your hair is distinctive as well. Might pay to keep your hood up."

Aleni nodded, pulling up the fur-lined hood and tucking her long white hair into it.

"And try not to look people in the eye too much."

She gave him a questioning look.

"I've never met a human with eyes that blue. They're... memorable. We don't want anyone looking too closely."

Surprised, Aleni hadn't realized her eyes had that effect. They were fairly normal for an elf. But Jacek's eyes, a light brown, did seem more common for the humans she had met. They mostly had more olive skin than she did as well.

Jacek stood next to the boarding plank and held an arm out to invite her to go ahead. "Age before beauty."

She couldn't help a small smile as she crossed the board in front of him.

With Bandur padding along behind them, they disembarked from the Gallant. Deems followed closely behind. When they were about to leave the pier, he called out to Jacek.

"Don't forget my offer, Jacek. It still stands."

The mercenary merely nodded and turned away. What was that about? Had the captain made an offer for her to Jacek? Or did it have nothing to do with her? She shook her head to herself. It didn't look like he was going to take him up on it, so she should just let it go. She knew she was being slightly paranoid, but her experiences so far warranted the vigilance.

The harbor was busy, with sailors and stevedores all around carrying crates and cargo either coming off a ship or being loaded onto one. Two other ships were moored in the harbor, looking in better condition than the Gallant. They must have missed the storm. Captain Deems would have quite a job ahead of him, getting his ship repaired.

Aleni looked back at the vessel, wondering if she would ever see the man again. She had liked him, even accidentally saved his life. Although, thanks to him she now knew of her burgeoning power. She had tried again in their cabin to lift something with her mind. But the best she got was getting the candle to wobble and nearly catching the room on fire. That hadn't been the best idea.

Hopefully, it would grow with time. Her parents hadn't told her much about gaining different powers. They probably assumed they had plenty of time. She would have to work it out on her own now.

As Jacek led her towards the main city center, Aleni observed how the humans lived. The buildings were roughly made, with little skill involved. Some looked like they were only just staying up, being propped up by makeshift posts or long straight tree limbs. She marveled that the inhabitants managed to stay alive in the cold climate. The houses appeared very drafty.

The people looked dirty and ragged. Most were very thin, especially the children, who stayed close to their homes - none played in the street. The adults they passed watched Jacek mistrustfully, holding their young ones close or shuffling them inside the shacks they called home.

Aleni walked behind Jacek, looking around her in astonishment. This was not a flourishing society. It was most certainly a far cry from the one she had grown up in. Passing an alley between two shacks, she noticed an oddly shaped lump in the snow. Stepping closer, she realized with horror that it was a body. A stick-thin dog sniffed around it, possibly looking to eat. Bandur let out a low growl. The dog in the alley backed up a few paces.

A large hand gripped her upper arm. She turned to see Jacek pulling her away. She hadn't even realized she had stopped to gawk.

"Leave it," he said.

"But won't someone want to know? They might have a family that need to be notified."

"They know."

"And they're just going to leave it there?!" She didn't even know if the body was male or female. What sort of society left their dead to rot in the snow in an alley?

Jacek met her eyes and nodded sadly. "It's just how it is. It's how it's always been. Eventually, someone from the family might come and take the body and bury it out in the woods somewhere. But that could be some time from now. There's no hurry. The snow will keep the body from decomposing."

"And what will keep that dog from eating it?" She pointed back towards the alley.

The corners of his mouth dipped. "Nothing. The dog will live a while longer. It's lucky."

Aleni let out an angry huff and shook off his hand. She knew it wasn't his fault, but she needed to feel angry at someone. With another look back at the body in the alley, she finally followed Jacek on.

After another five minutes of walking, they started seeing shops as they made their way through the streets towards the center of the city. What stood for shops were slightly better put together than the houses, but not by much. There was a butcher, with his table outside under a canvas awning, chopping at the carcass of a pig. He looked up at them with a scowl as they passed. Aleni lowered her gaze self-consciously, remembering what Jacek had said about her eyes.

The warm smell of baking bread gave away a bakery. Heartened at the aroma, Aleni was suddenly glad that there was something in this town that felt positive. Something that reminded her of home. She was sure the humans didn't bake the special bread that her people made, but it was a similar scent.

Jacek turned into the bakery, which sent a thrill of pleasure through her. She followed him into the shop, hoping for a taste of something fresh.

The baker stepped up to a counter with a slightly hopeful but wary face. Aleni knew Jacek could be an intimidating sight, with his height and display of weapons, but after seeing the city so far, she wondered if it was just a side effect of living here.

"What can I get you?" The woman asked. Not friendly, but receptive at least.

"We need some travel bread. Something that will last several days." Jacek said.

The woman, a short lady with angular eyes and slightly darker skin, nodded and stepped into the back. When she came out, she had two rounded loaves of dark brown bread. "These'll do. They're a hard bread, but they'll last a while. They're a half Olon each."

Jacek nodded and pulled out the money. "We'll take both of them."

The woman took the coin and placed the loaves in a soft sack and handed it out to him, which he went to grab. But that's as far as he got.

He reached for them and looked like he was trying to close his hand around the neck of the sack, but his hand didn't move. A grimace formed on his face. The woman, not paying attention, let go of the bag. Having watched closely, Aleni acted quickly. In a flash, she caught the sack before it hit the floor, snatching it back as though she had meant to grab it all along.

The baker raised her eyebrows at the quick exchange. "You here for the arena?" She looked both of them up and down. "Might make some good money there by the looks of you."

Jacek shook his head, his hand now cradled surreptitiously in the other, close to his chest. "Not this time. Just passing through. Can you recommend a good herbalist around here?"

She pointed north, towards the center of Amathnore. "Two streets north of the market, past the well. Bergan is his name."

"Thank you."

"Well, thanks for not robbing me." She gave them a flat look.

Jacek raised one eyebrow for a second, then gave her a nod. Aleni hoped they could leave the bakery with the woman a little less wary at least.

"Wow, that was a low bar for a good sale." Aleni commented on their way out.

"Unfortunately for her. Fortunately for us. She could have sold them to us for a lot more."

Once they were outside the shop, Aleni stopped him with a hand on his arm. "What just happened?" She moved to stand in front of him, one hand on her hip, the other holding the sack at her side.

"What?" His sullen look told her he didn't want to talk about it.

"What's wrong with your hand?" She demanded.

"Nothing. It's just the cold." He pushed past her, rubbing the hand in question like he had no feeling in it.

The cold didn't affect her too much. She felt it, sure, but even while she was walking back in the forest with no shoes on, her feet didn't get damage from the cold. Were humans really this fragile? They lived in a cold world. How did they survive? She suspected the cold wasn't the answer, but knew she didn't have any right to pry.

She watched him walk away down the street. He had asked the baker for a herbalist. Was there something wrong with him? Or was it really a cold thing like he said? Maybe he needed more of the 'warming tea'.

Let him have his secrets then. It was none of her business. As long as he kept up his end of the bargain and didn't turn her over to some greedy warlord. Or sell her back to Krodon. She shivered, and not from the cold.

"You coming?" He called back over his shoulder.

Sighing, she hefted the sack over her shoulder and ran to catch up.

The central market was bustling with the wealthier patrons of Amathnore. These people were dressed warmer. Women with fur hoods like her own, long woolen cloaks and warm boots. They wore trousers like the men and were hard to distinguish except for the curves on their chests.

The wealthier men wore their hair long like the women, but their clothing was bulkier. They didn't wear hoods, much like Jacek, who still stood out however, plowing through the crowd like a shark through water. His axe clanked as it hung from his belt, while his great sword on his back told everyone he was not to be trifled with. At the sight of him, people made way, obviously wanting to avoid trouble.

Over the sound of the crowd, her sharp hearing caught a sudden commotion to her left and a scuffle of feet. A shout of anger rang out, and a boy shoved through the crowd at a run. He bowled into Aleni, pushing her violently into Jacek. It was like hitting a wall. She put her hands out to catch herself and felt a slice of pain in her palm. Jacek stopped and turned back to see what was going on.

Aleni watched the boy disappear into the crowd again

without looking back. A man followed him through the throng, calling out to the boy to stop. It sounded like the boy was a thief. Once they had moved on, the crowd went back to their business as though nothing had happened.

"You alright?" Jacek looked blandly down at her.

She realized she was holding her left palm tightly. She pulled her other hand away to reveal a cut along the length of it. Blood was starting to seep out, but it wasn't deep.

"I'm fine. I think I caught my hand on your axe." She pointed with her head to the weapon on his hip. The blade was pointed backwards, and he kept it sharp.

"Let's see." He put his hand out to inspect the wound.

"It'll heal quickly," she said.

He looked at her with a question in his eyes. "Another perk?"

She nodded.

"Must be nice." He looked around before turning to carry on.

Yes, it was so nice being part of an endangered species. Aleni rolled her eyes at his back and used her sleeve to wipe away the blood that had beaded on the cut. She soon followed along silently in his wake, Bandur close behind her.

They spent some time at various stalls, picking out more rations of food for their upcoming journey. Aleni remembered to keep her head down, letting Jacek do the talking and haggling. It was his money anyway. It looked like being a mercenary paid well. He never seemed to be short of Olons.

"Freedom from your sins! Sleep well at night again! These will cure all your worries!" a voice called out from somewhere up ahead. Jacek kept moving steadily forward past the stalls. Aleni tried to crane her head to see what was going on, but she couldn't see past Jacek's massive form.

"For only ten Olons, you too can be released from your burdens. Burdens that may not even be yours! Our ancestors left us with generational curses! The Creed of Redemption can help!"

Jacek finally got clear of the crowd and reached the other side of the market. Aleni saw a man standing on a crate, holding up a small white stone in his hand, crying out more promises. She stared up at him in consternation. Was he selling something?

"You, sir!" The man, garbed in a black monk's robe, addressed Jacek, pointing at him. "You look like someone who needs to atone. I can help you with that."

Jacek shot him an annoyed look as he passed him, but kept moving. Aleni ran to catch up with him, grabbing his arm. "What is he talking about?"

He stopped, half turning to look at her then at the monk on the crate. "He's selling atonement stones. Magical stones imbued with elven blessings, apparently."

Aleni frowned. "Really?"

He scoffed. "No, not really. He's just a con man."

She looked back at the monk. People were gathered around him, listening eagerly it seemed. "He must be good, because people are buying it."

Jacek shrugged. "Well, he has the clout of a religion behind him. Some people will believe anything to make themselves feel better."

"There's an entire religion around this?" Her eyebrows shot up. She eyed the stone in his hand. Curious, she walked with purpose back to the monk.

"Don't -" She heard Jacek say in an annoyed tone, but he trailed off.

"Excuse me sir," she said to the monk.

"Yes, child?" The monk, his head shaved and polished so it shined, bent down a little with a kindly smile on his face.

Bandur, having followed her, growled at the monk. The man gave the dog a frown. Aleni placed a hand on Bandur's head and conveyed a sense of calm to him. The dog stopped his growl, but stayed alert on his feet.

"Can I feel the stone?"

"Of course, dear." He passed the smooth white stone to her hands. "Feel how holy it is. It could be yours, or your father's for only ten Olons."

As soon as she touched it, she could tell it wasn't magical at all. It was just a nicely polished stone. There was a rune carved into it, the sign of the stag. She wondered if the monk knew what it meant, or if it was just picked at random from some ancient elven text. Likely it was random.

She handed the stone back to the monk, giving him a small smile. He looked hopefully at her, then at Jacek, who shook his head. The monk must have decided he wasn't getting anything out of them at that point and turned back to the crowd, starting up his rhetoric again.

Aleni and Bandur joined Jacek again. Another question had been on her mind since they had encountered the baker. "What is the arena?" She asked.

Jacek didn't answer straight away, staring up at the afternoon sun. "It's a place where people fight to earn money. People come to watch it for entertainment. It's a big industry here in Amathnore. Krodon's father, Tarkan runs it. He's based here."

"Hmm, strange. You humans are odd." Aleni didn't quite understand the concept, but she wasn't sure she wanted to know all the details just yet.

Just beyond the market, Jacek turned into a two-storied building that had quite a few men coming and going from it. Inside, Aleni saw several women in low-cut dresses that showed more than any woman outside was showing. A fire roared in a large hearth directly across from the main entrance, which heated the room well. There was less need for layers in here, and Aleni figured out pretty quickly why that was useful.

"Are these people here to copulate with each other?" she asked Jacek. There had been no such establishment in the elven society, with most adult elves either paired off for life or courting their beloved. What exactly was this place?

Jacek gave her an amused look. The first she had ever seen from him. "This is a whorehouse." As though that explained everything.

"What is a whore?"

"It's a woman who sells her body to men to have sex with."

It was a second or two before she realized her mouth had dropped open in shock. Why would a woman do that? Did she not care for her body? Did she have no dignity? She had so many questions, but Jacek had turned away with a small smile on his face toward a busty woman who sashayed over to them.

"Hello handsome." The woman, a pretty blonde with dyed red lips ran her finger down one of Jacek's muscular arms. "How about we go upstairs for some fun?" She grinned up at him.

Jacek merely raised an eyebrow, but didn't move. "I would like to hire you."

"Well, of course, that's the idea isn't it?"

"How much for an hour?"

"Ooh, got some stamina, have you?" The blonde gave Aleni a sidelong wink while her hands ran over Jacek's leather-coated chest. "It'll be two Olons for an hour."

"I'll give you three if you take her and keep her safe upstairs in a room for that hour." He pointed to Aleni.

"Hey!" Aleni said, her hands going to her hips. "You can't leave me here!" What if he didn't come back? What if this was how he got rid of her?

The woman stepped back, dropping her hands. All pretense of seduction was gone. She shrugged. "That's easy money I suppose. Gives me a break."

Jacek handed her three coins and turned to Aleni. "I have some things I need to do and it wouldn't be safe for you to be with me. I'll be back." And with that, he left.

Aleni, her heart pounding, watched him walk out and wondered if her worst fears were coming true. She looked up at the blonde woman, who gazed back at her with a bored expression on her face.

"Come on, let's go upstairs. Maybe I can do your hair or something," she said.

Aleni clamped her hands down on her hood. She had a headscarf on underneath to cover her ears, but the hood helped to keep them hidden more. She followed the woman upstairs, but hoped she didn't have to fight her to keep her hands off her hair.

What had he dumped her in now? Could this woman be trusted?

❧ 10 ❧

Once Jacek was outside the brothel again, he checked the street for any soldiers. He had been on the lookout since arriving in Amathnore. He couldn't believe how much bother the kid had been since they left the ship. She was so curious about everything. Chatty. He had to remember she hadn't grown up in a society like this. But how different must it have been all that time ago with the elves, that they didn't even have whores? He wasn't sure he wanted to live in a society like that.

Not that he used whores much, just he couldn't believe every elf had all their needs met without needing public services like that. It was hard to fathom.

Bandur padded down the steps with him, but Jacek commanded him to stay and guard Aleni outside the building. The dog obediently sat at the bottom of the steps with a noble tilt to his head. He knew his job well.

The baker had said the herbalist Bergan was two streets past the market and after the well. He marched off down the street in search of the herbalist. Spotting the well, he looked around for a likely building. One such building, roughly put together with boards, canvas, and even glass in the windows, had the sign of a three-pointed cudweed leaf above the door. He crossed the street and entered the dimly lit main room.

Shelves from floor to ceiling were filled with ceramic jars with labels and various roots on dishes. Black mint, oglagrass, oya stalk, and of course cudweed leaf. Dried plants and herbs hung drying from the ceiling, brushing the top of his head. He knocked them away from his hair as he stalked through the store. Various herb smells accosted his nose, but the most pungent was a fungus of some sort.

Jacek browsed through the jars, reading the labels. His parents had taught him to read long ago but he hadn't had much chance to practice it over the years. Killing people didn't require much book learning.

The herbalist had better have the medicine he needed. Already his hand was locked in a rigid state. The kid had noticed straight away. Not much got past her keen eyes. She had surprised him with her speed in catching the bag. He was relieved she hadn't pressed any further with her questioning. He did not need her worrying that he couldn't protect them.

In the back of the store, he found a desk with all sorts of mixing bowls and jars of varying sizes where it looked like the herbalist mixed his potions. There was no sign of the man in question himself.

"Bergan!" he called out.

A noise indicated someone had heard him and soon a shuffling of feet came his way. A small old man emerged from the back rooms, his head down. Short and wiry, he sat at the desk and finally looked up at Jacek standing in front of him.

"Who are you?" The old man demanded, craning his neck to peer up with eyes almost hidden in the folds of his face.

"A customer. I need something."

"Really. What is it?" His voice was cracked and dry, in

desperate need of a good strong alcohol to smooth it out. Surely, he had something to help with that?

"I need the potion commonly used to treat Wasting Sickness. It's... for a friend."

The old man eyed Jacek's hand held at his waist. "Right. Well... you'll have to tell your friend I don't have it in stock." He turned back to the desk, grabbing a jar of sage and opening it to sniff.

Jacek clenched his jaw. This wasn't going to go easy, was it? "So make some."

"I can't. I don't have the right herbs here. The boy who gathers them for me went missing two days ago." Bergan didn't look particularly apologetic.

Grinding his teeth and trying to stay calm, Jacek figured the only other way was for him to get the herbs and make it himself. "Can you give me the recipe then?"

The herbalist reared back in indignation, spearing him with a dirty look. "I most certainly can not! A herbalists' medicines are a closely guarded secret. We can't just go around giving out the recipes. We would go out of business very quickly!"

Sudden rage erupted out of Jacek's gut and into his chest. He shot his good arm out and grabbed the small man by the throat, shoving him up against the wall behind him. The chair he was sitting on crashed backwards on to the wooden floor. Bergan's feet dangled a foot off it.

The little man's eyes widened, and his mouth opened and closed like a fish. He let out little choking sounds and slapped ineffectually at Jacek's arm.

Jacek wasn't even sure why he was this angry all of a sudden. Perhaps the fear that was constantly sitting in his gut due to the death sentence he had hanging over him. He knew if he didn't get this potion, he would decline very quickly and he may not be able to recover.

"Do you know who I am?" He growled at Bergan, letting his breath hit the man in the face.

Bergan frowned slightly, trying to shake his head, but Jacek's big hand held him fast.

"Take a closer look at the scar." He turned his face slightly so the scar was directly in the man's line of sight.

It took a few seconds, but realization finally hit Bergan and his eyes widened again in fear. He knew.

"So now you have an idea of what I can and will do to you if you don't give me that recipe. I'm not interested in selling it, I just need it for my friend." He said in a low, quiet voice.

"Alright!" Bergan said, his voice coming out in a squeak. "Just don't kill me!"

Slowly he let the herbalist down until his feet found the floor. He let go and Bergan doubled over, coughing and heaving in great gulps of air. Jacek crossed his arms across his chest, planted his feet and waited.

After much dramatic coughing and spluttering, Bergan straightened and peered up at him, seemingly evaluating the assassin's resolve to follow through with his threat. He should have known Jacek never threatened.

He promised.

Keeping his face blank, and his eyes hard, he stood in front of the herbalist while the old man wrote out the recipe on a piece of paper. Jacek took it from him and studied it. It consisted of six herbs and roots. All of which he knew he could find in the local forest.

"Do you have any of the ingredients here?" He asked.

"Only one. The yegopara stalk." The old man moved to a shelf and brought down a ceramic jar with the label. He lifted out a single stalk and handed it to Jacek. "Peel the fibers off the outside, slice it up finely and mash it into a paste with the other ingredients. Then dissolve it in boiling water to make a tea."

Jacek stared at the herbalist long and hard. "If any of this is incorrect, I will return. You will not be happy. Ever again."

Bergan narrowed his eyes and sneered. "I assure you, I take pride in my work. None of my potions will ever harm anyone. Not good for business." He rubbed at his reddening throat.

"It wouldn't be good for your health either."

"That'll be one Olon, thank you very much." Bergan lifted his chin at him.

Jacek handed over an Olon and walked out of the store, his boots thudding on the wooden floorboards, leaving the now sour-faced herbalist standing there fuming.

After picking up a couple more things in various specialty shops, Jacek made his way back to the brothel. A block before reaching it, he spotted a contingent of soldiers walking his way. He slipped into a side alley and watched the four men from the corner of a building.

Being an assassin had its downsides. Eventually you had to take contracts that angered the wrong person.

They were dressed in black leather and iron chest guards, carrying swords on their hips and pikes in their hands. Walking in a square formation, the men bore the eagle emblem of Tarkan. Warlord Tarkan ruled absolutely here in Amathnore. He controlled the trade, the thieves, even the whores. A sudden thought came to him that the woman he'd left Aleni with might find out what Aleni was and turn her over to Tarkan. But the kid knew to keep her identity a secret.

The soldiers were stationed in all major thoroughfares in northern Selendria, including Milliger's pass, which was where they would need to go to get to the Twilfell Basin beyond. He didn't know what Tarkan knew about Krodon's capture of Aleni, or his loss of her. As far as he knew, Krodon wasn't close with his father, even possibly seeing him as a rival for power. Still, he might use his father's resources to his advantage.

Feeling the need to get back to the brothel quickly, he waited for the soldiers to pass before leaving his hiding spot.

He made his way down the muddy lane to the brothel. The first thing he noticed was that Bandur was gone. That did not bode well.

Storming up the steps to the warm interior, he glanced around for the whore. There she was, sitting by the fire, her dress hiked up to display her legs for all to see. Jacek stormed over to her and grabbed her arm, pulling her to her feet.

"Where is she?" He pressed close to her face, looming over her.

The woman gasped, her eyes darting to either side of her. When her eyes finally focused on his face, she spoke.

"She's gone."

"What?" He shook the woman, frustration and fear clawing at his chest for priority. "Speak quickly, for your life depends on it." Had she figured out who Aleni was and sold her?

"She ran off on her own. Didn't say where to. You didn't pay me enough to chase her around the city."

Baring his teeth, he entertained the idea of throwing her across the room. But that would get him nowhere, except possibly in the sights of Tarkan's men who protected the brothel. They weren't here all the time, but it wouldn't take much for the madam to fetch them.

Letting her go, he rushed out of the warm bordello into the freezing cold again, his breath frosting out in front of him. He scanned the street in both directions, but there was no sign of the girl.

A tanner across the street sat under his porch smoking a pipe. Jacek crossed over to him, putting one foot on the step.

"Have you seen a young girl come out of the brothel over there? Sometime in the last hour?"

The tanner didn't speak, but jerked his thumb east, back behind his shop. Jacek thanked him and turned down the side street in that direction. Only a few people were walking this way, and Jacek asked each one if they had seen her. None had.

Heart racing, he moved along at a faster pace. He asked in at houses along the way, but he either got doors slammed in his face or just a blank stare. Only a couple actually said they hadn't seen her. Most people didn't pay attention to others on the street. It was a healthy way to live in this town. Ignorance was safety.

With a rock-hard feeling in his stomach, he wondered what he was going to do from here. He was getting closer to the arena now, just hearing the roar of the crowd and the occasional clash of weapons. But then another sound over the din turned his head.

Barking. He knew Bandur's bark like his own voice. The dog had been with him for five years now, after Jacek had rescued him as a pup from a cruel butcher who wanted him for dog fights. Jacek had taken the pup and left the man with no teeth. He felt it was a fair bargain.

The barking got closer and Jacek moved toward it, shoving people out of the way in order to see ahead. Finally, he rounded a corner and spotted Bandur running towards him. There was no sign of the girl. The dog reached him, barking furiously and jumping around restlessly.

Jacek squatted down to take the dog's head in his hands, but Bandur wouldn't let him. He kept moving away, as though he was trying to run off in the other direction, looking back at Jacek as if to follow.

Getting the message, Jacek followed him down the street.

As they neared the arena, he started to see vendors lining the street either side, selling street food for the spectators to take in with them.

The arena loomed up ahead of them, a high-walled construction built out of an ancient stone amphitheater built originally by the elves. Jacek figured it wasn't used back then for what filled it now.

Bandur led him to a small back entrance to the arena where they came upon a small hooded figure standing to one side, watching the proceedings within. Aleni.

Not wanting to give her a fright, Jacek stood next to her and waited for her to sense him. It didn't take long. She looked up at him and then turned back to the arena. A fight was currently on, between one man and three soldiers of Tarkan's.

The man was of average skill, but managed to keep the soldiers at bay for a short while until they eventually flanked him and killed him. The crowd roared in appreciation. It wasn't pretty, and with Aleni watching, Jacek saw it in a new light. He saw how violent it really was.

"Have you fought here before?" Aleni asked quietly, looking up at him again. Her light blue eyes bored into him, and he found he had to look away.

He let out a sigh. "A few times... a while ago. When jobs weren't coming in for a time. I had to earn some money, so I signed up as a contender. It was good money." He looked down at his feet, wishing she hadn't asked him that. Would she think less of him for it?

He risked a look up and saw her eyes narrowing slightly and her brows merging into a single line. She went back to watching the attendants in the arena carry the mangled body of the man away. A pool of blood had gathered in the mud where he had fallen. It would mingle with the already reddened mud where many had fallen before him.

A commotion behind Jacek made him turn to see what was going on. Soldiers of Tarkan's had entered the square in front of the arena, pushing people around. One who looked to be the leader, gazed around the square looking for something. Or someone. His eye stopped on Jacek.

The two stared at each other for several seconds, not blinking, sizing each other up. The soldier had a sword at his hip, but he hadn't drawn it yet. Three other soldiers roamed around the square, grabbing people and looking closely at their faces before letting them go. They were definitely looking for him.

Finally, the lead soldier drew his sword and shouted something at his men, pointing with the weapon in Jacek's direction.

The herbalist. It had to be. The self-righteous piece of shit. He must have known Tarkan's men would have wanted him. Even if he didn't, it cost him nothing to tell them the Red Hunter was in town. He would have pointed them in a direction at least.

"Hey kid," Jacek called back over his shoulder.

"What?" She sounded a little sullen. There was no time for an attitude right now.

"Run!"

He grabbed her arm and took off, pulling her along behind him until she got the message and started running with him. Jacek looked back to see the soldiers give chase. They ran down the muddy street past small street vendors with temporary stalls. Jacek grabbed the pole of an awning on one and yanked it down. It fell with a crash across the narrow street. The soldiers behind them tripped on the sudden impediment, sprawling on the canvas and wooden poles, along with the vendor himself.

Aleni kept the pace up well. She was fast, he'd give her that. Bandur loped along easily beside her. She turned right down the next street, Jacek's long legs catching up to her quickly. He spotted an alleyway on their left and pushed Aleni towards it, guiding her in. They ran between the buildings, the cold air rushing against Jacek's face.

Out the other side of the alley, they came out on another street running parallel to the last.

"Which way?" Aleni asked, panting.

Jacek looked down the street both ways, spotting a pile of barrels further down to the right. Perfect. He raced towards them, grabbing the middle one and tipping it so the whole pile fell. Shouts of alarm and annoyance rang out around him as the barrels rolled all over the street, hitting some people and knocking them over. Others were forced to dodge them.

"Quickly, back!" Jacek ushered Aleni back to a small gap between two buildings, just big enough to run between. Using the chaos of the barrels going everywhere, they slipped away behind the buildings.

They ran down between a long line of shacks and shops, heading north. Jacek heard a shout behind him and turned back to see a soldier running up behind him, waving a sword over his head. The gap they were running through was not wide enough to swing it. Jacek stopped and pulled out his knife.

As the man and his sword got closer, Jacek trapped the longer weapon up against the wall with his knife in his good hand and kicked straight out with his foot to catch the soldier in the chest. The man let go of the sword, flew back and landed flat on his back; the wind knocked out of him. His sword fell to the snow. Satisfied he'd bought them some time, Jacek turned back to follow on Aleni and Bandur's heels.

Exiting the rows out onto another street, they turned left and then right again at the next intersection. Jacek glanced back to see if they were being pursued still. He couldn't see any soldiers yet, but he heard the squelching of heavy foot-steps in the mud back around the corner.

Halfway down the next street, Aleni pointed to some crates stacked against the front of a sturdy building. She looked back at Jacek, who nodded. They needed to get some altitude. Aleni practically flew up the crates, barely using her hands. Bandur followed her, used to climbing with Jacek.

Jacek had a slightly clumsier climb since his left hand was still not working properly. But he managed to clamber to the top and step onto the snow-covered roof of the building. Aleni waited for him, but when he was fully on the roof, she started for the other side, keeping low.

Bent over, Jacek followed her, leaping from rooftop to rooftop. When they came to the end of the row of houses, they lay down to peer over the edge and figure out their next move.

Down below in the street, they watched as three of the soldiers met, conferring with one another.

"We'll have to be very careful here." Jacek whispered. "If we're patient, we can get past them without a fight."

Aleni was silent but wide-eyed.

The soldiers parted and went off in different directions to cover ground in looking for them. One walked back down the street they had just been on. Another went off to the right and turned north. The last went right as well but back down a south-leading street.

Once all had moved on, Jacek crawled over to the far-right edge of the roof and rolled off, twisting and landing on his feet. The thick mud helped to soften the landing. Snow from the roof fell all about him in his own personal little storm. He looked up in time to see Aleni jump lightly down and land with her knees bent. Once more he marveled at her grace and lightness on her feet. Especially for someone so young. She would make a good assassin. He had had to work hard at moving silently for someone so big. She just did it inherently.

Holding out his arm and patting his chest with the other, he waited until Bandur leaped down into his arms, the dog once again showing his complete trust in his master.

Checking both ways of the north-bound street, Jacek led the way crossing over to the other side where a brewery was located. A water barrel sat against the side of the building, and he jumped up on it to grasp the roof of the brewery. Muscles straining in his good arm, he struggled to pull himself up. Just when he thought he couldn't make it and would have to drop down again, a force pushed up under his dangling feet, propelling him up onto his stomach. Taken by surprise, he hung there for a second before he got his leg up under him and rolled his body onto the roof.

Looking back down, he saw Aleni gazing back up at him, her palm up in the air. Slowly she lowered it and then leaped onto a vertical beam going up the wall and shimmied up to join him.

Jacek stared at the girl. He hated that he had needed help, but was a little shocked that she had given it. Her power seemed a little intermittent at this point. What triggered it? Maybe she didn't even know. She ducked her head at his scrutiny.

"You're welcome," she said.

"I don't need your help."

"Sure you don't," she threw back at him.

With a snarl he got to his feet and made his way over the rooftops, ignoring the kid. He assumed she was behind him, but as usual, she made no noise. The last intersection appeared before them, with the road leading out of Amathnore ahead. On the opposite side, a stable offered horses for sale. Jacek had bought from them before. In the middle of the intersection, the lead soldier stood guard, his hand on his sword pommel.

Jacek ground his teeth. He could just shoot the soldier with his bow, but he didn't want to leave bodies behind, which might induce Tarkan to hunt him further. They didn't need that kind of heat right now. This was bad enough. He mentally kicked himself for having to be heavy handed with the herbalist. But he hadn't seen any other way. It was all once again because of his stupid illness. Everything he did to try to remedy it just made everything worse.

Sighing, he retrieved a smoke bomb from his pouch. They would need to move fast once he threw it. He gave Aleni a look that he hoped said, be ready. She nodded, gripping Bandur's scruff.

He lined up the shot and threw, watching as the thin ceramic casing smashed and released the powder and liquid that combined to create the smoke. The soldier looked down and started coughing, raising his hand to his mouth.

As one, Jacek and Aleni leaped down. Aleni must have used some power to help Bandur get to the ground safely. She let the dog go and they all took off across the square. While Aleni and Bandur circled the smoke-encased soldier, Jacek rushed at him, his knife held aloft. He brought the handle down on the top of the soldiers' head, knocking him out cold. The body crumpled to the ground.

Without losing stride, Jacek joined Aleni on the other side, where they entered the stable. The stable hand came rushing forward, probably at the sound of the scuffle outside. Jacek produced several Olons of his dwindling supply and pressed them into the young man's hand.

"Two horses. Quickly."

The man opened two stalls, where a tall dun stallion and a smaller white mare were stabled. He rushed to put bridles on them, while Jacek threw a blanket from the stall door over the dun.

Once they were ready, they threw themselves up on their mounts and rode out of the stable at a gallop. Turning onto the road leading out of town, Jacek looked back to check if they were being pursued. Only the soldier left lying in the square was to be seen, fading clouds of smoke dissipating around him.

He hoped that meant they had made a clean break.

❧ 11 ❧

Krodon hated the city of Amathnore. He hated the stench, the sight of the slums, the sounds of the poor people, and most of all he hated the sprawling fortress on the eastern side. This was where he had grown up. Where his father kept his court. Where his mother died.

His ship made landfall by midday on the third day of the voyage. The sailors had managed to skirt the edge of a storm and come out unscathed. Stepping onto the dock, he gritted his teeth at the necessity of being here again. When he left over three years ago, he hoped he wouldn't have to return for a long time. Or at all.

But his plan was too important to put feelings first. He needed that girl back. And with her moving through his father's territory, it forced him to have to use his father's resources to find her. If that's what it took, he would humble himself before his tyrant of a father and ask.

A contingent of ten men followed dutifully behind him. He stalked through the city toward the fortress, determined to get it over with.

At the gates of the keep, two guards stood in his way,

demanding to know who they were. Filled with self-impor-tance, the guards tried for a fierce mien but only achieved a vaguely maligned stance.

"You must be new." Krodon said. "Step aside before I kill you where you stand. I am Krodon, Tarkan's son." He lowered his chin and stared through his eyebrows at the first guard, who shifted his feet uncomfortably. The man looked back at his fellow guard, flicking his head back at the castle. The other man ran off, presumably to check with a superior.

Krodon sighed, knowing he would get nowhere by bullying his way in. His ten men were nothing compared to what his father could bring to bear.

The chill wind blew in off the ocean and tugged at the furs sitting across his shoulders. With the salt tang came the odor of dead fish, no doubt reinforced by the nearby shacks and what passed for meals produced inside them. Krodon couldn't stand being anywhere near the common people. He clutched the hilt of his sword with impatience, his palm creaking over the leather grip.

After a few minutes the call came back to let them through. They were led through the courtyard, up the main steps and through the entrance to the castle. Along the way, sets of guards stood to attention in their black leathered armor topped with shining steel breastplates. Steel was rare in Selendria, so the overt use of it in armor was a show of wealth and power. Of which Tarkan had the lion's share.

On entering the main throne room, with its sunken floor in the middle and red and black trimmings, Krodon was flooded with memories. Right over there, by the west window was where he had punched his fist through the glass in a fit of anger at his father. Right after his father had beaten his mother to death on the steps leading to the throne.

Right there.

Krodon stared at the spot, the flagstones still discolored from the bloodstain. His mother, the only one who had showed him love, who tried to shelter him from his father's wrath, had begged him to stop while he beat her. But in the end, her face a pulpy mess, had died staring at her son, love still in her eyes.

"My son," Tarkan said, breaking the spell.

Krodon lifted his face and finally looked at his father again after three years. Time had aged him a little more. Or maybe it was the drink. His round face was mostly hidden under a thick bushy black beard, with his crooked nose sticking out of the middle of it. Intelligence peered out over the top of shadowy bags hanging under brown eyes. His black hair stopped just below his shoulders, half of it tied back with a strip of leather. A rounded belly protruded out of the huge stone chair he called a throne. He'd had it carved out of a boulder that had once been the pet rock of a giant from the northern steppes. Tarkan had lost a fair few men in killing the giant, after which he took the boulder as a trophy. As well as the giant's head.

"Father." Krodon clasped his hands behind his back and tried to look at ease. Bored even. He eyed the large body-guard to the left of the throne, a mountain of a man who did not look at ease. He looked ready to fight.

"It's been a long age since you've deigned to darken my door. What have you been up to down there in the south?" Tarkan leaned back on the throne, his hands resting lightly on his large belly.

"As if you don't know." Tarkan would have had spies keeping an eye on him. He didn't trust anyone, let alone his only son.

"I want you to tell me." This was a test, for sure.

Krodon swallowed. "I've been building up men to serve me. Just a small force, nothing too big. I've subjugated the small town of Roguevale, where they pay tax to me for protection."

"Protection from what?"

"They've had problems with Goblin raiders. They're coming out of the hills and pushing further into inhabited land. I think they're desperate for food. My men keep them back out of the town."

Tarkan nodded approvingly. "Good use of a local problem to profit. I see you've learnt at least one thing from me over the years. You might not be a complete loss."

Krodon, despite his history with his father, found himself filling with a little pride at the backhanded praise. He puffed his chest up, but tried to keep his face neutral. However, the action was not lost on Tarkan, a slight smirk playing on his lips. Then Krodon remembered Tarkan's strategies. He first built someone up and then ripped them back down again.

"Is this your entire force?" Tarkan asked, gesturing to the men before him. His tone indicated he was not impressed.

"Of course not. Why would I bring them all with me?"

"I figured ten men might be all you could pull together."

Krodon clenched his jaw, not even bothering to answer him. He wasn't going to let him bait him into something.

"Why are you here now?" Tarkan finally moved on.

"I'm looking for the Red Hunter. He stole something from me and I want it back. I was hoping your men had seen him. He was reported heading for Amathnore."

"The Red Hunter? Hmmm." He put a finger dramatically to his lips. "Now it's funny you should mention him. My men did just see him this afternoon. I'm told they chased him through the streets."

Krodon's heart quickened. Could it be that easy? Could his father have captured him already?

"Yes? And?" He tried to keep his tone modulated.

"He gave them the slip."

"What? Why didn't you pursue him further?" Krodon let a little anger creep in. Frustration was pushing at him, making it harder to keep calm.

"They were only following up on a claim that he assaulted a local herbalist. I had no bigger reason to capture him. What did he steal from you?"

Krodon kept his mouth shut. He didn't need to know. "I want access to your resources in tracking the Red Hunter down."

Tarkan laughed, a deep, throaty sound that was ominously far from a happy sound. "You are no match for the Red Hunter! He is the foremost killer in this land." He pointed a finger at Krodon. "If he took something from you, then you deserve to lose it. There is no getting that back. Call it a loss and go home, son." Tarkan waved his hand in the air dismissively.

Krodon clenched his fists, rage boiling in his gut. How dare he? The coward had never fought his own match before in his life. He just used his fists on defenseless women instead, calling it a win. Well, he would show him.

"You think I'm incapable father? Well, let's see." He took a deep breath. This was harder to say than he thought. "Fight me. Show me what you've got." He took a step back, gesturing to his men to back up and give them room. "Come down from your pathetic throne and challenge me!" He shouted the last two words, trying to goad him into accepting.

Tarkan merely smirked and flicked a finger from the side towards Krodon. The huge bodyguard next to him stepped forward, looking eager. Oh, so he had a champion, did he? No matter. He would finish him first.

"Gattas will fight you, if you are insistent on trying to prove yourself. But know that you will look all the more stupid once he puts you on the ground," Tarkan said.

Krodon threw off his cloak, throwing it to one of his men, who caught it deftly. They had backed up to the sides of the court, trying to look confident. This hadn't been the plan, but this was what was happening now.

Gattas stepped down onto the sunken floor, flexing his gratuitous muscles. His skin, a deep bronze, gleamed over toned and bulging biceps. His torso, wide at the shoulders and narrow at his waist, displayed overbuilt pectoral muscles pushing their way out of a sleeveless thick leather jerkin. There probably weren't any sleeved clothes that would cover those ridiculous arms.

Drawing his sword from his hip and swinging it all in one movement, Gattas pushed forward with long strides and a snarl on his face.

Krodon drew his own sword and caught Gattas' strike with a clash. Despite the bigger man's size, Krodon had his own strength, and the two pushed backwards and forwards in a measuring dance. Knowing that the big man represented his fathers' strength, Krodon bared his teeth at the champion.

With a final push of his blade, Gattas shoved Krodon's sword to the side and lashed out with a left hook to Krodon's face. It caught him square on the chin, throwing him to the ground.

Shaking his head to recover from the blow, he sensed movement and rolled back instinctively. Gattas' sword point hit the stone floor with a spark right where his head had been. Jumping to his feet, his sword still in his hand, he blocked another swipe toward him. The two traded strikes, blocking and parrying each in turn. Gattas pushed his size advantage, trying to get Krodon to trip on the steps, but Krodon was well aware of his footing and danced away.

Seeing the frustration in Gattas' eyes, Krodon wondered what his next move would be. They were still trading blows, but it was getting nowhere. Krodon grinned at him, knowing he was just as good a swordsman.

A foot flicked out towards him, catching his knee. Gattas hadn't given anything away, and it took Krodon by surprise. His leg crumpled, and he went down on the knee which pinged with pain. Before he knew it, Gattas hit him in the face again, the massive blow making the room sway. Krodon glimpsed his men shifting uneasily on the sides of the room, their hands on their swords.

Just then, the fight was momentarily interrupted by the throne room doors opening and twenty of Tarkan's soldiers parading in to take up space on the opposite side to his men. If there was going to be a battle in here, the odds did not look good anymore. Not something Krodon was happy with.

Gattas threw his foot out to connect with Krodon's chest, who tried to catch the foot, but he was too strong. He flew back, landing on his back.

Enough of this.

From a small pocket at his belt he produced a ring. He slipped it on his middle finger and instantly a flood of energy flowed through him. He sat up and spat blood before grinning at Gattas, who looked perplexed. The champion turned his head back to Tarkan, who nodded and flicked his hand at Krodon.

Shrugging, Gattas moved forward again, reaching down to grab Krodon by his coat.

He didn't get any further. Krodon caught the champion's wrists in his hands, gripping them like a vice. Gattas struggled to release his hands, but couldn't. Something else was helping Krodon now.

Power flowed out from the ring, one he'd had activated before the elven girl was taken from him. He stood, still holding the big man's wrists. With a twist of his hands, the bones in Gattas' arms cracked audibly. The champion roared in pain, sweat breaking out on his brow.

Releasing him, Krodon lifted his hands, palms toward Gattas. Using the magic, he wrapped it around the champion and lifted him up over his head. Gattas' eyes widened. He couldn't move. Krodon kept a tight hold with the magic.

Krodon flung the champion at the steps before Tarkan. The muscular man landed heavily, his shaved head bouncing off the stone, stunned. Krodon quickly followed up with a tendril of power to wrap around the man's throat, choking off his air supply. Gattas gasped and grabbed vainly at the invisible thread around his neck.

The whole time, Krodon stared at his father, wanting him to witness his power. He wanted him to feel helpless, like he once did as a child; wanted him to know what his son had become.

Without looking at his victim, Krodon moved his fingers and the tendril of power snapped Gattas' neck. The big man lay still in front of Tarkan with his head on an angle, eyes blank.

Tarkan leaped to his feet, outrage written on his face. At the same time, his men drew their swords. Krodon's men also drew their weapons, readying themselves. Both companies waited for orders from their commanders.

Krodon had eyes only for his father. He stalked back and forth, watching the older man.

"What have you done!?" Tarkan demanded.

"I've won, that's what, father."

Tarkan, his fists clenched and his chin down, breathed heavily in and out, the breath hissing between his teeth. "I should have put you down as a pup. But your mother pleaded with me not to." He pointed at Krodon. "She argued that I could train you up to support me and we could take over Selendria together. And I stupidly listened to her. Until I put an end to her whining finally. But still I stayed my hand. I thought you could be useful to me. But I was wrong. You are nothing. You will never be anything! I will put you down now for good!" Spittle flew from his mouth, his rage unchecked. "Men!"

Tarkan's men rushed forward, moving down into the sunken area of the room. Krodon's men moved in to meet them with a crash. Krodon held a shield of power around himself and moved through the soldiers, swords bouncing off an invisible sphere.

Tarkan himself drew his own sword and stepped over Gattas' body. On the stairs, father and son met. Krodon caught Tarkan's sword with magic from the ring and ripped it out of his hand. He threw it to the side.

His father tried to swing a punch in to hit him, but he just hit the shield instead. Snarling in frustration, he screamed wordlessly at Krodon, who just smiled weakly. He swung his fist at Tarkan's face, where it connected with a crunch. Bone and flesh gave way under the strength of his power. Tarkan dropped to the steps, raising his hands to ward off another attack. His cheek looked concave, the surrounding skin ripped open from the blow.

Krodon pounded his fist down on his father's face again and again. Around him, the fight between the two groups of soldiers raged on. But all Krodon could see was his father, growing bloodier and bloodier. Flashes of his mother's face that day flew through his mind as his fists rained down.

Finally, when Tarkan's face was no longer recognizable, Krodon stopped, his breath heaving. He staggered to his feet, staring at the pulpy mess that used to be his father.

"Stop!" He yelled, his voice echoing through the room.

The crashes and clangs behind him came to a sudden end. He turned to face the men.

"Tarkan is dead." He paused, letting the news sink in to

the soldiers in black. "I am now the warlord of this castle. Everything that was my fathers' is now mine." He pointed to the soldiers. "Pledge your loyalty to me and I will be merciful. Defy me and die here, right now." He turned his finger to point to the ground.

Tarkan's men looked around at each other. Within moments they were all filing up in front of him, kneeling in obeisance. Krodon's men put their swords away and stood to attention, their heads held high in pride.

Once all the soldiers had pledged to him, he released them to go and spread the word throughout the fortress. He had to plan the search for the girl and the Red Hunter. He had an entire army now to hunt them down. They wouldn't get far.

He walked out of the throne room, leaving his father's body lying on the stone. The blood trickled down the steps to mingle with the faded blood of his mother.

_ 12 _

They rode fast for several miles out of the city. Jacek only slowed when he was certain they were not being followed. It was heading into evening when he finally pulled them back to a trot and then down to a walk to let the horses rest. The road took them through a valley of low hills, twisting and turning between them. The setting sun left a fiery trail behind it, disappearing into the hills. The kid looked tired from the run. He guessed that while she was a good rider, she wasn't used to spending so much time in the saddle.

He thought back to the events of the afternoon. Tarkan's men weren't well trained, but there were a lot of them. They could be quite a worry going forward. Tarkan had a lot more resources than Krodon. He would have to factor that in to their plans.

Then there was the new dynamic of Aleni's powers. Where did they fit into it all? Could he rely on them in the future? He had to admit, they'd been useful. He couldn't normally take Bandur up on a rooftop with him. He gazed down at the black and tan dog next to them, his tongue lolling out of his mouth, panting heavily from the run. Bandur had followed the girl up those crates like it was nothing. She definitely had some connection with him.

Which would make it harder when they would inevitably have to part ways in the future.

It was then that his left hand started to shake. It had been numb since Amathnore, but now it definitely trembled. His arm ached right up to his elbow. Looking at it made him feel like an old man so he tucked it into his jerkin to keep it still.

"Is your hand still not working?"

He startled slightly at the sound of her voice. They'd been quiet for so long and it felt odd to have the silence broken.

"It's fine. It's none of your business." He knew he sounded gruff, but he didn't want her prying into it.

"You have said that before. But you don't look well and I am worried." Her accent thickened slightly as she spoke and the formality of it seemed rehearsed. Had she been practicing that in her head? Or was it just the fact she wasn't a native speaker?

"There's nothing to worry about. It's under control. Worry about yourself." He shifted on the horse's back, trying to ease the ache in his backside. "Tell me about your powers. You seemed to have them better under control back there. Could you call on them again if you needed them?" That seemed like a better topic of conversation, since she was so keen on chatting.

She looked down at her hands. "They are... what is the word? Come and go?"

"Intermittent? Inconsistent?"

"Probably one of those. Or both. I am still learning some of your words. I tried back on the ship to use them in the cabin to practice, but I could not get them to work. But in the heat of the moment, it seemed natural. Now... again, I cannot." She looked frustrated with herself. He knew the feeling when it came to his own body.

"I'm guessing this is something your parents would usually teach you about?"

She nodded. "I know from watching other members of my clan that magic comes slowly as they reach a certain age. And they must learn to control it, like any other skill."

"Does everyone get the same magic?"

She shook her head. "No. Some will be gifted at healing, others will be better at reading minds or lifting objects."

His ears perked up at the mention of healing powers. "But you can't heal, can you?" He knew it was risky to ask, but at this point he had to.

"No, of course not. My own body will heal by itself rather quickly, and I will not get sick like you humans seem to, but that is a passive power we are all born with. Some elves theorized that it wasn't even magic at all, but just a feature of our makeup. Built into our cells like feathers on a bird."

Jacek thought about it for a bit. He knew from what his parents had taught him that the world his people originally come from had more scientific knowledge than they had here and now. A lot of knowledge had been lost because they were exiled and cut off from their people. Some had been retained, but they couldn't use it because they didn't have the industry here to facilitate it. He often wondered what Selendria would have been like if his people had come willingly, bringing all the wonders of the old world with them. There were some stories that had been passed down, but it was impossible to tell what was a myth and what was truth. Stories had a tendency to get embellished over time. His own legend was a prime example.

"It does make sense," he replied. "I'm sure your elves were very smart people. They lived for a long time, didn't they? So, they would have had a lot of time to develop scientific and medical knowledge."

"Yes, our scientists and mages were extremely smart. They were always coming up with new ways to improve our living standards. We had indoor plumbing and heating. I don't think you have those here, do you?" She turned her head to look at him.

"No. But I believe it existed in the world we came from. And more."

"Did the Arena come from your world too?"

There was silence between them for a few seconds. Eventually Jacek spoke. "The arena was invented by Tarkan. He had a thirst for blood that needed to be slaked. Once it was built and running, he found many other people thirsted for it as well."

"Did you?" There it was. Hesitation in her voice. Accusation hiding behind it.

"I did what I had to do to earn money. I'm not proud of it." He looked out across the low foothills, trying to find something to look at other than her. "There's something you have to understand in this life. Most of the time it's kill or be killed. If you want to survive, there are things that must be done."

"Kill people for sport?"

He winced. "When you put it like that it doesn't sound so good."

"It sounds horrible."

"Alright it's horrible. I admit, it wasn't the best decision I ever made. But this is what I do for a living." He hated saying it out loud, but it was best that she fully understood what kind of person he was. "I kill people for money. I steal for money. And I'm good at it." There. Maybe now she wouldn't get too attached and would be happy to move on on her own when this was all over.

Then why did it feel painful to admit it to her? When did he start caring what she thought of him?

He opened his mouth to say something more when he heard the distant thudding of galloping hooves. They were getting louder. He twisted on the dun to look back down the road. Four riders rushed toward them, their mounts kicking up the dirty snow behind them. The black leather and silver breastplates gave them away even at this distance.

"Tarkan's men!" Jacek wheeled the stallion around to face them.

"Shouldn't we run?" Aleni asked.

"There's no point now. The horses are tired as it is, and we have nowhere to go. The only thing we can do is make a stand." He took his pack off and threw it on the road. He rolled his shoulders to limber up.

"But your hand! You are not up to a fight." She turned her mount to join him, but she didn't look happy.

"Never mind about me," he growled as he pulled out his knife and handed it to Aleni. She took it hesitantly. "Just in case," he said.

Drawing his axe and kicking his heels into the dun's flanks, he took off toward the oncoming soldiers at a gallop. As he neared them, he sized them up. They rode in a tight square formation, swords out and focused looks on their faces. Amateurs. Three of them were right-handed and one was left. The lefty was in the back.

Jacek held his axe aloft in his right hand, looking for all the world like he was going to smash into the middle of the soldiers with his horse. He had only seconds before the clash. Then it would be chaos.

At the last moment, he swerved the dun to the left. He pulled his leg up to push off the horses' back and leaped into the midst of the tight group. His size and momentum took them all down to the ground, horses and people falling together in a tumble of arms and legs. The horses screamed in fright as they fell. With most of the soldiers having their swords on their right, they found their weapons stuck under the pile of animal and human bodies.

On top of the pile, Jacek had sunk his axe into the neck of one of the front soldiers as he landed. Blood spurted out, and the man screamed in pain and terror. Jacek scrambled to his feet and jumped away from the pile of people. One of the soldiers had managed to get to his feet as well and faced him now with his sword pointed out in front. He looked to have a few years' experience under his belt. He was at least holding the sword on the right angle. Should he give this one a chance?

The man lunged toward him, stabbing out with his sword. Jacek knocked it to the side with his axe while jumping back out of the way. Once again, the soldier pressed in, swinging in a wide arc at Jacek's head. He blocked it and stepped in to kick at the man's knee. Too late he saw the punch coming in from the other hand and barely got his weak arm up to deflect. The blow still hit his jaw and knocked him sideways. He staggered to the right, stunned, but kept his feet.

From the corner of his eye he saw movement, and only just got his axe up in time to block the sword coming down. Still the blade tip bit into his left shoulder and a spear of pain forced a grunt out of him.

Gritting his teeth, he bunched his leg muscles and pushed back with his axe, forcing the soldier to stumble backward. Pressing in, he followed through with a brutal overhand stroke and embedded the axe head deep in the collarbone of the soldier. The man roared in pain and dropped his sword. Jacek tugged the axe out as though the man was a block of wood and finished him off with a strike to the head. The body collapsed to the road.

Breathing heavily and with the countryside around him

spinning from the blow he'd taken, Jacek stumbled back to assess the situation with a glance. The last two soldiers looked down at what was left of their comrade in horror. Their mouths agape, they fixed their eyes back on Jacek.

"I'm sorry, were you two close?" Jacek said.

The younger one gritted his teeth and charged at him. Belatedly, the other followed suit. Eventually he was forced to give ground at the wild incoming thrusts from the younger enraged soldier. Jacek tried to block each one while looking for an opening. Normally he would be able to use his sword in his other hand but that wasn't an option now. He really didn't like this new reality he lived in. Maybe this was how he would die. At this point, it was far better than the alternatives.

When he was about to step to the side to dodge a downward strike, the other soldier stepped in to stab at his right hand. He tried to jump back, but the sword nicked his fingers. The axe slipped out of his hand.

He had only one choice at that point and very little time to do it. He launched himself at the younger soldier, his hand outstretched to grab his neck. The soldier deflected his hand in time but fell under the weight of the big mercenary. As he went down, he heard barking and a low growl. Bandur was wading in to the fight.

The two wrestled in the dirty snow for dominance. At any moment Jacek expected a sword to come down on his back from the last soldier. But with growling from Bandur and what sounded like something in his mouth, no blade bit into him. He heard a yell and a scream and the sound of a body falling. Was the kid alright? He had no chance to look around.

He discovered it was difficult to grapple with only one working hand. The soldier was on top of him now. Twice his elbow came up to collide with the side of Jacek's head. He was starting to hear ringing in his ears, and he wasn't sure if it was because his brain was being jostled inside his skull or because he was about to pass out from exhaustion. His body had had enough and he knew it.

Shaking his head to clear it, he rolled the young man over with a deft move of his leg and pushed his forearm down hard on his throat. A gurgle emitted from the soldier as he choked for air. He batted at Jacek's head with his hands but the assassin just leaned back further. Both their breaths were coming in gasps now - the soldier trying to get air and Jacek with exhaustion.

With a final push and a twist of his arm, he broke the young man's neck.

Heaving for air he leaned on the soldiers' chest for a moment. After several seconds he pushed himself up and got to his feet. The last soldier lay dead on the road behind him. He was on his back, lying in a pool of blood that was growing around him. His sword arm was bloody with the sleeve ripped. Bandur stood next to the body, growling. His mouth was stained red.

Aleni stood over the soldier, Jacek's knife in her hand. The blade dripped with blood.

"Did you -?" Jacek pointed at the man on the ground.

She looked up at him with wide eyes. "He was going to kill you. I had to do something."

"Huh." He hadn't actually thought she had it in her. He had only given her the knife as a way to protect herself if he failed. Perhaps he had underestimated her. She didn't look happy about it though. Her mouth had dropped open, her top lip curled back. She obviously didn't plan on doing it again anytime soon.

His head was still buzzing like an angry bee. Aleni was starting to look fuzzy, even though she was only standing a few feet away. His stomach tilted and the surrounding hills moved slightly.

"Are you alright?" Aleni asked. "You don't look well."

He tried to speak but his mouth wasn't working right for some reason. Finally, his vision blanked out, and he remembered nothing more.

Aleni sat on her horse, watching Jacek gallop toward certain death and wondered where she could run to. If she remembered rightly, this road led into a forest. Maybe she could lose the soldiers in there? Fighting Jacek would slow them down and give her time to get away. But something rooted her to the spot as she watched the fight play out. She couldn't bring herself to turn the horse away. One soldier died very quickly in the ensuing mess and Jacek put another down in a quick spar. Aleni urged her horse in their direction, starting to hope that maybe he might prevail. He looked haggard but was somehow holding on.

Aleni wasn't stupid though. She knew something was wrong with him. What she didn't know was why he wouldn't admit it to her. Was it pride? She didn't put it past him. She had known many older male elves who had been driven by pride. It wasn't a strictly human failing.

She gripped the knife in her hand like it was a rope from which she hung. Her lifeline.

When she saw Jacek's axe fall from his hand, she dismounted and ran towards the men. A voice inside was screaming at her to run away. She had no business being in a fight with grown men and swords. But something drove her forward. Bandur ran alongside her, sticking close.

Jacek was on the ground struggling with a soldier on top of him. The other soldier stood behind them, his sword at the ready. When they rolled over and Jacek's back was exposed, the soldier raised his sword.

Aleni put out her hand to stop him with her magic. The soldier hesitated, as though something had brushed him. But she felt the magic falter. It wasn't flowing through her now like back in Amathnore. Straining at whatever sat inside her, she tried to force the magic out through her fingers. But it was no use. The man gave her a puzzled look, then moved to strike Jacek again.

Bandur barked and rushed in to grab the man by his sword arm with his sharp teeth. He growled and pulled on the soldier who cried out in pain and fear.

Aleni ran forward and jumped on the soldier's back. As she did, she plunged the knife down into the top of his back, just below the nape of his neck. He cried out and his legs folded. Aleni rode him down to the ground, twisting the knife as they fell. Kill or be killed. She knew from their encounter with the goblins that she was dead without Jacek.

She stepped back from the soldier. He lay on his side, not moving. With her foot she rolled him onto his back and checked his throat for his life pulse. Nothing.

Aleni looked down at the bloody knife still in her hand. What had she done? Who was she becoming?

Hearing a sickening crack, she looked over in time to see Jacek finish off the other soldier. Wavering, he got to his feet. He surveyed the man on the ground, blinking rapidly.

"Did you - ?" He asked.

"He was going to kill you. I had to do something."

He let out a huff of breath. Her mind was still in a slight state of shock, but she noticed Jacek was looking pale. Paler than usual. His eyes bounced around and his hand twitched at his side.

"Are you alright? You don't look well."

His legs gave way suddenly, and he dropped to the ground. Aleni rushed to his side. His body twitched and contorted. She had never seen anything like it. His eyes rolled up in his head and gurgling sounds came from his throat.

Her own body trembled as she tried to hold his arms still. But his muscles were too strong as they jerked back and forward. She didn't know what to do. Was he dying? Did he get stabbed somewhere? She tried to look for injuries, but all she could find was a cut on his shoulder and a shallow graze across the fingers of his right hand. They didn't look serious.

Her own breath burst in and out as she watched him. He looked completely helpless, his body it seemed had taken over, pushing out his mind. It was as though he was being controlled by something else. Aleni feared he would never return. Somehow, that thought alone was scarier than the fact that Krodon was chasing her. She had no idea what to do.

"Jacek! Jacek, talk to me! Come back!" She gripped his shoulders, desperately trying to snap him out of it. But the convulsions continued and he made no indication he heard her.

Bandur stood over him, looking lost. He let out a whine and flicked his eyes between Aleni and his master. Aleni sensed he knew something was wrong. She felt it through their connection. She put a hand on the back of his neck, more for her own comfort than for his.

"It'll be alright. He'll be alright." She kept saying it over and over.

After a long minute the convulsions calmed. His body settled, and he lay still with his eyes closed. Beads of sweat sat on his forehead. Was he dead? Aleni held her hand under his nose. Faint warm breaths still hit her skin. She let out a breath she didn't realize she was holding.

Aleni looked around. It was getting darker now, and he might be unconscious for a while. She had to get him somewhere safe. The road, now covered with bloody snow and dead soldiers, was not ideal.

She retrieved Jacek's horse and his bag. Inside, she found a good length of hemp rope. Walking the stallion to where Jacek lay, she tried to lift him, but only got his head and shoulders off the ground. She heaved and pulled, but she was too small and he was far too big. Sitting back on the snow, his head in her lap, she wondered what she could do. He needed to be up on the horse so they could move.

Could she use magic? It hadn't worked when she tried it before. And even if it did, she had no idea how heavy an object she could lift with it. Clenching her jaw, she knew she had to at least try.

Calming herself, she tried to reach deep inside herself for the elusive power. She closed her eyes and imagined a ball of pure magic, white and incandescent, churning inside her. It built up heat as it grew and burned. Like scooping out a ball of snow, she gripped it with her will and pulled it to the surface.

Despite the frigid air around her, beads of sweat formed on her brow. Slowly she wrapped Jacek in the magic. Without moving a muscle, she willed him to lift up in the air. Inch by inch he hovered up and onto the tall dun stallion, who miraculously stood still the whole time. Carefully she positioned him on his stomach over the horses' back.

Letting out a whoosh of breath, she let go of the power and opened her eyes. She stood and surveyed him lying limply on the horse. Yes, she hadn't just imagined it. It was real.

She tied him to the horse to make sure he didn't fall on the way. It was long past sunset now, but she could see fine in the dark. She hoped she could find the forest and somewhere safe to make camp.

Leading Jacek's horse, she rode off down the road.

Kamde forest lay sprawled on the western side of the northern continent. From the coastline nearly to the Milliger river, the densely packed Bove trees created a protective canopy over the area. Less snow coated the ground here, and it actually felt warmer to Aleni.

She led them deep into the trees and eventually found a nice little hollow to make camp. Soft needles covered the ground in the little ring of trees, making a nice mattress for Jacek to rest on. Aleni got him settled on a fur pelt with his head slightly elevated and a blanket covering him. He slept soundly on. Bandur settled himself to lie at Jacek's head.

She then took his waist pouch and searched through it. If he was sick and knew about it, he might have some medicine. Pulling out a folded piece of paper with a small pouch of herbs, she opened it up. Written on it was a list of ingredients for some kind of medicine. Also in the pouch was a small empty material bag with the last few dregs of a mixture. She held the bag to her nose. Her sense of smell picked out a few different herbs she recognized. They must be the ones on this list. Her people had their own names for herbs, but she thought she could figure out which was which between the bag and the list.

First though, she collected broken branches and dried needles for a fire. She had watched Jacek put one together enough times that she knew she could emulate it. When the fire was crackling away, she set out to find the herbs.

It took her over an hour to find them. She kept smelling the little bag to pick out the various plants and compare them with ones she found. She had learned herbal lore from her grandmother, who insisted she be able to identify various plants and what they could be used for. It was all part of incorporating nature into the way they lived. She was grateful for the lessons now. Hopefully they would keep Jacek alive. For how long, she didn't know.

13

When Jacek came to, he heard the crackling of a fire before he saw anything. His eyes took longer to start working. Slowly he cracked them open, only to squeeze them shut again at the bright light of the fire. It took some time before he could open them without stabbing pain hitting the back of his eye sockets. Next to him sat Aleni, cross-legged on the ground, stripping leaves from a pile of plants in front of her.

He blinked a few times and focused on her. He lay silent, just watching.

"How do you feel?" she asked after a while.

At first, he couldn't find the words to answer. He just stared at her, his brain refusing to work.

She stared back at him, her eyes pinched in a question. She waited.

"Head hurts," he finally croaked out.

She offered him a canteen of water, holding it while he drank slowly.

"What happened? Where are we?" Jacek gazed around at the small clearing, lit up by the crackling fire. The tall trees ended in a thick canopy high above them. They were a perfect protection from the icy elements above. The little hollow was almost cozy.

Aleni answered him after putting the canteen down. "You had some sort of episode of convulsions. I brought you here where you could rest. You slept for some time."

She had brought him here all by herself? She was so small. How had she managed it? He looked at her in a new light. Maybe she was stronger than he had thought.

"How long have you known you were sick?"

Jacek didn't meet her eyes, instead staring up at the tree-tops. Here it was. She knew now. There wasn't much point in hiding it any longer. If she used it against him, he would just have to deal with it. Despite that, the old fear still rose inside him. Here goes nothing. "For about two months now. It started with numbness in my feet. I went to a herbalist, and he told me it was the Wasting Sickness."

"What is that?"

"A disease that will slowly get worse over time. My muscles will seize up, like my hand here." He nodded to his left hand under the blanket. "And eventually it will get harder to breathe until I can no longer draw breath."

"It will kill you?"

"Yes."

"I'm sorry."

"You're not to blame." He met her eyes now. "This is my burden to bear, not yours."

"Is that why you didn't tell me?"

"I didn't tell you because it's none of your business." He knew the words were cutting, but he couldn't help himself. He suspected she was starting to get attached to him, and he had to put a stop to it.

Her face crinkled in response. "Whether you like it or not, we're working together now. When something happens to you like what just happened, it *is* my business. I could have left you on that road to die in the cold. But I didn't. It took a lot of effort to get you here and keep you warm and safe. It seems you need me just as much as I need you. You need to remember that!" She got to her feet and stomped to the other side of the fire, where she sat stiffly and continued preparing the herbs.

Jacek was silent for a long time. He lay looking up at the canopy while she worked. Bandur whined and snuffled at his hair.

He knew why he feared connection so much. Because he had lost everyone he had ever been close to. His parents - killed when he was nine years old. He still missed them, even after all these years. His friend Ham when he was on the streets of Omel Ortheiad after they'd died. Ham was the smallest of the street kids and Jacek had protected him from the older ones. Until one day Ham had betrayed him. Not because of malice, but through weakness of character.

"People are not to be trusted," he finally said, speaking softly into the night. "You can tell yourself you are a good judge of people's intentions. That you can tell if someone will betray you or not. But how can you tell, when that person doesn't even know? The world is a harsh place. And people will sooner or later be put in a position where they have to choose between survival and friendship." He turned to look at Aleni. "The will to survive is a strong one. It's built into each one of us. So, people cannot be trusted."

"And what of honor?" Aleni asked.

He scoffed. "There's no such thing as honor. Not in a world of thieves and murderers."

"I come from a different world. A different time." She raised her chin and looked down her nose at him. "To an elf, honor is everything."

He narrowed his eyes at her.

"You are afraid I will use this knowledge of your illness for my own gain. You believe it makes you vulnerable. But when you trust someone else to help carry you through that, you are no longer vulnerable." She lowered her chin to bore her aqua colored eyes at him. They almost glowed in the dark. "Will you put your trust in an elf?"

That was a good point. She wasn't like everyone else. He wanted so badly to let down his walls and trust her. It sounded less exhausting. And he wasn't sure he had the energy to go on on his own.

Maybe he might just have to risk it.

❧

It was late at night when Krodon got the message that one of his father's patrols was missing. He was getting the feel for his new throne room when the messenger entered the dimly lit hall. Tarkan's body had been taken away several hours earlier, but the puddle of blood and the surrounding splatters still decorated the base of the steps. Krodon wanted to revel in it a little longer. Just to honor his mother's memory. In his mind, it felt right.

Outside the hall, the corridor echoed with rushing footsteps and people calling out. The fortress hummed with activity. The word was being spread that the old warlord was dead. Krodon had the men he'd brought with him monitoring the reaction of Tarkan's troops. So far, the soldiers were receptive to the change in power.

Rooms were being prepared for Krodon and his men. He thought maybe he might send for Arlette and bring her here to Amathnore. She had lived here up to the age of five. He missed her already and wished she was here. Traslek had stayed behind to care for her while Krodon was gone.

"Sir, report from the northern city guard!" The messenger

said. He was a young man with dark hair and skin with a nervous mien.

Krodon didn't bother replying. He sat still on the throne and waited, staring at the messenger.

The boy stopped just short of the blood puddle. His eyes lingered on it, his mouth gaping open to talk but no words made it out.

"Get on with it!" Krodon said.

The boy jumped, his eyes widening. "Ah. Oh, the guard reports that a patrol is missing. They traveled the northern road out of Amathnore to the forest several hours ago and haven't returned. Men have been sent to find them."

Krodon knew that was the direction the Red Hunter and the elven girl had gone in. Had they taken refuge in the forest? It was a dense and wild forest, one two fugitives could easily get lost in. But if the patrol had come across them on the road, it was possible they had been taken down by the Hunter. They could have been ambushed. Despite the mercenary's reputation, he still found it hard to believe four trained soldiers had been bested by one man.

"Voss." He turned to a soldier in red and black leather who was standing off to one side. Voss was trained personally by Traslek. His loyalty could be vouched for completely. "Put together several units of four men each. Two of mine and two of the old guard." He was reluctant to speak his father's name in front of his men again. Time to move on.

"Send them out to patrol the edge of the forest and surrounding areas. I want the Red Hunter and the girl found and brought back to me alive."

"Sir." Voss said. "What condition would you like them in?"

"Feel free to rough the mercenary up, I don't care. But the girl is not to be touched."

"Yes, sir." Voss smartly turned and marched out of the hall.

The messenger was left standing there, seemingly lost as to his next move. He hadn't been dismissed yet.

"I have another job for you." Krodon said. "I need you to go to my fortress near Roguevale and report to my lieutenant, Traslek. Tell him what's happened here."

"Uh, yes, sir." The boy looked unsure.

Krodon frowned. "Is there a problem?"

"Um. I'm sorry sir, I don't know how to get to your fortress." The boy shuffled his feet and looked anywhere but at Krodon.

Krodon stared at him for a long while, seething. He didn't care if the boy didn't know. How hard was it to ask for directions? What kind of people did his father have in his employ?

"Then find out!" Krodon yelled, getting to his feet.

The messenger actually physically jumped back. He started panting heavily, frozen to the spot.

"Get out!" He yelled again. The messenger ran. Krodon returned to the throne, wondering if he should get a cushion for it. Or would that make him look weak?

14

Aleni told him she was making up the medicine for him. Jacek felt around for his pouch, but couldn't find it under the blanket. He scanned around and saw it sitting on the ground next to him. "You looked in my pouch?" Heat flushed through him. The thumping in his head intensified.

The kid didn't look perturbed. "I had to see if you had medicine for what ailed you. I'm guessing you ran out but were planning to make more?" She nodded to the herbs in front of her.

"I got the recipe from a herbalist in Amathnore. He didn't have any more in the shop with him." She cared enough to make it for him? He wasn't sure how he felt about that. His chest loosened a little at the thought.

Boiling a pot of water over the fire, Aleni threw the herbs in and brewed a strong tea. While that bubbled away, she put a simple meal together from their packs. The fresh bread from the baker and some dried meat and cheese.

When the medicinal tea was ready, Jacek drank it slowly while Aleni tended to the cut on his shoulder.

After they had both eaten, Aleni insisted Jacek sleep

through the night while she kept watch. With his body feeling so weak, he didn't put up an argument. He knew he was no good to her or himself if he was dead on his feet.

Bandur kept a watch as well, he knew. The dog stayed close instead of wandering off to hunt like he normally did. The night was quiet as Jacek slipped off to sleep.

In the morning, he awoke to find the fire had gone out. Aleni was sitting against one of the trees on the other side of the hollow, her head slumped to the side in sleep. The horses grazed outside the ring of trees. Bandur sat upright and alert next to him.

He rose and rolled his bedding up, trying not to wake the girl. She murmured and twitched in her sleep. He tried to ignore it as he packed up and erased traces of their campsite. His hand felt better this morning. The cramping and shaking had eased. He flexed it experimentally. The medicine had done its work. Better than the original, in fact. He wondered idly if the kid had infused it with some sort of elf magic. He had no idea if she could even do that, but if she had, it had worked well.

Aleni cried out suddenly and he whipped around, scanning for attackers. But she was still asleep. Her face contorted. Was she trying to escape from something? The dungeon?

He kneeled in front of her, not sure whether he should wake her. Every night she was plagued with these nightmares. They only seemed to be getting worse. She cried out again, her voice raw and visceral, wrenching at his heart.

He gripped her shoulders gently and shook her. "Kid! Wake up."

She wrestled weakly against him. He held firmly but gently as she squirmed, aware of his strength against her lithe frame.

"Come back, Aleni. You're safe," he said.

Her eyes came open with a start and met his. "Jacek?" A sheen of sweat coated her pale face.

"You were dreaming. A bad one." He let her go, awkwardly aware that she might not want to be touched. He stood and went to his pack, finishing with tying it back up.

Aleni got to her feet, rubbing her forehead. Her gaze was lost in the middle distance. Jacek watched her carefully, frantically hoping she wasn't going to run on him again. She moved to her pack and retrieved a cloth to wipe her face. When she had freshened up, she stood and gathered her things. Without a word they mounted the horses and rode off.

They moved through the forest, heading northeast. Neither spoke as they rode. Bandur ranged out from their positions, looking for game for breakfast. The tall trees clung closely together, making it hard to see much further ahead. Jacek was often bending to the side to try to see around trunks and bushes. There was a risk of them running into another patrol. Surely the men from the day before had been found by now.

He kept a close eye on Aleni as they plodded on. The dense trees prevented them from moving very fast, forcing them to ride single file. She rode in front, but her stiff upright posture indicated she was upset. He wasn't entirely sure if it was because of him or because of her nightmare.

As they came to the edge of the trees, the sudden bright sunlight hit their eyes and blinded them for a few seconds.

Without warning, hands grabbed him from the right and pulled him off his horse. Surprised, he hit the ground hard and soon found himself on his knees, held fast by men on both sides. Soldiers.

Once his eyes adjusted to the light, he saw there were four of them. Two wore the black of Tarkan's men, while the other two wore the red of Krodon. Had they actually joined forces? Jacek hadn't thought Krodon and his father were civil enough to achieve it.

His weapons were soon stripped from him and thrown in a pile to the side. He struggled against them. One soldier threw his weight into his fist and drove it into Jacek's stomach. He curled over, gasping for breath. Another blow rained down from above, hitting him in the head. He tenses his muscles, readying himself as more kicks and punches came at him. At a disadvantage on the ground, surrounded by superior numbers, he had to bide his time. Finally, the attacks stopped. He would be bruised later on, but nothing seemed broken. While two men held him, one in red and one in black, a third in Tarkan's armor stood a few feet away with a bow drawn and pointed at him.

"What do we have here?" One of his captors said. "That was a lucky break. Of all the places you could come out of the forest, we happened to be near it. Heard your horses before we saw you."

Jacek struggled against the hands holding him but the two men weren't taking any chances. Their grip was firm. The last was looking at Aleni in a not so friendly way. He motioned with his sword for her to dismount. She silently obeyed. Bandur growled, taking up a position near her, but Jacek commanded him to hold still. He didn't need him getting shot with an arrow.

"What is this?" Jacek asked, trying to draw attention to himself. "Am I right in seeing you're a mixed group of Krodon's and Tarkan's men? Are they working together?"

The man in front of Aleni laughed. He had shoulder-length fair hair and a large brown birthmark over his left eye and down onto his cheek. His red fur-lined coat was dirty and strained at the seams.

"Tarkan is dead. Warlord Krodon killed him. Welcome to

the new army of Krodon's." He held his arms out expansively. "He now controls everything that was once his father's. Including his men." He nodded to the other men in black.

Jacek's stomach went rock hard, his heartbeat spiking. If that was true, there would be many more men out there looking for them. How could they avoid them now? Everything in him wanted to run and hide. He had no reply for the soldier.

The soldier in red turned back to Aleni. "Now girl, what's got Warlord Krodon so determined to find you? What is it about you he finds so alluring? Must be some sweet pussy down there!" The men all laughed.

Jacek glanced at his pile of weapons on the ground not far away. Two steps to get to them. If he could only break free and avoid the arrow that would come flying at his head from four steps away, then he could help her.

Aleni had gone whiter than usual. She was only a child. She probably had no idea what they were talking about. The pressure in Jacek's head grew with every word.

"Leave her alone, she's just a child." Jacek growled at the man.

The man glanced at Jacek, then back at Aleni. "A child that can entertain the Warlord better than any whore!" The group snickered.

"What the hells are you talking about?"

The man frowned at him. "You don't know? Krodon took her up to his chambers most nights. She would spend the night with him." His grin dripped with lust.

His blood ran cold as he took in a shaky breath. He stared at Aleni, who wouldn't meet his eyes. She was so little. How could a man as big as Krodon... his mind recoiled from the image.

She started backing away, her eyes blank. His mind tried to process this new information. There was no way she would have entertained him willingly. Which meant she was forced. Was this what the nightmares were about? His heart broke and he turned his head to the side, closing his eyes tight.

"Now it's my turn to get me some!" The man lunged forward and grabbed Aleni by the arm, pulling her toward him. Strangely, she didn't fight back. The soldier pushed her to the ground onto her back and straddled her.

Jacek started to writhe against the men holding him. "Don't you fucking dare! Get off her!" His voice came out in a hoarse roar.

The man on Aleni pointed back at Jacek. "Hold him tight!" He started fumbling with her clothes. Aleni just lay there as though dead. Jacek silently willed her to start fighting back.

"Don't forget," the bowman said. "The warlord didn't want her touched."

"I won't mark her. He won't know. You won't tell him, will you, sweetie?" The ugly man loomed over her face.

Jacek bucked and twisted, letting out a wordless roar before pulling the man on his left in front of him. A whizzing sound reached his ears and the man let go, an arrow in his back. Jacek used the momentary confusion to launch a weak left hook at the other soldier's face. The man twisted slightly and the blow glanced off his cheek. He followed through with a right knee to the groin to double the soldier over.

By now the archer had nocked another arrow, so Jacek used his former captor as a shield, lifting him slightly off the ground by his throat. The man gagged and grabbed at his wrist, but Jacek used his full height and strength and charged at the archer. He held the soldier in front of him, roaring all the way.

The archer was so surprised by this sudden turn of events that he didn't have enough time to move. All three men fell in a tangle of limbs and weapons. Jacek scrabbled around in the mess until he felt the hilt of a knife strapped to a hip. He yanked it up and immediately back down again to plunge it into someone's back. One of the men screamed. Again and again he stabbed into flesh. He didn't know who, but didn't care. One of them was dead, that was all that mattered right now.

The archer struggled underneath his comrade, trying to get his own blade out. Jacek slashed the knife across the archer's throat, opening it up with a spray of blood in his face.

He got to his feet and in a few strides crossed the distance to the man sitting astride Aleni, who was watching it all with fear in his eyes. The man better know what was coming. Jacek imagined his bloody face made him look like something from a nightmare sweeping down on him.

Jacek grabbed him with another roar and pulled him up. He drove the bloody knife into the man's groin, all the way to the hilt. The soldier's eyes went wide and his mouth dropped open, his voice lost in the certain pain. Jacek yanked the knife out indelicately and threw him down on the ground where the man belatedly tried to protect his manhood. Blood gushed out onto the grass as he screamed. He wasn't going anywhere soon.

Chest heaving, he turned to Aleni, who was still lying on the ground. Her eyes were blank and her body still. Had the man killed her?

Frowning, he moved to her side. He lifted her head to look closer. "Hey, kid! You alright?"

Her eyes were still unfocused, her mouth slack. He felt for her heartbeat at her throat. It was still there, pulsing hard and fast. "Kid!" He shook her by the shoulders. "Snap out of it!"

Her eyes squeezed shut and she started breathing shallow and fast. Damn, she was panicking. Her breaths got shorter and shorter, the whites showing in her eyes.

"Breathe! Just slow it down and breathe!" He demonstrated by breathing in through his nose and out through his mouth in slow, controlled breaths. She copied him, her face starting to get a little more color.

"Jacek? Did he -?" Her breath hitched in her throat. Her hands felt around at her waistline and gripped the top of her trousers, which were still mercifully in place.

"No. You're alright. I stopped them. Most of them are dead. One wishes he was." He gently pulled her up to a sitting position so she could see for herself.

The soldier with the birth mark writhed on the ground, groaning and holding his groin. The pool of blood around him was growing rapidly.

Jacek pushed the handle of the knife into her hand. She needed to finish this. She stared down at the gruesome implement.

"Finish him." Jacek said.

"Why?"

"For yourself. For closure. You'll feel better for it."

"I'll feel better once I've taken a man's life?" She shook her head. "That doesn't make sense."

"Trust me, it'll feel good."

"But he didn't do anything to me. Why should I?"

Jacek breathed out and squeezed her shoulder. "Because somebody once did. And it affected you."

"I'm fine."

"No, you're not. You were really out of it just then. You went somewhere in your mind so you didn't have to be here."

Dropping the knife, Aleni pushed herself to her feet and walked a short distance away.

Bile burning at the back of his throat, he got up and went back to the groaning soldier and finished him off. He took no small satisfaction in the act.

He gathered up his weapons and strapped them back on.

When he returned to Aleni, she was bent over, throwing up. Her white hair hung long over her face. He itched to hold it back out of the way for her, but feared she might not be comfortable with that. When she was finished, she wiped her mouth with the back of her hand and straightened.

"So now you know." She said in a whisper. "My secret. My shame."

"Hey." He spun her around by the shoulder, kneeling in front of her. "That is not your shame. It was not your fault, you hear me?" A growl crept into his voice. He hadn't intended to sound so rough. "That was Krodon's shame. He's a monster. It was his fault alone. You couldn't stop him. Don't you ever think otherwise!"

Tears formed in her eyes and spilled down her face. "He - he -" She couldn't finish.

Feeling hollowed out, frustration warred with wanting to do something to ease her pain. But what? What if he did the wrong thing? What if he made it worse? He was a man, just like Krodon. If he hugged her, she might be terrified. The last thing he wanted to do was traumatize her further.

Instead, he found himself moving back to his horse. Maybe he should just pretend it didn't happen. He scooped up some snow from the ground and scrubbed his face clean of the blood. "Come on kid, let's get a move on."

Sniffing, she nodded and went to her own horse.

15

It would take them two days to get to Snowmelt, a small village on the Milliger river. From there, the only way through was Milliger's pass. They would have to find out in the town if it was currently controlled by Tarkan. Or was it Krodon now? Jacek took some time to get that through his head as they rode. Krodon had finally stepped up and ended his father. Tarkan was dead.

This was a huge development. But a dangerous one. Tarkan might have left them alone, eventually. Krodon would not. Whatever he wanted the kid for, he was not going to give up easily. She might be running for the rest of her life. Or until she outlived the warlord. Or killed him. He watched her, riding beside him astride the white mare. She looked exactly like he had imagined elves would look like. Serene, regal, graceful. Marred only by the brokenness now residing in her eyes.

She stared blankly ahead, her posture stiff again. She was not present. She was somewhere else. Jacek had no idea what to do to help her.

"How did you get me to the forest?" he said. She needed to be distracted at least.

She blinked and turned her head to face him. Her icy blue eyes did not meet his, focusing on his beard.

"What?" She said.

"I mean, I'm not a small guy. How did you get me off that road and into the forest?"

"Oh. I, uh, used magic."

His eyebrows shot up. "You got it working again?"

"I had to focus a lot. It took a lot of energy. I'm not sure I could do it again. But I had to move you."

He had to admit he was slightly impressed. Impressed that she would go to all the effort. She could have left him on the road to die in the cold. He hadn't exactly been kind to her. Maybe she *was* worth trusting?

They skirted the edge of the forest for as long as they could, keeping an eye out for the new patrols. Nobody appeared.

By nightfall they came upon the Milliger river. It was high at this time of the year, fed from icy springs in the mountains to the north. The water raged past, fast and dangerous. Jacek knew they would have to stay on this side, even if it was riskier with the patrols.

"Let's camp in the forest for tonight." Jacek said, nodding to the trees. "It's too exposed out here."

In the dark, Aleni found them a sheltered circle of trees further in from the edge. It was too risky to have a fire, so they bundled up with all the furs and blankets they had to get through the cold night.

"You sleep." Aleni said. "I'll watch."

"You need sleep too. You watched last night."

"I don't need as much sleep as you. I can meditate." Her manner was evasive again.

Jacek couldn't see her well in the dark, but he knew she

could see him fine. She sat up against a tree, holding her blankets close under her chin. He couldn't hear her shivering at all, but her breath sounds seemed short. Was she agitated about something? Was it because of the men earlier?

He knew it wasn't his business, but he found himself asking. "Is there some reason you don't want to sleep?"

She was silent for some time, watching out through the trees. When she spoke, it was barely above a whisper. "If I close my eyes, I see him."

A knife pierced his heart at the words. He hung his head, not knowing what to say, but he had to say something.

He raised his head again to face her. Tried to look in her eyes. "I'm sorry, Aleni. You should never have experienced that." A slow anger bubbled in his gut as he spoke. He would have to be careful to keep it contained around her. It surely wouldn't help.

There were no more words between them so Jacek settled down to sleep.

In the morning, he got up and put a small cooking fire together. Less chance of being seen during the day and in the forest. Aleni was nowhere to be seen, but he trusted now that she wasn't far.

He had water boiling and was just putting his medicinal herbs in the pot to steep when she returned with Bandur. In her hands dangled two fat rabbits. Had she hunted with the dog? He'd never been able to keep up with him, so he normally left him to go off on his own. Bandur always brought something back for him.

"Did you just -?" He pointed to Bandur and then the forest.

She stopped and stared at him. "Yes. Why?"

"You can keep up with him?"

She glanced at the dog. "He's not that fast. It was easier hunting together. We could come at the rabbits from two directions. He chased them towards me, and I snuck up and grabbed them." She held up the result in front of her triumphantly. A small smile played on her mouth.

His eyebrows shot up. He'd noticed she was fast and silent on her feet, but that was ridiculous. To sneak up on a rabbit? He shook his head.

"I knew elves were quite different from us, but I didn't expect this." He held his hand out for a rabbit. She passed it to him and he laid it down to start skinning it. Aleni kneeled down close by and watched, looking interested.

"You want to learn how to do it?" He cocked his head at her, mildly surprised. She wasn't like any young girl he'd met before.

She nodded. So he showed her.

Later, the rabbit meat bubbled in a stew over the small fire. Jacek was keeping an eye out through the trees for any signs of patrols close by. Only the horses, tethered close by, made any movement. Up above, the rustle of the trees told of a growing wind. It looked like a storm was on its way. The sweet, pungent zing of the coming rain filled his nostrils. They would need to reach Snowmelt before it hit or they would be in trouble.

He checked the stew. It was ready. They needed to eat quickly and get moving. He passed a bowl of the stew to Aleni and they ate in silence.

Once they had packed up their gear onto the horses, they mounted up and were on their way. Snowmelt was half a day away by horseback. The forest soon disappeared and the terrain merged into lower growing scrub and bushes. Raindrops tinkled on Jacek's sword handle in the scabbard across his back. Soon they were both drenched. Even Bandur looked wretched.

Jacek picked up the pace, kicking his horse into a canter. Being soaked through and cold was not a good combination.

Dark clouds rolled in from the east, bringing the clash of thunder and flashes of lightning with it. The sun became entirely covered, darkening the sky.

At least the growing rain made them harder to spot from a distance. They might actually manage to get to Snowmelt without being seen.

⚜

Aleni was miserable. Her only set of clothes and furs were soaked through, making the fur smell and the material chafe. She had to keep shifting her seat on the horse to keep her backside from going numb. Not only was she tired, she was jumpy and irritable. Jacek had been kind since he'd found out about what had happened with Krodon, but talking about it out loud had brought it all to the surface again.

When it had happened, she had managed to shove it to a corner of her mind and build a wall around it. It wasn't quite forgotten, but it didn't dominate her thoughts every moment. Now, disturbing images flashed through her mind more often. Occasionally she caught herself physically flinching away from the memories. Out here in the wilderness with nothing to do but ride, her mind was left to itself to run unchecked.

A few times Jacek had tried speaking to her, but over the sound of the rain it was difficult. She ignored him, urging her horse faster. Snowmelt finally came into view. At first it was just outlines of low wooden buildings through the misty rain, but soon horses and a few people rushing across the muddy street materialized. Aleni was not familiar with the town. It didn't exist in her time. The humans must have built it entirely themselves. They slowed the horses to a walk and rode in side by side. She pulled her dripping hood lower over her face.

Jacek pointed to a tavern down the street on the left.

Indicated by a hanging sign with a bunch of grapes that swung and creaked in the wind, the inn was a very basic construct of wood and slate. Leaving their horses tethered outside, they untied their bags and climbed the steps to enter the warm taproom. Bandur, his coat dripping and smelly, followed them in.

Lit by flickering light from tallow candles, the taproom was filled with the sound of patrons chatting and gaming. Tables scattered across the room, with men drinking and eating at nearly half of them. A huge open fire crackled and spat on the eastern wall. Outside, the wind whistled past the closed shutters on the windows. The sudden warmth was almost painful on Aleni's frozen skin. Under her feet, rushes covered the floor, soaking up water from her drenched and chafing clothes.

Jacek led the way to the bar.

"Welcome to the Romantic Axe. I'm Lotho. What can I get ya?" Lotho was a rotund man with reddened cheeks and a thin film of dark hair. He leaned on the bar with both hands. "Ya look a little damp there. Looking for rooms? We have some upstairs."

"Yes, and we'll need stables for our horses outside." Jacek thumbed back over his shoulder towards the door. He took his coin purse off his belt to count out coins.

"I'll send my boy out to get them." Lotho leaned over the bar to look at Bandur dripping on the floor. "That your dog?"

Jacek glanced down and back up. "It is." He flicked another Olon on the bar. "And he's staying inside with us." Aleni watched as his eyes hardened. That seemed to be enough for the bartender who straightened and nodded readily. He probably didn't want any trouble. And Jacek, with his multiple weapons strapped on, looked like trouble.

"Go dry yourself by the fire." Jacek said to her.

Aleni crossed to the fireplace with Bandur. The heat radiating out from the hearth warmed her instantly. She found herself closing her eyes to it and letting the heat seep in. When she opened them, she found her clothes steaming. Bandur decided then would be a good time to shake the excess water off.

"Bandur, couldn't you have done that outside?" She scolded the dog. He stared at her then turned in a circle and settled himself in front of the fire. She sighed. He had it easy sometimes.

Aleni turned to face the room. She lowered her hood, but made sure the cloth was still tied around her head to cover her ears. The room was noisy, people chattering and laughing with each other. One table was playing some sort of dice game where someone was losing badly and being loud about it. Aleni focused in on that to distract herself from the fact she was surrounded by a room full of strangers. Men. The only thing holding her together was the presence of Bandur and Jacek.

Jacek was talking to Lotho in a low tone. Aleni had no idea what they would be talking about. He didn't seem like the type to chat to strangers.

When her backside was a bit drier, Aleni sank onto the nearest stool at a table. Her stomach growled, reminding her they hadn't eaten since that morning. Hopefully, there was food being served here too.

"Well, aren't you beautiful!" A voice came from above her.

She looked up to see a young man standing next to her chair. He swayed on his feet and smelled like something fermented. He had rough cropped dark hair and a sleepy disposition.

"I'm Hobard." His words seemed a little slurred. Could he possibly have a speech impediment? She just stared at him, frozen to the spot. If she offended him, would he get aggressive?

"What'sh yer name?" Hobard frowned at her.

She couldn't speak, couldn't move. Flashes of Krodon entered her mind again. Her breath caught in her throat and her vision narrowed. What should she do? She couldn't think. Her muscles were frozen.

Hobard reached down to put a hand under her chin. Before he touched her, there was a swish in the air to their right and with a thwack a knife embedded itself in the table a few inches from Hobard. A few inches from his crotch, to be precise. The room went dead quiet.

Jolted out of her immobility, Aleni whipped her gaze to where Jacek stood at the bar. His arm was out in front of him, having just released the knife from his hand. He walked with deliberate steps over to them, pulling his axe out from the loop on his belt.

"Touch her, you lose a hand," he said, his bass tones rumbling like rocks falling in a pile.

Hobard stared up at the assassin with wide eyes and a slack mouth. "What's it to you?" Aleni wondered if he was mentally deficient as well.

"Walk away. Right now," Jacek growled.

Hobard looked around at the other men in the tavern who collectively stared at the three of them in horrified fascination. The young man must have been bolstered by the presence of his friends, because then he said something really stupid.

"I saw the bitch first. She's mine. Go find your own."

Aleni held her breath. They didn't need to draw attention to themselves. If a fight broke out, it could jeopardize their stay here.

Jacek's knuckles cracked as he clenched his free hand. "Boy, if you don't stop, I'm gonna rip your head off and shove it in the last place you want it." He took another step forward.

Aleni shot to her feet and put her hands out between them. "No, he's not!" She said to Hobard.

"Whose side are you on?" Jacek said, his head cocked to the side.

"I just don't think there's a need for bloodshed here. Hobard is obviously mentally slow. His friends are going to take him home now." She deliberately looked around at the other men in the room. "Aren't they?"

A couple of other young guys got up from their table and stepped forward, their eyes wide. They grabbed Hobard by the arms. He struggled a little, but they convinced him to walk away. They kept a wary eye on Jacek over their shoulders as they went.

When they had left the tavern, Jacek pulled his knife out of the table and returned it to the sheath at his hip. He sat and stared at Aleni.

"What?" she asked.

"That was some bit of diplomacy. Normally there's no talking a drunk man down and you just have to beat it out of them."

"That wasn't diplomacy. It was common sense. What is drunk?"

"You don't know what drunk is?"

She shook her head.

"It's how people get when they drink too much ale. Or mead or wine. It's alcohol. It affects their minds. Makes them do dumb things."

"Why would you want to drink something that makes you dumb?"

Jacek shrugged. "I suppose the feeling they get when they drink outweighs the effects. Some people drink to forget."

"I suppose that makes sense then. He was acting pretty dumb. But it's also sad. I wonder if he was drinking to forget. Do you drink alcohol?"

"No. I can't afford to act dumb. I'll end up dead."

"Because you have no friends to take you home?"

"Ouch." His mouth twitched upward.

Aleni couldn't help her own smile.

Soon Lotho brought over plates of hot food. Some sort of roasted meat and vegetables with warm bread. It smelled delicious. He left and then returned with two drinks. The one in front of Aleni steamed and smelled of spices and something tart.

"What is this?" She lifted the cup and sniffed at it.

"Mulled wine." Jacek said.

"Is it alcohol?"

He wavered his head back and forward. "Technically. But it's not a very potent wine. One cup won't make you dumb. It'll warm you up." He sipped at his own cup.

She took an experimental sip of the warm drink. It was somewhere between tart and sweet, somewhat fruity, and warmed her throat as it went down. She decided it was a pleasant experience.

"Is that what's in yours?" She nodded to his drink.

"This is called Dire Sip. It's not very popular. Only for the brave." He smiled and took another gulp.

"Can I try?"

Jacek's eyes flicked between his drink and her, eventually settling on her. He pursed his lips and passed the cup over to her. She took it and sniffed at it. It wasn't heated at all and smelled earthy. She took a small sip.

It had a bitter, acrid taste, and she spat it out to the side after a couple of seconds. Coughing and spluttering, trying to get the taste off her tongue, she gagged.

Jacek laughed, banging his hand on the table. It was the first time she had heard the sound from him. It wasn't altogether an unpleasant sound, but it did seem foreign coming from his mouth. Like his tongue wasn't accustomed to it.

"That's disgusting!" Realizing her reaction was giving him joy, she played it out for him. "How can you drink that?" She pawed at her tongue, trying to wipe it clean of the taste.

With a grin still on his face, Jacek took the cup back and drank more. "I told you. It's only for the brave."

"More like for the foolish," she added with a smile of her own. She liked this side of him. He needed this. How long had it been since he'd laughed? "I'm plenty brave, thank you very much!" She pointed to her chest.

Jacek nodded with sincerity. "That you are." He sat forward in his chair. "The bartender told me the pass is guarded by Tarkan's men. I'm guessing word hasn't reached here yet that Krodon has taken over. So we have to assume the men there will be looking for us."

"So, what do we do?"

"We go over the mountains."

"Those mountains are huge!" Aleni remembered them well.

"We have no choice. If we are to get to this city you say is under the mountain around the Twilfell basin, then that's the only way we can get there. Unless you want to trek all the way *around* the mountains, but they cover the entire width of the continent. And I don't think I have that kind of time." His voice went quieter on his last sentence.

Aleni reached across the table and put her small hand on his giant one and squeezed. "I'm sure we can find something in Y'ha Taesi that will heal you."

His eyes widened at her words and at her touch. He didn't pull away.

"I know that's what you're really looking for. It makes sense. There should be stones there that have the power you seek." She patted his hand and pulled back, returning to her food.

"What if the artifacts there need activating? Do you know how?"

She had to admit, she had never had to activate anything magical in her life. Nothing from her time had ever had to be 'activated'. Her people just used stones and artifacts to store power for use when they had to focus on something else. Her own father had used a ring in the war that held power for a shield. As far as she knew, they didn't have to do anything to them to use them. But apparently the humans here couldn't use them. Maybe the power of the stones had died with her people. Maybe this was a fool's errand. What if they couldn't find anything to cure him? Her gut roiled at the thought.

She gave him another smile. "I'm sure I'll figure it out."

❦   16   ❦

At the break of dawn Jacek arose and readied their gear. Checking out a window, the storm had broken overnight and the sun was peeking out from behind the clouds. In the distance however, gray menacing sky promised further rain.

He had slept in a separate room to Aleni, as Jacek thought she might want some privacy for once. A bath had been ordered for her, which she had taken to with glee.

Bringing her pleasure seemed to warm his heart somewhat. It was a curious feeling. One he hadn't felt in a long time. Not since his parents had been alive. This young girl, vastly alone and having endured degrading abuse, seemed to be worming her way into his life. He wasn't sure yet whether he was comfortable with that or not.

Before he knocked on her door, it opened and Bandur padded out. Aleni stood there, dressed and looking slightly more refreshed. Her eyes still looked heavy from lack of sleep, but her face was clean and she looked pleased to see him at least. He hoped she had got some sleep last night, but he wasn't about to ask.

"Ready to go?" he said.

"Yes." She slung her bag over her shoulder and closed the door behind her. Downstairs in the taproom there was a cluster of men at the windows looking at something outside. Curious, Jacek joined two men at a window facing the street.

"I heard he beat his father to death in a rage. Left him a bloody pulp." One man was saying to the other. "A messenger from Amathnore came through late last night and told us what happened. Apparently Krodon wanted people to know he's in charge now."

At hearing the name, Jacek's heart quickened. He peered out through the dirty glass and saw rows of mounted men riding through the street. Most were in the black and burnished steel of Tarkan, with the red of Krodon's men scattered throughout. As the men rode past, Jacek's heart beat faster and heat flushed through him. Near the end of the column, one man stood out from the rest.

His long black hair was uncovered in the morning cold, but the heavy furs adorning his shoulders and torso made up for the lack. He rode a huge black destrier covered in a red and black caparison.

Krodon the warlord.

Jacek breathed in and out heavily, his chest feeling like it was about to burst. His jaw clenched and his hand went to his axe at his hip. A small warm hand covered his, and he turned to see Aleni at his side.

Her eyes pleaded at him. "Don't."

He clamped down on his tongue. The monster riding past held his head upright and proud. How could he live with himself? Didn't he have a daughter of his own? He should have slit his throat back when he had the chance. "I could put an arrow in his head right now and be done with it."

"And what would that achieve? I admit, I would like to see that, but we would both be killed as soon as you did. You might be the world's best assassin, but even you can't fight all those soldiers." Aleni pulled on his arm to convince him further. "Let's get out of here. Before they start searching buildings."

He glanced back at Krodon, imagining in his mind taking the man's head off with his blade. But she was right, there were too many other men around who would avenge his death. They would both die. Finally relenting, Jacek gritted his teeth and turned away. Lotho was just coming out of the kitchen, a barrel balanced on his shoulders. Jacek crossed to him and caught his attention.

"Where's your back door?"

Lotho pointed out through the kitchen. Jacek put a hand on Aleni's back to guide her along in front of him. Bandur followed close behind, his claws clicking on the wooden floor. Out behind the tavern, they found themselves in a dirt yard with the stables on one side. Their horses had been well tended by the looks of them. They had even been brushed down. A young boy of about ten years ran up to them and opened the stall doors.

"They're lovely horses," the boy said.

Jacek didn't reply, but flicked him a half-Olon for his services and together they bridled the animals and threw riding blankets over their backs. Once they'd strapped on their bags, they led the animals out of the stable. So far, Krodon's new soldiers weren't deviating from the main street, so slipping out the back unseen was relatively easy.

There were only a few houses behind the Romantic Axe tavern. Snowmelt was tiny compared to Amathnore. They slipped between the buildings with the horses and made it out to the fields beyond without alerting any soldiers.

The sunken fields were Selendria's way of growing food in the cold. Great pits were dug out of the ground and covered with a sheer fabric to keep the snow off and the sunlight in.

In this way food was still able to be grown through the colder parts of the year, albeit less of it. The sunken pits lined up in rows that went on for at least a mile out of Snowmelt.

Skirting the edge of the fields, they eventually mounted and rode on. In the distance, the northern backbone ranges sat as a blue backdrop for the land stretching out ahead of them. The sky began to loom gray and threatening overhead. More rain was coming. They spent a couple of hours riding in silence. Aleni moved her horse next to Jacek's and finally broke the quiet.

"Thank you," she said.

Jacek assumed she must be talking to him, although he couldn't imagine why she said it. "Um, your welcome? What for?" he said.

"For being angry."

Of all the things he thought she might be thankful for, being angry was not even on the list. What did that even mean? Certainly no one had ever thanked him for his anger before. It was normally cursed instead.

She looked at him. "The fact that you were angry at Krodon means you care. It means a lot to me that you would risk getting killed just to avenge my honor. Even if it was stupid." She gave him a shy smile.

"Oh." He didn't know what to say. He supposed that made sense. It was also alarming to realize what that meant for him. He had been willing to assassinate a high-risk target just for her. It *was* stupid. What had he been thinking? He'd never been compromised by emotions before. What made him the best was the lack of emotions. Could he be losing his edge with Aleni around? The thought terrified him.

He nudged his horse faster, moving up through a canter to a gallop. Behind him, Aleni did the same.

It was mid-afternoon by the time they reached the foothills leading up to the mountain range. The hills spread out for miles and were sparsely populated with shrubs and gorse. The occasional leafless tree stood sentinel over the plain.

They pushed the horses up the hills, knowing they would have to set them loose at the base of the mountain. Jacek wanted to save his legs as long as he could. There would be a lot of climbing to come.

The ground was covered in a thin layer of snow that made it slippery to walk on. The horses were finding it harder and harder to find purchase. The animals snorted and heaved, trying their best to go on. When it looked like the horses couldn't go on, Jacek decided they had to leave them.

"We can't push them any further," he yelled. The wind was picking up and the occasional sliver of ice drove into his face.

Aleni stopped her horse and twisted back to look at him. Her eyes told him she didn't want to let them go. But she dismounted anyway, dropping lightly to the ground.

Jacek untied his sack of belongings from his horse's back. He then undid the clasp on the blanket and folded it up to put in the bag. The bridle came off after that and it, too, went into the bag. He gave the horse a pat and then pushed it away, shouting and clapping to scare it off. The big black beast snorted and made off down the slope.

Aleni had the blanket and bridle off hers, but was holding on to its head, speaking softly to the mare. Jacek slapped the horse's rump, making it jump, but it didn't run.

"Come on!" he said.

"Let me thank her for her labor." The young elf looked back in the mare's eyes. Something must have passed between them, because the horse lowered her head once before turning away to trot back down the hill.

"Did that horse just understand you?"

"I believe so, yes. Do you not talk to your horse?"

"If I do, it's usually to yell at it."

"Then that's your problem." Aleni raised her chin. "No horse will want to talk with someone who only yells at them. If you speak respectfully to them, they will respect you."

"It's an animal."

"So is Bandur."

"That's different."

"How?"

Jacek struggled to come up with a decent reason. Bandur and he seemed to have an understanding, but Jacek couldn't articulate it.

He just sighed and shook his head and started walking up toward the mountain. The wind got stronger and the rain more frozen, hitting them with little chips of stinging ice. Jacek was forced to wrap a cloth around his face and head. Aleni pulled her hood down over her face further to combat the growing sleet.

As they climbed further up the hill, the ground started giving way to rocks and trees. The trees here weren't very tall, but they kept the snow off the ground at least. The going got easier the higher they went. When they reached the base of the mountain, the climb got steeper. But they soon found a little trail made by mountain animals and followed it upward.

After an hour of climbing, Jacek found his legs were starting to seize up. Stabs of pain protested the exercise, but he pushed on. Aleni was ahead of him and still seemed to be moving easily. He wasn't going to stop as long as she could carry on. He was the adult here after all. Even if she was technically three hundred years old.

He ducked his head to step under a spider's web spanning two trees and pulled his furs tighter. The cold bit into his skin and permeated his muscles. It was getting harder and harder to move.

The wind whistled through the higher rocky slopes. The trees creaked and groaned under the pull of the wind, bending and straining. The path underfoot was made of packed dirt and rocks. It jutted out from the mountainside about four feet. Jacek took another step and suddenly the ground under his back foot gave way. With a strain he pulled his weight onto his front foot and jumped out of the way of the slip. Aleni stopped and turned back to see what had happened.

He stared down at the gap in the path behind them. That was a close one. They would need to be careful going forward.

"Why don't we find somewhere to camp for the night?" Aleni called back. He watched her eyes take note of his shaking legs. "I'm getting tired."

He looked up at the gap in the trees. The sun had well and truly set, although they hadn't seen it for some time because of the weather. They would struggle to travel much further in this, anyway.

He met her eyes for a beat, then waved his hand to keep moving. "Next place we find, we'll stop." Relief filled him at his own words. His legs were getting embarrassingly shaky.

Fifteen minutes later they reached a plateau halfway up the mountain. Surrounded by evergreens, the area was about fifteen feet across, with sheer rock going up one side and a massive drop on the other. At one end a cave entrance led some depth into the mountain. Jacek retrieved a torch from his pack, lit it, and stepped into the opening, warning Aleni to stay outside.

The flickering torch steadied as he stepped further into the cave, away from the wind. The light showed a low ceiling of rock, but it looked solid. No cracks showed or water dripped down from above. The hollow space went back nearly twenty feet and spread seven feet wide. Just enough space for them to get shelter for the night. He called Aleni to come in. She stepped inside with Bandur next to her, dripping.

The dog decided to shake just then, making Aleni squeal at the shower of water. Jacek kept his smirk to himself.

He placed his pack down and stared outside at the wind-driven sleet. It would turn into snow soon. He needed to get a fire going. It would be hard finding dry wood in this weather, but he had to try.

"I'll go find some firewood," he said.

"I'll help you. It's getting darker out there. I can see better than you."

True. He didn't bother answering, but stepped out into the wet again. Bandur stayed inside the dry cave, probably thinking he was guarding something. He was just being lazy. Jacek didn't blame him.

He scoured under the evergreens for bits of broken branches that were dry. In the end he reluctantly had to use his axe to cut off some lower boughs that were dry enough to burn. It was not that sort of axe. But if they were going to make it through the night, it had to be done.

He returned before Aleni and started setting up the fire just inside the entrance with some stones to ring it. Next, he broke up the bits he had and laid them out in a careful design so they would catch. Then he threw on some dried needles for a starter. It took a couple of tries to get the needles to catch from his flint. He was leaning down and blowing on the pile when Aleni returned with an armload of wood.

He sat up and stared at her gain in surprise. "You did well."

She lifted her shoulder up and down before carefully dropping the wood next to the fireplace. "It wasn't too hard. I grew up in a forest. I know where to look for dry wood."

"Tell me about that," he said.

"What, finding wood?"

"No, growing up in the forest. With your people."

She huffed out a sigh and sat down next to the fire. Jacek

kept feeding wood into the growing flames. Aleni pulled out food for their dinner and poured water from a canteen into a pot. Jacek retrieved the collapsible pot stand from his pack and set it up over the fire.

While they waited for the water to boil, Aleni talked. She spoke of her parents, seemingly noble people who had lived for hundreds of years before giving birth to her. Jacek couldn't imagine what that would be like. What sort of wisdom would they have from all that life experience? For some reason it made him feel inadequate. He knew he wasn't her father, but at the moment, he was all she had to look up to. He had never particularly wanted kids, but he didn't mind the thought of it right now.

She wove a picture of magnificent idyllic forests, green with life and full of birdsong. Of tall, strong elves who excelled at everything they put their hand to. They lived off the land, only taking what they needed, and always giving thanks to someone they called the all-mother.

Jacek sat with his back against the cave wall, eating his food and listening to the kid talk. She seemed calmer as she remembered her childhood. It sounded like a happy one. One where she was loved and safe. It made him realize all she had lost since waking up from the magic stasis. There was no going back. It was like she was from another world. But instead she was just from another time and culture.

It was several seconds of silence before he realized she had stopped talking and was just looking at him.

"Sorry. My mind wandered," he mumbled.

"What were you thinking about?"

"My own parents."

"Where are they?"

He took a deep breath in. "They're dead. Killed when I was nine."

Her eyes took on a deep sorrow. "I'm sorry to hear that. Who killed them?"

He shook his head. "I don't know her name. She was a young woman who was traveling through the small town we lived in. She had been attacked and needed help. My parents were known as the local 'do-gooders', so people sent her to them. They took her in late at night and cared for her."

When he paused, she leaned forward, her blue gaze intense. "What happened?"

"The next morning I came back from getting water from the well and found them stabbed to death on the floor of our house. The woman was gone. I still don't know why she did it."

Saying it out loud for the first time in a very long time made him realize it was still fresh in his mind. It still hurt just as much as the day it happened. Time wasn't really the great healer. He had been running from it ever since that day. Since he ran out of that house and never looked back.

"What happened to you after that? Where did you go? Did someone help you?"

His heart wrenched at her innocence. No one would help. No one was expected to help. He was on his own from that day. "I lived on the streets after that. Ran with some kids occasionally. That was where I met Ham."

Why was he blabbering his mouth off like this? He'd never talked to anyone this candidly before. Why now? Jacek didn't know, but now he'd started he found he didn't want to stop. There was this irrepressible urge to be known.

"Who was Ham?" Aleni prompted.

"He was the closest thing I had to a friend. He was the smallest in the group. He didn't talk much, but he was good company. Maybe that's why he was good company." He lifted his gaze briefly to Aleni. She didn't blink. Oh well.

"I had a little hovel underneath the floorboards of a

ruined house. It was dry and out of the cold. And it was all mine. I only showed it to Ham.

"Ham got picked on by one of the bigger boys in the group. Arth was a bully. But I was bigger than Arth. Bigger than all of them. I didn't get picked on. So, I stood up for Ham. Punched Arth right in the nose one day. Gotta say, it felt good." He couldn't help a small grin.

Aleni mirrored him with her own smile.

"I walked away after that. Left him with a broken nose and something to think about. When I returned to my little house later, it was in flames."

"What?" Aleni said, sitting back on her ankles, her back straight.

"Arth and the rest of the kids were standing in front of it. Arth just smiled at me. Standing behind him was Ham. He wouldn't even look at me."

"Oh Jacek, that's horrible. How could he do that to you?"

"I guess he was more scared of Arth than me. Maybe they all were. Maybe I'm just a monster."

Aleni scooted closer and gripped his hand. "You're not a monster. I think underneath the hard exterior is someone who cares. A lot. That's why you stood up for Ham. What Ham did was a reflection of himself, not of you." Her cool eyes bespoke earnestness.

Jacek coughed and sat up straighter. "How did you get to be so wise?"

Her grin was impish. "I'm three hundred and twelve years old, remember?"

17

By the time Krodon stopped in Snowmelt, the people had come out of their houses, staring at the soldiers in the column. His men were at the far end of the main thoroughfare, and from there Krodon ordered them to spread out and look for any signs of the Red Hunter and the girl.

Houses were ransacked to the screams and cries of the families within. Those that screamed the loudest were silenced. Forever. Krodon sat comfortable in his new leather-made padded seat strapped to the warhorse. Tarkan had had it made. Much more comfortable than a padded blanket. He found he could easily sit in this for hours. He was the only one who had one though. His men did not need the luxury.

"Sir!" One of his men approached from the southern end of the town.

"What is it?" He had to twist in his seat to see the man.

"I've got a report from one man who saw the two last night. Fits the description, and they had an interaction."

"An interaction? Bring him to me."

The soldier left and returned with a skinny youth who was

half pushed towards Krodon. His knees were kicked in until he kneeled in the mud at the warhorse's hooves.

"I've been told you saw the Red Hunter last night."

"Yes, sir." The young man groveled at the show of power around him. "In the tavern. I didn't get their names, but the girl was extremely beautiful and I tried having a conversation with her. The man interrupted and threatened me."

"He is the Red Hunter himself. Your life was in his hands."

"Oh, well I didn't know his name then, but the girl, she stopped him."

"Then you have her to thank for your life. You were a fool to engage him."

"I- I guess so, sir. I was drunk."

"Indeed. Do you know where they are now?"

"I believe they were staying in the tavern overnight, but I haven't seen them this morning. Maybe the bartender knows."

"Bring me the bartender," he ordered the soldier holding the young man.

"Right away, sir." He stalked off down the street with an air of importance.

Krodon caught the eye of another soldier standing nearby and motioned for him to take the young man away. What he did with him after that was open to interpretation.

Soon the bartender was brought in front of him. A sniveling pig of a man, he was pushed to the ground by the soldier behind him. The rotund tavern owner craned his neck to look at Krodon, who sneered at him in disgust. He had very little time for people like him.

Krodon leaned down a little to look the man in the eye. The saddle creaked as he moved his weight on it. "Tell me where they went."

"I don't know!" The bartender was actually shaking on his knees.

"Then this is going to be a bad day for you."

Her hands ran over the soft cloud of a bedspread. It was always the bed. This was how it started. After the cold stone of the dungeon, the bed was a benign torture in itself. Sinking into its silky depths, the covers caressed her skin. It was like the promise of the after-world.

Then it turned into hell. He was there suddenly, huge and looming over her. A shadow of evil with strong grasping hands. Fear washed through her like a massive wave, drowning out all thought. Her heart pounded in her head. A large hand grabbed her foot and pulled her toward him. Struggling. Then pain bursting through her head, leaving her senseless. More pain, of another kind. No, she didn't want this. How could she stop it? She screamed. She sobbed, begging for it all to end.

Then it changed. Something was different. Something didn't fit. Something that wasn't part of the usual events. A gentle hand took hers. A voice, far away at first. She couldn't hear what it was saying. It was indistinct, but gentle. It grew in volume.

There. It pierced through the darkness surrounding her and flew to her muddled brain.

"Aleni. Wake up."

She fought the hands that grabbed at her. But they held firm.

"I'm here, kid. Wake up."

Jacek. It was him. His voice. Aleni opened her eyes to see his bearded face leaning over her, his brows crinkled. She sat up. The calloused skin of his right hand gripped her soft one. She hadn't just dreamed that.

"Hey, there you are. It was just a dream." The big mercenary sat back on his ankles, releasing her.

Feeling the sudden urge for comfort, Aleni leaped forward and wrapped her arms around his waist, holding on tight. She sensed him stiffen. He hesitated, but after a beat she felt his arms go around her shoulders carefully.

"It's alright. You're safe," he said. "It was just a dream."

She released him and sat back on her sleeping furs. "It's not just a dream."

His jaw muscles twitched. His eyes didn't quite meet hers. "Memories?"

She nodded. "Krodon wanted to breed with me. Did... I mean. To make more elves." Her words stumbled over themselves, not quite coming out right.

Jacek sucked in a large breath through his nose. He looked like he was trying desperately to hold himself in. A rush of feeling flowed through her chest at seeing this big man care. He reminded her a little of her father. Rhothomir had been the noblest and strongest of the elves. Over a thousand years old, he was wise as well as strong. He had doted on Aleni and made her feel safe.

Jacek made her feel safe, too. In his own strange, gruff way. He probably didn't even intend to. It certainly didn't make sense, considering he had drugged her and kept her at arm's length all this time. She knew he had his own reasons for having her along with him. He wasn't an altruistic soul. He was definitely a violent killer. There was no getting around that.

But underneath it all he was gentle and kind. He cared. That was what mattered.

"To build his army with elves instead?" Jacek said.

"I guess so. But it would take a long time for that to happen. Elves aren't particularly... what is the word? Flowering? Fruitful?"

"Fertile."

"Yes, fertile. My parents were at least a thousand years old before they had me."

His eyebrows shot up. "That's a long time to wait for children."

"Elves are a patient people."

"No kidding."

Aleni wrapped her arms around her chest, hugging herself. "Do you think if I killed Krodon I would finally feel better? Maybe the nightmares would end?"

Jacek sighed. "Perhaps. I'm not sure what will make you feel better, but if you want to learn how to defend yourself, I can teach you that."

"Fight like you?" Her heart lurched.

"Possibly. We can make a start at least." He had never taught anyone before, let alone someone half his size. It would be a challenge.

"Tomorrow?"

He stared out at the darkness outside the cave. The wind was still whistling out there, and by the light of the campfire, Aleni could see a layer of snow building across the entrance. They were lucky the wind wasn't blowing straight in.

"Alright, we can start tomorrow." Jacek finally said. He threw another piece of wood on the fire, making sparks jump and fly up. The flickering flames made the light in the cave dance and shift. "But first you need sleep. Proper sleep."

"Do you still have those herbs for sleeping?"

He stilled. Possibly remembering what he had done with those herbs? He flicked his eyes up to meet hers.

"I- I didn't dream when I drank it."

He raised an eyebrow. "Fair enough. I'll make some tea."

While he got the tea ready, Aleni lay back down. Bandur padded over and curled up next to her, his fur now dry from the fire. She snuggled her face into the dog's fur and flung an arm over his body. He gave a contented snuff and closed his eyes.

"He likes you," Jacek said.

"I like him too. He's very calming."

"That he is. Here." He handed her a steaming cup. "I've made it a little weaker than before. You won't sleep as long, but hopefully it'll be without dreams."

"Thank you." She took a sip. The now-familiar taste was no longer bitter to her tongue. "Do you miss your parents?"

He nodded. "All the time." His hand went to a pocket inside his coat. He withdrew a small wooden musical pipe. It looked well-crafted and worn by the years. "This was my father's. He taught me to play. It's the only thing I still have that reminds me of him." He ran his fingers over the holes down the length of it. Three in total.

"Will you play?" she asked.

He sat back against the cave wall and brought the pipe to his lips. Aleni settled in and closed her eyes. Soon a languorous, lilting melody rang out through the cave. The song was reminiscent of love and loss, ringing in the air like a delicate touch. Aleni didn't know the song of course, but she could imagine characters searching far and wide for their lost love.

She drifted off to sleep with Jacek's song in her ears.

◈

When sunlight creeping along the cave floor reached Jacek's back, he opened his eyes. He had tried to stay awake to keep watch, but the climb up the mountain along with his aching body was too much for his lagging energy levels. He was feeling old this morning.

He watched the kid while she slept, her relaxed face in stark contrast to the previous night. Thinking about what the warlord had done to her made his stomach turn. She was a child. Innocent. People like him deserved only one thing. And Jacek would be glad to give it to him. He'd seen victims like her on the streets when he was a kid himself. Street girls who got caught by the wrong people out late at night. The girls had never been the same again.

He got up and moved to the entrance of the cave. A thick white blanket canvassed the wide mountain shelf outside. Breathing in the fresh air, he noted a slight tang to it. Lazy flakes drifted out of the sky and settled on the firs and rocks surrounding the area. It looked like it was settling in for the day. Traveling up the mountain would not be easy. Today might be a good day to rest for a while. No one was following them up here.

After going outside to relieve his bladder, he retrieved a pot and filled it with snow. Bandur passed by him on his way out for his morning hunt. He wasn't sure what the dog would get up here, but hoped he found something.

Stoking the fire up from the still-burning coals, he put the last of their wood on to build it up further. Once the flames reappeared, he hung the pot over the fire to melt. Then he got to preparing their breakfast.

The smell of his medicinal tea brewing must have woken Aleni. She stirred and sat up, wiping her eyes of sleep. After a few moments of watching him with the food, she pushed her blankets back and stood, stretching.

"How did you sleep?" Jacek asked.

Through a yawn she spoke. "Good."

"No more dreams?"

"No, none." She moved closer to the fire, holding her hands out over it.

That was good. Jacek knew what it was like to have bad dreams. They had plagued him a lot when he was younger. Driven by the unconscious fear that the woman who had killed his parents might come back for him. It wasn't until he had learned how to fight and take care of himself that they had gone. Maybe in teaching her how to defend herself, it might help her nightmares.

After they had eaten and put everything away, they moved to a cleared space in the cave and stood facing each other. Thankfully, the rocky ceiling was high enough that Jacek didn't have to duck his head. He first showed her how to stand in a fighting stance, balanced and ready to move.

"Now, the first thing to remember is where the vulnerable points are on a person. Only three places on the body that even a large, muscular, trained man cannot condition to take a hit. Everywhere else, he can build up muscle to protect. Don't bother hitting them in the stomach or chest, or even arm if you're trying to inflict damage. The three points are eyes, groin and knees." He pointed to each spot on his own body.

Aleni watched carefully, nodding along.

"So, for self-defense, particularly someone your size, you need to focus on those points first. You can use a kick, a punch, or your fingers. Fingers to the eyes is very effective. Even the toughest opponent will still stop all attack and focus on the fact that a finger just gouged their eye."

"Ew." Aleni gazed at her own fingers, her mouth contorted in disgust. "I'm not sure I can do that."

"Would you rather be raped or killed?" He knew he was being a bit harsh considering her state of mind, but if that's what it took to get her over some personal aversions, then he'd be that person.

Her eyes snapped to his, a little wild. "Again? No."

"Good. Then you'll do it. Now, show me a fist."

He took her through some basic punches and kicks, and where to aim them. They drilled for most of the morning, as the snow grew outside. The sun was slowly blanketed out by the gray clouds, leaving the cave darker than before. By midday, they had to stop and go out to fetch more wood for the fire. Bandur returned eventually with a squirrel in his mouth and sat down to chew on it.

After eating a quick lunch of dried meat and bread, they got back to it. Aleni had been quiet while they ate.

"You alright?" Jacek asked her.

She nodded. "I'm just worried I won't be able to move at the right time. Whenever something has happened, like outside the forest and in the tavern, I freeze. The fear takes over and I can't move."

Jacek thought for a moment. "Let's try something." He stepped outside into the freezing snow and crossed the wide shelf to one of the trees. Using his axe, he cut a straight limb off the tree three feet long and stripped it of all smaller branches. Returning to the cave and Aleni, he held it like a sword in front of him.

Aleni's eyes furrowed. "What's that for?"

"I'm going to swing this at you. All you need to do is jump out of the way. You'll need to jump backwards to avoid it."

"That's it? Jump backwards?"

"That's it."

"What's that going to do?"

"You'll see."

She moved into a fight stance again and waited for him. He swung the branch quickly from right to left in front of him. She leaped out of the way. He continued to swing it at her, getting faster and faster. Soon her breathing was coming in quick gasps. But he noted she moved quickly, learning fast.

"Do you feel that?" he asked.

"My heart beating out of my chest?" She placed a hand over it.

"That's fear."

"I know what it is."

He dropped the stick and drew his axe.

"What are you doing?"

"Dodge this." He moved in closer and swung it at her.

Once again, she moved quickly and jumped back. The blade narrowly missed her stomach. She gasped, her eyes widening. They repositioned, and he swung once more. "Duck as well." He aimed a little higher.

Again and again he attacked her. Each time she managed to jump back or duck to avoid the sharp axe head. He moved with speed and accuracy, but always having full control of the weapon, making sure not to hurt her just in case she didn't quite move fast enough. His fears were unnecessary however, as she moved blindingly fast. It was possibly an elven thing. He'd certainly never seen a human move that fast.

Finally, they stopped, both breathing heavily.

"How do you feel now?" he asked.

"What do you mean?"

"You moved. Every time. Even though you felt fear."

Her eyebrows raised as the realization sunk in. She bent over and rested her hands on her knees, taking in big deep breaths. "I did, didn't I?" She straightened. "I did it. I didn't even realize." A small smile played on her lips.

Jacek put his axe away. "It's called stress conditioning. I can train you to act even in the most terrifying of situations. It will help you to control the fear. Fear will always be there, but the key is to feel it and act anyway. Let the training kick in."

"Do you ever feel afraid?"

"Of course. Only a fool doesn't feel fear."

She stood there, thoughtful for a moment. "What is your worst fear?"

"We're not talking about me right now. Focus. The next thing you need to learn is how to handle a weapon."

Pouting, she got back into her ready stance.

"The best way to disarm someone with a weapon is to attack the hand holding it." He untied his leather knife sheath from his belt and removed the blade. Handing the sheath to Aleni, he instructed her to hold it by the open end.

"I'm going to stab you, and you will jump back and at the same time swipe the sheath across the top of my hand." He demonstrated with the point of his knife just above his left hand.

"You're going to stab me?!" She gave him an incredulous look.

"If you jump out of the way in time, I won't." He raised an eyebrow at her. He had full faith that she could move in time. And he wasn't going to hold back. That would be an insult to her.

She let out a breath and nodded.

He lunged at her, stabbing the knife out at her stomach. She leaped back and raked the sheath across the top of his thumb. He indicated her success by dropping the knife. It clattered to the stone with a ringing clang.

She grinned up at him, her blue gaze twinkling. "I did it."

"Yes, you did. Now, again."

With grunts and huffs of breath, they sparred for the rest of the afternoon, only stopping for water. Bandur sat curled up on Jacek's bed furs by the fire, watching them between naps.

Jacek was impressed with how fast Aleni learned. She picked up whatever move he taught her and executed it with finesse and grace. Her confidence was growing.

When they next stopped for a rest, chests heaving for air, Aleni spoke between gulps of water.

"I wish I knew this before Krodon took me. I could have fought harder. Maybe then I wouldn't feel so ashamed."

Jacek closed his eyes at hearing the words. "It's not your shame to carry, Aleni. It's his."

"But maybe I could have stopped him." She stared him right in the eye.

Replacing the lid on his canteen, he dropped it and darted at her, hands outstretched. In a split second, he had her in a tight hold. One arm locked around her throat while the other held her left arm down and behind her back, twisting it.

$\mathbf{\mathscr{H}}$ 18 $\mathbf{\mathscr{H}}$

"I could kill you right now. Snap your neck like a twig. Elf or not." He breathed into her ear. "Could you stop me?"

He could feel her heart racing at the pulse in her throat. Her breaths came in short gasps. His heart clenched knowing he was the cause. But she had to get this.

She pulled at his arm around her throat, trying to pull it away. But he held firm just short of choking her. Like a rock, unmoving.

Eventually, she stopped fighting. Her body went limp, and he found he had to hold her up. "I can't." Her voice choked on the words. "I can't stop you." Defeat hung in those four syllables.

He loosened the hold before speaking. "If you had fought him harder, he would have killed you. Even unintentionally. He's not known for his self-control." He made sure she was standing on her own before turning her to face him. "It took more strength not to fight him. It was a matter of survival. You have nothing to be ashamed of."

She hung her head and looked down at her feet.

"Remember seeing him in the village?"

She nodded.

"I was going to go out there and kill him. You showed strength in stopping me and convincing me to run. Survival. You reminded me of that."

She lifted her gaze, but rested it on his chin instead. Lost to memory. "I never thought of it like that." Her eyes finally came back to the present. "Well, shall we get on with it?"

"You're not tired?"

"No. Are you?"

"Yes." He flexed his right hand, which was going numb. "I'm not as young as I used to be."

"I thought I was older than you." A cheeky smirk decorated her delicate face.

"You, little one, will be eternally youthful I suspect." He crossed back over to the fire and sat down, his aching legs protesting at the movement. Time for some more medicinal tea.

❧

Training continued throughout the next morning. Jacek played his pipe again the night before, enjoying Aleni's ethereal voice as she composed words in Elvish to his music. Even though he didn't understand what she was singing, he still felt carried away by the sound. All his pain lifted as her voice soared through the notes.

The snow had stopped early in the morning, revealing the sun again. Several inches of packed snow began to succumb to the rising temperature. They were sparring again when Aleni spoke up.

"How would I defend against someone holding me like you did yesterday?"

"The choke hold?" Jacek lowered his axe. He had a leather

covering over the blade just in case, but so far it hadn't been necessary.

"Yes, that. How would I get out of it?"

"Use your teeth."

"What?"

He mimed grabbing an arm around his own neck and pulling down. "As soon as you can, pull down on the arm and bite the forearm or bicep. Bite down as hard as you possibly can, as though you're eating raw meat. Take a chunk out of it."

She scrunched her nose up.

"Again, remember, it's your life here."

She rolled those intense blue eyes. "Fair enough." She squared up, rolling her shoulders. "Alright, try me."

He stepped in and put an arm around her neck in the same position as the day before. She gripped his forearm and pulled down on it, getting it away from her neck. At the same time, she bit into his leather forearm guard. He could almost feel her teeth clamping down on his arm. If not for his hardened leather armor, she probably *would* have taken a chunk out of his arm. She seemed to take things very literally. He would have to be careful of his instructions in the future.

"Wow, you took to that one quickly." He rubbed his arm, checking to make sure she hadn't actually bit through. She was stronger than she looked.

Going through it a few more times, he was finally satisfied she had it. When they took a break, he stepped over to his pack and rummaged through it for something. Withdrawing a dagger in a sheath, he stood and held it out for Aleni to take.

"I got this in Amathnore. For you."

Her eyes widened. "For me?" She tucked her white hair away behind one of her pointed ears. He had to admit to himself he never tired of seeing them. Both odd and elegant at the same time, they reminded him she was not like others. Not like him. Which was actually a good thing.

Stepping forward, she gingerly took the dagger from him. She drew the blade out from the leather sheath, examining it in the light near the entrance. It was a little smaller than Jacek's own, about six inches long. The wooden handle was carved expertly to fit in a smaller hand with a flowing leafy design adorning it.

Even if she did go her own way once their arrangement had come to an end, she would have some way of protecting herself. And with the skills she had picked up so quickly already, he had no doubt she would be fine. He pushed away a tingling of apprehension as it flitted across his chest and gazed out at the world outside. The previously hard packed snow was now dotted with little puddles of water. Soon they would be able to leave.

"I love it." Her voice came out in a whisper. She looked up from her examination with a smile. "Thank you."

He ducked his head, not knowing how to respond. All the years he'd spent alone he felt acutely.

"Let's spar again. I want to try it out."

"As long as you don't try it out inside my kidney."

She shrugged. "No promises."

Shaking his head with a small smile, he moved to their makeshift sparring arena and readied himself with his own knife. Aleni held the knife out in front of her with a casual but firm grasp. He gave her a nod, and she lunged.

Several hours later, Jacek decided it was finally time to move on. They packed up their gear and put the fire out. Bandur almost looked sad at having to move from his warm spot. He reluctantly pulled himself to his feet and followed them out into the cold. Aleni had her hood back up on her head, holding it close to her face to keep the icy breeze off.

Jacek's feet sank several inches into the snow at every step, making the going slow and arduous. Aleni seemed to flaunt her small size and glided over the top of the ice as though she was walking on clouds. Jacek shook his head to himself. There were times his size came in handy. This was not one of them.

They trudged up the mountain, hiking up a narrow track that switchbacked up towards a summit. The sun couldn't quite touch them on the southern face they were climbing, forcing Jacek to hold his arms close to his body in an effort to stay warm.

At one point they startled a herd of mountain goats, who took off at speed in all directions. Some managed to jump to tiny ledges below the track and somehow looked comfortable and stable in perching themselves there. Aleni marveled out loud at the animal's agility.

By mid-afternoon, they took the last few steps to reach the summit of the mountain. The sun was high in the sky by then, allowing for some warm basking on a large rock. The chill wind tugged at the ends of Aleni's hair.

The valley below stretched out before them like an exquisite painting. A vast forest lay at the base of the mountain, meeting the Milliger river on the north-eastern side. The river fed from a large waterfall on another tall snow-capped mountain in the distance.

Aleni pointed to the mountain. "That's where Y'ha Taesi is."

"That's a mountain." Jacek commented.

"It's inside it," she said with a hint of exasperation.

"Right."

Aleni sighed. "It doesn't look the same."

"What doesn't?"

She gestured expansively. "The whole land. While it is beautiful, it's white and barren. Nothing like my world."

"This is still your world." Jacek wondered why she insisted on thinking back to the past. It was gone now. Nothing was going to change that.

She turned her gaze on him. "No, it's not. All this used to be green and alive. Apart from the forest down there, everything else is dead. Including my people. My family." She looked away, Jacek just catching the sparkle of a tear in the corner of one eye.

Jacek held his breath. Emotions. What should he say? He had so little experience with females. Let alone children. All he knew was from his own experience of loss.

"You have to let it go. Move on. Stop dwelling in the past." He didn't intend on the words coming out with a hint of panic, but they were out now.

The searing look she shot him spoke volumes. "Don't ever tell me to let go of the memory of my family. You have no idea what they meant to me."

He gritted his teeth at the sudden surge of anger in himself. He knew plenty about family and loss. But he probably shouldn't have said that. He let out a breath and scrubbed his hand over his face, wanting to explain himself. His arms hung heavy and his belly knotted.

"Aleni..."

"No." She put up a hand, palm out. "You don't understand. Elves are very tightly connected through emotions and spirit. With them gone, I feel it so strongly. Like a part of me has been cut off. You can't replace them."

"I'm not -"

She cut him off. "You probably think I can be like your daughter or something. You've certainly been treating me like it. Well, I'm not. We're not even the same species! You don't even come close to my own father!" Her words came out hot and cutting.

Jacek hadn't been trying to be her father, he had just tried to be nice to her. She had no one else. Why couldn't she see that? He gave her a long, pained look. She stared back, her eyes narrowed and flinty. After several heartbeats he turned away.

A stone skittered off down the slope as she kicked it away before stomping off. She might be over three hundred years old, but she still had a lot of maturing to do. Jacek looked down at Bandur sitting at his feet. The dog met his gaze with large watery brown eyes, his expression almost an accusation.

"What? I didn't see you stepping in to help."

Bandur merely cocked his head to the side and let out a tiny whine. Jacek gave him a pat behind the ears, finding comfort in the silky fur. What he would give for Bandur to be able to talk.

The way down was easier on Jacek, although it used a whole different set of muscles. The snow had mostly melted on this side of the mountain, leaving loose stones and packed earth on the trail. He heated up quickly in his fur-lined leather armor, the sun baking it till it creaked. Aleni walked a fair distance in front, her hood off and head high with her arms crossed, despite the uneven ground. That was most likely what a huff looked like.

Well, let her have her anger. Hopefully she'd get over it soon. He did understand it, but it wasn't easy being on the pointy end of it. He would take a sword fight any day over dealing with a moody pre-teen. At least he knew how to handle a sword. He wasn't quite sure which one did more damage though.

Birds called to each other overhead, a good sign that the weather might be settling. They were nearly at the end of the long cold months. The next three months were usually warmer, although in the last couple of years those months had been getting shorter. When he was a kid, they had been longer. Selendria's unbalanced ecosystem seemed to be getting worse over time.

Movement above caught his eye, and he looked up to see rocks spilling and bouncing down from the cliff face ahead.

Right above Aleni.

19

Before he had the chance to move or call out, the earth underneath Aleni's feet gave way suddenly. In a space nearly five feet long, the hard path just dissolved. With a cry, she fell to her side, sliding along with the debris cascading down. Jacek sprang into a run, Bandur barking alongside him.

Rocks continued to fall, bouncing and cracking against each other. Aleni rolled onto her stomach, her hands scrabbling to grab hold of anything that was still holding fast, but everything moved with her in the landslide.

A particularly large rock plummeted towards her, hitting her on the top of her head. She went instantly limp, sliding further down off the edge along with the dirt and rocks. Jacek leaped, landing hard on his stomach on the part of the path that stayed firm. His arm shot out and just managed to grasp the cuff of her sleeve with his fingers. Her slide halted, but he barely had her.

Letting out a grunt, he snatched hold of a small sapling on the side of the trail for purchase, trying not to get caught in the landslip himself. His body lay half off the trail, his left leg dangling out over the edge of the cliff. His semi-numb fingers strained at clenching even her slight weight. Below the slip, a sheer cliff dropped off, with large boulders far below. Dirt, rocks and bits of trees plummeted towards the ragged bottom like a waterfall. If he let go, she would fall to her death. Even her accelerated healing most likely wouldn't help with that.

Arm muscles straining, he gritted his teeth and lifted carefully. A ripping sound came from her shoulder. The seams were giving way. He was running out of time. Her head hung limply to the side, blood staining the crown of her alabaster hair. Bandur continued to bark, making his heart beat faster.

"Bandur! Shut it!"

The dog whined, but obeyed.

Knowing he had only one chance to get this right, he planned through his next move in his head. If he could fling her up toward him, he could let go momentarily and get a better grip on her arm. His fingers weren't going to work for much longer.

His cheek pushed into the wet dirt, he took a couple of deep breaths. Bunching his muscles, and with a wordless outcry, he lifted with everything he had. Aleni hoisted toward him a foot more. Just enough for him to let go and make a grab for her upper arm.

His fingers dug into the loose dirt underneath her. Tiny stones caught in his palm, but his hand closed around her slender arm. That was better. He let out his breath in a pant. Now he just had to maneuver himself back onto the trail.

An inch at a time, he wriggled back from the edge, pulling Aleni with him. He just hoped like crazy that the stretch of trail he was lying on wouldn't give way as well. His shoulder muscles strained at the awkward weight. He then felt a tugging on his pack strapped to his back. Looking over his shoulder, he found Bandur had his teeth sunk into it and was pulling. The dog wasn't big enough to pull them both, but Jacek appreciated the support nonetheless.

With a final groan he rolled over on to his side, still gripping her arm. Bandur let go of the pack and backed away. Aleni's chest was now back on solid ground, anchoring her weight in place. He let out a sigh, but still held fast. He didn't put it past the mountain to suddenly give way again.

Getting to his knees, he finally got both hands under her arms and lifted her off the slope. He swung her into his arms, cradling under her back and knees. He took a few steps back from the edge, hugging the cliff face behind them. Aleni's eyes were still closed, her body limp. Jacek got down on one knee, resting her against the other. She still had her pack on, but it wasn't too bulky, so he left it on her. Parting her hair, he inspected the gash on her head. He could see white bone through it and it was bleeding profusely. He had to get somewhere safe so he could lie her down.

The debris from the slip finally settled in a conglomeration of rocks, dirt and small trees. Jacek figured the melting snow must have loosened the soil and rocks. Unfortunately, he was on the wrong side of it. He would have to risk the crossing.

Eyeing up the gap, he figured he could probably jump it. It was about five feet across. He was over six feet tall, it shouldn't be too hard. Except he was carrying Aleni as well. While she was small in comparison, she was still an extra weight and would put him off balance. There was also the chance that the added weight of him landing might set off another slip. He would just have to move fast.

Gauging the distance, he stepped back a little more and lined up his run. He repositioned Aleni so her head was over his shoulder, her body held close and secure. Taking two slow deep breaths, he took a step and ran.

He pushed off just before the edge of the slip, realizing as he did it was unsettled earth. His heart lurched as his feet left the ground, the second he was in the air feeling like an eternity. If the ground was loose on the other side, they were done for.

At last his foot came down on soil. It sunk in a little, but the ground underneath held solid. His breath heaved out in relief. He stepped away from the edge and turned to look back for Bandur. A blur of black and tan fur flew towards him, landing easily. The dog's tongue lolled out to the side, his mouth panting.

"Yeah easy for you, with four legs. Try it on two that are aching and half numb." It felt good to be able to talk out loud with Bandur again, without the risk of being overheard. He knew he tended to complain more with the dog, but it wasn't like the mutt was going to judge him for it.

He shifted Aleni back to a more horizontal position. She was still unconscious, her hair matted with crimson. Her head hung limply. He needed to keep moving.

Picking up the pace, he hiked as quick as possible down the mountain. The trails on this side were a little wider than the southern slopes. Twisting and turning however, the path presented with large rocks and trees that had to be navigated. Jacek almost dropped Aleni in a couple of places, slipping on moss-covered rocks.

As he got lower, the exposed path finally gave way to the cover of the forest. The tall evergreen lashrimmon trees with their soft wide leaves shushed in the wind higher up. Down underneath them, as the forest thickened, it was more sheltered.

Finding a flat spot, Jacek removed Aleni's pack from her back and gently lowered her to the forest floor. The ground was covered in a soft bed of green moss, making a comfy mattress.

From his own pack he retrieved a needle and thread along

with a clean bandage. Being a man of violence, it always paid to have such supplies handy. He'd lost count of the times he'd had to stitch himself back up after an unfortunate encounter.

Resting her head on his lap, he inspected the top of her head again. It looked nasty. He pushed the wound closed and started sewing it shut. It was good she was still unconscious for this, as it would be painful. She was going to be in a lot of pain as it was.

After he finished binding the wound closed, he wrapped the bandage tightly around her head. Hopefully it would be enough to stop the bleeding. He grabbed her sleeping furs and got her settled with one over her and one bundled up under her neck. Now he had to start a fire, making sure she stayed warm.

Leaving Bandur to guard Aleni, he hiked out in search of dry wood. As he searched, he thought back through the events of the day. The argument they'd had. It was his fault, he knew that. He should never have told her to move on. She wasn't ready. Her grief was still so new to her. He had to remember, he'd had more than thirty years to deal with his grief. How had he felt right after it happened? He ran from it. It had nearly ripped him apart. He'd lost himself in violence and death in order to cope. She at least faced it. She needed time to process it.

He was stupid sometimes when it came to emotions. He had to admit it. If he hadn't said those things, she wouldn't have stormed off ahead of him. And then maybe she wouldn't have been caught in the landslip and lying now under that tree with her head split open. He wished he could go back and change what he'd said. But it was too late now. He wouldn't blame her if she decided to leave again. He just couldn't seem to keep her safe.

The soldiers outside the forest had caught them because he was off his guard. He should have been aware of them.

And even in Snowmelt, he had been about to go off on a rampage of killing which would have surely got himself killed and her recaptured. She was the one who had held him back. And now, he had nearly lost her again. Could still lose her if she didn't wake up.

Was caring about someone this much really worth the heartache of losing them?

❧

Aleni became aware of a screaming in her head. Was it her? What was she screaming about? As she lay with her eyes closed and her awareness building, she soon realized it wasn't an audible scream. Pain resided in her. Like it had just decided to move in. She had no way of knowing how long it was staying, but if it carried on too long, she might just start screaming out loud. Never had she felt pain like this before. It pulsated through her head in time to her beating heart.

There was little sense of time, so she had no idea how long she lay there. It was all she could do not to cry out or moan to express the pain. When she finally found the energy to crack her eyes open, she was glad to find the sun had gone. The light would have been too much to handle at that point.

Vision blurry at first, she blinked a few times to focus. Lashrimmon trees soared up into the air, creating a gentle ceiling overhead. A few stars peeked through the gaps, twinkling their light from far away.

Hearing a shuffling on the ground to her right, she turned her head to see Jacek hovering over her. The pain intensified at the movement and she squeezed her eyes shut in response. "Ow." She breathed slowly and deeply in an effort to get it to calm. It worked back down to a dull roar soon enough. "What happened? Where are we?" Her voice came out in a rasp.

"The path gave way in a slip. You were hit on the head by

a rock. Got a nasty gash. We're now in the forest on the other side of the mountain." Jacek said.

She reached back to touch her head gently and found a rough fabric covering it. "Yeah, I can feel that." She attempted to sit up, but wavered as the surrounding forest moved just a little too unnaturally. She felt a steadying hand on her shoulder.

"I'm alright. It will heal quickly."

"I hope so. We're very vulnerable right now. If Krodon were to find us here, we would be done for. He would easily kill me and take you back."

"Thanks for the reminder." She managed to finally sit up without the world tipping and stared at him. A fire licked at the darkness, creating dancing shadows on Jacek's leathery face. The scar that bisected it was raised enough to have its own shadow. That must have hurt when it happened.

"How did you get that scar?"

He passed her a canteen of water. "Drink. Elf or not, you still need to replenish your fluids. You lost a lot of blood."

Aleni took the canteen and drank deeply. The fresh cold water must have come from some nearby stream. "You didn't answer my question."

"An unfortunate memento of a fight with a giant." He paused for a moment, staring out into the dark woods. "Actually, it was a troll. But everyone called it the Giant of Beremor. I didn't disabuse anyone of that notion. A little fearsome reputation never hurt anyone. It was certainly good for business."

"Did it hurt?"

"Of course. But I managed to get myself to a healer who stitched me up reasonably well." He touched the scar, running his finger down it. "I think it adds to the good looks, don't you?" His eyes twinkled, crinkling at the edges.

She returned the expression along with a smile. An expansive feeling grew across her chest. She felt bad now for being mad at him earlier. She could barely remember what it was about.

"How do you feel?" Jacek asked.

"My head is pounding." She placed a hand on her temple, pushing on it. "Could I have some warming tea, maybe?"

Jacek shook his head. "Too risky with a head injury. It thins the blood, making you bleed more."

"Oh."

"I have some broth for you though." He passed her a bowl of steaming liquid. "Try and get that down."

When Aleni had drunk all she could, she passed the bowl back and reached to pat Bandur. The dog raised his head and crawled closer. He stared up at her in adoration. She sensed his feelings, some concern along with relief. He understood what was going on.

"Rest. Bandur and I'll keep watch." Jacek said.

Aleni lay back down carefully and Jacek covered her with the fur. As she closed her eyes she listened to the crackling of the fire and the hoot of an owl somewhere nearby. To try and block out the pain, she listened closely for any other sounds. As she focused hard, she could hear moles in their underground den close by. The scratching of a squirrel climbing a tree. The talk of the trees as they chatted to one another. Lashrimmon trees in particular were terrible gossips. But their nattering lulled her off to thankful sleep again, where the pain didn't follow.

20

When she awoke again, the light cascading through the gaps in the trees pierced her eyes and stabbed at the nerve endings until she blinked a few times to adjust. The pain wasn't as bad now as the night before. Her body had had some time to heal.

Sitting up, she felt a slight sickening in her stomach. Hopefully that would pass soon. She had never felt anything like this before. Was this how Jacek felt all the time?

With that thought, he strode into their campsite just then, a young buck over one shoulder. He looked over to see her awake and gave her a small smile.

Groaning, she pushed herself to her feet. The ground moved farther away then back closer as she swayed slightly.

Dumping the buck on the ground, he rushed over and grabbed her arm. Her head felt cold and spots of light pricked in her vision. She gripped Jacek's arm until she felt her head settle.

"You should stay lying down." He sounded a little annoyed. "It's far too soon for you to be on your feet."

"I told you, we heal quickly."

"Had lots of head injuries, have you?"

She had nothing to say to that. This was her first serious injury - period.

"I didn't think so." He sighed. "At least sit. I'll take a look at it."

He guided her back down to sit on her furs, leaning against the tree behind. The bandage was unwrapped and the top of her head inspected with care. "How..." Jacek shook his head.

"What?"

"It's almost closed up. I could probably take out the stitches tomorrow." He sounded incredulous. He then stared closely at her eyes. His brown gaze was narrowed and his eyebrows knit together in worry.

"What are you doing?"

"Your pupils are a little big. Not a great sign. How's the head feel?"

"Still sore, but better than yesterday."

"Any nausea?" He must have noted her puzzled look and added, "Feeling sick to the stomach."

"Some."

He nodded. "You're very lucky."

"What is luck?"

"Good fortune. Pretty much based on chance. It's just a superstitious thing."

Puzzled, she said, "And you believe in this?"

"Not really. It's just something people say."

"What do you believe in?"

He sat back on his feet, then winced and repositioned to sit on his backside. "I'm not sure. I suppose I believe in what I can see and touch. Some people believe in gods, but I think that's just a way for them to cope with life. To have some hope."

"Hope is important. It doesn't matter how you get it. My parents taught me that." She fidgeted with her hands. She recalled now their argument on the mountaintop.

Jacek was silent for a moment before he spoke. "I'm glad you have good memories of your parents. I'm sorry I said those things yesterday."

While it was good to hear him say it, she still felt bad for her own response. "Do you remember much of your parents?"

He sucked in a breath. "There are good memories, but they have faded over the years. The only memory still vivid is the one of them lying on the floor in a pool of blood." He looked down at his feet. "I'll never forget that."

She closed her eyes in sadness at the thought of him as a little boy seeing that. "I'm sorry that happened. Did you ever catch the woman who did it?"

He shook his head. Aleni couldn't see his eyes, but she suspected they were watering. He probably wouldn't want to admit how much it still hurt. The big tough assassin who missed his parents. They might be different species, but they had more in common than differences. They both bled when cut, and they both longed for connectedness. As Aleni studied his lined and weathered face, she realized with a jolt that she didn't want him to die. Without being aware, this man had come to mean more to her than just a traveling companion. She cared about him.

Underneath the gruff exterior was a man who cared back. She had seen that in the little things like how he'd trained her to defend herself. She ran her fingers over the carved wooden hilt of the knife at her belt, feeling the ornate etchings under her fingers. It wasn't something her own father would have ever bought for her, but from Jacek it meant a lot. Tears pricked at her eyes at the thought of losing him to his illness.

"I'll get this buck butchered and prepared for the journey." Jacek got to his feet slowly. He looked like he was in pain himself. "We won't have time to dry it, but the cold does help to keep it fresh for longer."

"Should we get ready to leave?"

"No." He pointed back at her. "I want you to rest."

She sighed. He might not be her father, but he did sometimes act like it. She supposed she shouldn't hold that against him. It was nice that someone cared. Even if it was an old gruff assassin.

She rested for most of the day, as instructed. But she had a growing sense of impatience at their delay. She was anxious to reach Y'ha Taesi and see if anyone was still alive. Perhaps they had been hiding out all this time? If Jacek had never heard of it, maybe no one had found it. The closer they got, the more she hoped it was true.

By the time dusk infused the forest with a reddish light, her head was feeling clearer. She still had a headache, but the dizziness was gone. Mostly. It only appeared when she stood up suddenly. Jacek led her to a nearby stream where she carefully washed the blood out of her hair and off her face. The water was icy cold, but it felt good to be cleaner.

Back at the camp, Jacek started packing his gear away. "Do you feel up to moving on? You're looking better."

"I do feel a lot better," Aleni said. "Will we be walking through the forest?"

Jacek looked around, although the growing shadows probably hid more for him than for her. "This forest isn't safe. Bandits live here. But I suspect Krodon isn't far behind. He probably went on to the pass after the village. We can't risk traveling out in the open. So, we'll have to head west through the forest until we get to the edge of the Twilfell Basin."

"Are you going to be able to navigate through this forest in the dark? There's no moon out."

"It won't be easy, but I suspect you might be able to help

with that." He gave her a half smile. "You can see in the dark, can't you?"

"How did you know?"

"I've hunted many creatures over the years. I can tell when they can see in the dark."

"You got me. However, I'm not great at direction. You'll have to point me in the right one." Her gaze went to his leg. "Are you going to last long on that leg?" His gait had been getting worse, and she noticed a slight hitch to his step on the way back to camp from the stream.

He went quiet, glancing down at his feet. "I'll be fine."

"Don't forget your medicine." She pointed a finger at him.

"Yes, mother."

The journey through the forest was slow. Aleni kept her senses on full alert, knowing if they got caught by bandits, Jacek might have trouble with them. More than once she heard footsteps crackling on leaves off in the distance and ordered him to get behind a tree to avoid whoever it was. He was quick to follow her instructions.

Bandur stayed close, after a command from Jacek. They couldn't risk the dog running into anyone. Aleni also found, after a stumble from Jacek on a tree root hidden in the dark, she had to point out obstacles to him just to make sure he didn't trip. It was odd seeing him out of his element. Human vision seemed to be quite the weakness. He couldn't hide his growing limp. His leg must have been hurting a fair bit. The illness was progressing. For the first time she discovered she actually wanted them to find a cure.

Aleni couldn't imagine having that fear of impending death. Death itself was such a foreign concept for an elf.

Ironic, since they were all supposedly dead. Fervently, she hoped not.

They hiked all night. The constant movement kept them from getting too cold, but after a few hours, Aleni noticed Jacek's breathing hitch every few steps.

"Let's stop and rest," she said, halting. She estimated it was about three hours before dawn, and she hadn't seen or heard any movement for at least an hour. They were either going in the opposite direction to any bandits or it was just too late for them to be up and about.

"No, we keep going." Jacek let out a long breath, but stopped nonetheless. "We're not too far from the lake."

"You can barely stand."

"I'm fine." He looked like he was trying to stare her in the eye, but she knew he couldn't see her. His eyes lined up more with the top of her head.

"You're not."

He breathed in through his nose. "Then it's probably best we get to where we're headed sooner rather than later, right?"

He did have a point there. If his illness, this wasting sickness, was degenerating quickly, they had no idea how much time he had. For all they knew, he could drop dead in the next hour.

"If you don't rest, even for five minutes, you might not make it there. And I really don't want to have to bury you in these woods. You're... large."

"There's a better place to bury me?"

"I could just dump you in the lake. Much easier."

"It's nice to have someone who cares."

She caught the smile, wondering if he remembered she could see him just fine.

Jacek sighed, his shoulders slumping. "Five minutes. No more. Then we keep moving." After feeling around for a nearby tree, he carefully lowered himself to sit at its base. Bandur came to sit at his side, plopping his head on his master's knee. Jacek patted his friends' head. Taking a drink from his canteen, he then passed it up to her.

"Why do I feel like you're looking after me now?" he said.

"Because I am." She took a drink and handed the canteen back. "You looked after me, so now I look after you. Seems fair." She shrugged.

He gave a grunt and then went silent.

Once the five minutes was up, they moved on. An hour later, they came to the edge of the forest. In the distance sat a large body of water overshadowed by a huge snow-capped mountain. Bigger than the one they had just climbed over. It soared up into the sky like an arrow piercing the blanket of stars. Aleni knew it as Galellias. The covering over Y'ha Taesi.

"Ah, it's good to see again," Jacek said.

"Good. Now I don't have to lead you everywhere." Aleni feigned an annoyed look and walked out in front, eager to get to the mountain.

The pace picked up after that. Another three-quarters of an hour had them at the lake's edge, standing on the rocky shore. Bandur went immediately to the water and started lapping.

"So that's where you were born." Jacek stood with his arms crossed, staring up at the massive mountain.

"Yes. We lived in another forest to the north until I was ten, when we returned here. My parents wanted me to have a traditional upbringing. Unlike some other children my age who were raised entirely under Galellias here."

"Galellias?" He kneeled down and scooped up water to splash on his face.

"'*She who covers*' I believe is the translation."

Wiping his face and beard with both hands, he stood again. "Fitting. Where's the entrance?"

Aleni pointed at the waterfall feeding into the lake from snow melting higher up on the mountain. Cascading down from near the top of the mountain, it fell into a number of catchment pools on the way down, eventually dropping into the lake below. The sight, even at night, was breathtaking. "The entrance is hidden behind the falls. We'll have to find a boat to take us across." Aleni glanced around, but there was nothing nearby.

"Let's have a look."

Following the curve of the lake's edge, they made their way along the shoreline, keeping an eye out for anything they could use to build a raft. Aleni pointed out a few larger pieces of dried wood that would float, but Jacek dismissed them, saying they were the wrong shape for what they wanted.

Finally, Aleni spotted a building in the distance, high up off the shoreline. She pointed to it, but Jacek couldn't see it yet so they crept closer. The porous stones under their feet creaked and crunched, making enough noise that they had to go slow in case someone in the building was watching.

As they got closer, they realized it was a house. By the look of the skilled construction, someone wealthy lived there. The roof actually had ceramic slates on it. Most of the roofs Aleni had seen in Amathnore were just wooden slats. The logs used to construct the walls were well cut and fit together.

"Who lives here?" Aleni asked.

Jacek shrugged. "No idea. More importantly, they have a boat." He pointed to a spot further down the shore, in front of the house. A small wooden dinghy sat alone on the beach.

"Perfect!" Aleni surged forward.

"Wait -" Jacek whispered.

But Aleni didn't care at this point. Home was in sight and there was a means of getting there finally. She rushed down the beach to the dinghy, Jacek lagging behind. As she reached the little boat, she placed her hands on it, feeling the planed wood under her fingers. She looked up at the house, hoping no lights were lit. It sat dark and silent.

"Do you think the people will come after us if we steal their boat?" she asked as Jacek approached.

"That is the least of my worries. Besides, we'll just borrow it. We can return it once we're done in the city." He eyed the boat up and down. It was about ten feet long, with wooden boards across it at intervals for people to sit on. Two oars sat on the bottom, running the length. "How heavy is it?" He hefted one end. It didn't feel light.

Aleni moved down to the stern where it had a flat end. Two wooden handles were attached to lift the boat. She grabbed each handle and tried to lift, but it was too wide for her to get a decent grip and lift at the same time.

"Can you try your magic?" Jacek asked.

Aleni bit down on her bottom lip. She hadn't tried in a while. Not since she'd had to lift Jacek onto the horse. But she had to. Jacek's shoulders were sagging, and he was leaning heavily on the side of the dinghy. Closing her eyes, she set her focus internally. She took a couple of deep breaths in and reached down for the ball of pulsating light. As soon as she mentally touched it, a spear of pain shot through her head, targeting her still-healing wound. An involuntary cry came out and she bent over, clutching her head.

In a second, Jacek was beside her. "Are you alright? What's wrong?"

Pulling away from the magic ball inside her, the pain shrunk back to a dull ache. She gasped and straightened, opening her eyes.

"What happened?" He held a hand out, just shy of touching her shoulder.

"My head." Her hand went to it, over the hood. "As soon

as I tried to access my magic, my head exploded with pain. Maybe my injury is blocking it somehow?"

"Don't try then. Looks like you have more healing to do. Listen to your body." He squeezed her shoulder gently. "We'll have to get the boat to the water the old-fashioned way."

21

Jacek moved to the front of the boat, aware with every step that the stony beach was not the most ideal ground for sneaking around on. The stones ground against each other with his weight, moving and sliding around, making his footing precarious. He gritted his teeth. This was not going how he planned it. Bandur ran around the area, playing in the water and leaping out, dripping. He was acting like a puppy again, suddenly full of life and energy. No one would have thought he'd just walked all night through the woods. The sight of the display of energy made Jacek's body ache even more.

Pain was shooting up his right leg from the ankle to his lower back. He longed to just lie down flat, but he couldn't stop now. Who knew how far behind Krodon was? Considering their delay in the mountains, he may be only a few hours behind them.

He grabbed the prow of the dinghy with both hands, his back to the water and lifted. The boat raised a few inches off the beach. His arm muscles screamed at him to rest, but he bit down on the protests and shut off all but the focus to move. Aleni lifted from the inside of the stern, just under the lip of the edge. Her smaller stature meant she couldn't lift it very high, but she strained at it anyway.

Inch by inch they stepped together down the beach. Jacek glanced back over his shoulder at the water lapping at the stones. About forty or fifty feet to go. They kept moving.

Aleni stumbled, dropping her end. The bottom of the boat gave a horrible scraping sound before Jacek stopped. The sound echoed around the area, carrying over the water and bouncing off the sheer mountain face. He ducked down, hoping the people in the house hadn't been wakened. Aleni took his cue and scuttled around the side of the dinghy, staying low.

They listened, waiting for any sign of life at the house. The chill breeze whisked over their heads, carrying the promise of more snow to come. The only sound was the water washing over the stones behind them.

"I think we're clear," Jacek said after a minute. "Let's move. Daylight is coming."

Aleni returned to her end and lifted again. Jacek took a deep breath and bunched his arm muscles, ready for the weight. He lifted and stepped backwards, making sure to land each foot carefully before lifting the other.

After agonizingly slow progress, Jacek's foot splashed into water. Not wanting to get his leather boots wet, he placed the boat carefully down and stepped to the side. Bit by bit he lifted it forward until he felt the water lift the front. Aleni, arms straining, lifted it forward the rest of the way. Finally, she jumped in and moved quickly to the front of the boat. Jacek jumped in after her, tapping the back of the boat with his hand to call Bandur. The dog ran towards them and leaped in.

Jacek fished the oars out from under the seats and positioned them on the oarlocks each side of the dinghy. Seated in the middle of the boat, he had his back to the bow and dipped the oars.

He had to admit, he didn't have much experience rowing a boat. His father had been a fisherman, but he had only ever fished from the shore, never in a boat. Would he look too inept in front of Aleni?

As it was, when he looked back at her, she wasn't watching him. Her eyes were glued to the waterfall crashing down on the far side of the lake. He bore down and aimed for there.

As they neared the frothy cascade of water, the mist rising up around it engulfed the little dinghy. Jacek breathed in the water-saturated air, the roar the only thing he could hear. A slight echo bounced back at them from somewhere behind the wall of water.

He twisted in his seat to see ahead. Aleni made a curving motion with her hand. She obviously wanted him to navigate around behind the waterfall. After some tricky maneuvering of the paddles, he managed to steer the little boat around the waterfall without filling it with water.

The morning light was growing finally, but as they entered a water-filled tunnel, the darkness closed in again.

It took Jacek half a minute to let his eyes adjust to the tunnel. Low light filtered in through the entrance, but the main light source came from the thousands of glow worms on the rock ceiling. He stared up at them in fascination. He'd only ever seen glow worms once, and never in this number. Like stars in the night, they were almost close enough to reach up and touch.

"Wow." Aleni breathed. "I forgot about the calhenrim."

"You've seen them before?"

"Yes. But it's been a long time."

"We call them glowworms," Jacek said.

"Glowworms. Ha. But they're not worms?"

Jacek shrugged. "I didn't come up with the name."

"Fair enough. I'll stick with calhenrim."

"It does sound nicer."

Jacek's arms ached, forcing him to take little rests as they floated along. Row, rest, row, rest. The boat moved through the tunnel smoothly, water lapping gently at the sides. The water here was like glass. Clear, flat and still. The dinghy glided through it with little noise. Jacek and Aleni both stared up at the glowworms as they floated underneath the insects.

After navigating through a few twists in the tunnel, they eventually came out onto a vast underground lake. The cavern ceiling pushed up away from them alarmingly fast, making them both crane their necks up to try and find the top of the cavern. It seemed lost in the darkness high above. Stalactites hung down, appearing out of the black like javelins. Jacek twisted in his seat to take in the sight. The lake itself stretched out for a mile in each direction, with the far side meeting the edge of a stone landing. Beyond the landing Jacek finally got a glimpse of Y'ha Taesi, the last intact city of the Elves.

Elegant spires rose up into the ceiling of the cavern, born out of graceful buildings below. Jacek didn't even realize a building could be graceful, but in this instance, it was the only word. There wasn't a sharp angle in sight. Everything was curved in some way. A few buildings even looked like trees, but were obviously carved from stone. The craftsmanship was breathtaking.

Aleni was quiet as they drifted toward the city, but Jacek could imagine what might be going through her head. This was the first familiar place she had seen since waking up in the magic chamber. The place of her birth. Hopefully it triggered happy memories and not sad ones.

The boat grated against the stone of the landing gently. Jacek drew the oars in and placed them across the seats. Aleni and Bandur jumped out while Jacek waited for her to hold on to the front of the dinghy.

Once they were all ashore, Jacek pulled the dinghy up onto the landing further so it didn't drift away.

"Now," Jacek said, "where would one find magical artifacts with the ability to heal?"

Krodon loved the fact that his butt didn't hurt so much on the new saddle. He wondered idly if he should have more made.

Shadows faded under the trees as the sun got closer to rising. They had ridden through Milliger Pass nearly an hour ago. The gap in the mountains was guarded by Tarkan's men. Krodon had left a couple of his own men there on the way through to manage it. Tarkan's men had been updated on the events that had happened in Amathnore and had taken the news fairly well. Not that they had a choice. Krodon's smile grew at the thought of his power growing so quickly. Why hadn't he done this years ago?

The sound of two horses thundered towards them from the road ahead. His scouts were returning. Quicker than expected. Had they found something?

The men slowed as they approached, walking their horses to Krodon's place in the line of men. Krodon put his hand up to halt the column. The call rang out down the line until it reached the front.

"My lord." The first man bowed slightly on his horse. He was a little out of breath.

"Report." Krodon said.

The second man spoke up. "We spotted the Red Hunter and the girl getting into a boat on the Twilfell Basin." He pointed back down the road they'd come.

"How long ago?" Krodon asked.

"About ten minutes ago. It's not far from here at a gallop."

"You." Krodon pointed to the nearest soldier, a man who had been acting as his right-hand man for this trip. "Get twenty men and follow me. Leave the rest here. We're going to take out the Hunter once and for all." He dug his heels into his warhorse and took off at a gallop, the mountain overlooking the lake looming in the distance.

❧

Jacek stared up at the tall buildings in awe. There was a sense of being in the presence of giants, even though there was no one in sight. The city lay quiet and undisturbed, ostensibly for three hundred years. Together, they walked between the buildings, down a long street leading into the city proper. Lining the streets at set intervals were tall poles with lights at the top. Jacek figured they must be magical in nature in order for them to still be working after all this time. They let out surprisingly good light for such small devices.

Illuminated by the magical lanterns, piles of bones covered in a thick layer of cobwebs and dust displayed what was left of the elves of Selendria.

Aleni's hand went to cover her mouth as she stared all around her. Had she hoped they would still be alive? She seemed shocked at seeing the evidence firsthand. Jacek had no idea what to say to her. What could he say? She was the last survivor of an extinction level war. There were no social protocols for that. None that he knew of, anyway.

Jacek moved to one of the piles and examined the bones closer. He noted there was no sign of injury on them. He would have expected to see bones sliced through or damaged from weapons in some way. It almost looked like this elf had just laid down and died. Jacek didn't know the details of the war with the humans. That knowledge only their ancestors knew. The ones who had sent the prisoners through the portals. They hadn't deigned to pass that information on to the criminals.

He rose to his feet again and kept moving.

Aleni had told him the mage collegium would be the place to look for artifacts. Despite her apparent shock, she kept moving and led him through the city unerringly to a large building with a silvery curved roof that centered in a pointed apex. What was it constructed of? Jacek had never seen a building made of silver.

Steps led up to the main doors which Aleni pulled open with a flourish. They opened easily and silently, which Jacek was surprised at. Three hundred-year-old hinges should have been a little rusty. Apparently not these ones.

Inside, Aleni looked a little less sure of herself. The antechamber was large and high-ceilinged. Benches sat against each wall, between doors leading off to other rooms. The floor was that same silver color as the roof outside, albeit under a layer of dust.

"I haven't actually been inside here before. It was forbidden for children."

Jacek raised an eyebrow at her. "And you never snuck in?"

"Of course not!" She gave him a dirty look. "Why would I do that?"

"Because that's what kids do when they're forbidden something."

"Human children maybe."

"Surely Elvin children can't be that much different."

"It seems they are." She lifted her chin and made for a doorway on the far side of the room.

They explored through several rooms, finding nothing but more bodies and dust. Finally, in a room beyond a large ornate door in the center of the building, they found what they were looking for.

Lining the walls were a honeycomb of racks holding hundreds of scrolls. At one end sat a desk covered in papers, where a skeleton sat on a chair behind it. Cobwebs covered the remains, which had one hand resting on the desk, over a partially written document. To one side of the desk sat a white fist-sized stone. Jacek lifted it to examine. It had a rune on it that he couldn't decipher.

"What does this mean?" He held the stone out for Aleni to look at.

After a quick look at it, Aleni went back to her perusal of the room in general. "It's the symbol of someone's name. Pyrravyn. He was the high mage of the elves. The most powerful magician we had." She studied the bones, which were brown with age. "Maybe this is him. That would make sense."

Pulling out the papers under his hand, she started to read. "'These are the last days of the elves, I fear. We have fought long and hard, but the creatures who came through the portals have bested us. I am dying, along with every other elf in Selendria. I have tried to capture a healing spell in an elrydd stone to try to boost its efficacy. But it is no use.'" Aleni stared at the stone in Jacek's hand. "That must be it there."

"You mean... this could heal me?" Jacek stared at it hard. "I don't feel any different."

"It's probably dormant after all this time." Aleni held her

hand out for it and Jacek dropped it into her palm. She rolled it between her hands, cupping it firmly.

"Can you activate it?"

Her brows furrowed into a single line. "I'm not entirely sure how. This just feels like a normal stone. Like the one in Amathnore, with the monk. I don't sense anything magical within it. But my parents never taught me anything about the art of elrydd."

"El-rid?" Jacek echoed.

"The art of imposing magic into an inanimate object. I only heard about it in passing." Her eyes met his as she passed the stone back to him. "I'm sorry Jacek. I know you wanted a better answer than that." She lowered her gaze back to the paper and continued reading.

"'We tried everything we knew, but the creatures infected us with some sort of sickness. It takes away our ability to heal rapidly. We have no idea how they have done it, and possibly with time we could find a cure. But our time is up. The infection has spread from the front lines throughout our people, like ants carrying poison back to their queen. We have been annihilated in a most cowardly way.'"

Aleni's eyes widened at the revelation. Jacek found himself surprised too. He had had no idea.

"'The creatures sent through a poison gas that covered the area for miles. Elves everywhere immediately began to die. We are being exterminated.'"

Tears formed in Aleni's bright blue eyes, pooling and then dripping down her cheeks. She dropped the pages back on the desk. She hung her head and slumped against the desk.

Should he say something? Jacek looked around the room. Anywhere but at the young girl.

"Your people did this." Her voice came out in a whisper, breaking on the last word.

Jacek whipped his head back to watch her. Her face was

hidden underneath the fur-lined hood of her coat, her white hair hanging limp out the bottom of it.

"What sort of creatures are you?" She lifted her head to look at him again. Her eyes were now cold, dead. Lip curled, she spat out, "what did the elves ever do to the humans to deserve such treatment? Why all this killing? What possible reason?" She flung her hands out wide.

For the first time, Jacek felt the full shame of what his ancestors had done. As far as he knew, they had just wanted the land for themselves. Overcrowding on their home world had led to finding other solutions. Scientists had discovered they could open portals to other worlds and the rest was history. Although it seemed the official history had been edited by the victors. He wondered what the rest of the inhabitants of Selendria would think if they knew the truth. Not that this had been their decision.

It seemed when the powers that be saw Selendria as a cold and hostile world once the elves were gone, they decided their criminals could be exiled there. He'd bet a thousand Olons it had been originally intended for the rich and powerful.

Knowing there was no satisfactory answer, Jacek stayed silent. The weight of history bore down on his shoulders, shot at him by this lone young girl. He imagined she felt extremely alone right now. He squeezed the stone in his hand. Now this magic was his only hope.

"I can't even look at you," she said, turning her head away. "I should never have come with you." She stalked to the doorway, running a hand over Bandur's back as she went.

"Aleni." Jacek knew he had to say something, he just didn't know what.

She stopped and raised a hand. "Just leave me alone. Don't follow me. If I associate with you, it would be like stomping on the memory of my people."

With that, she walked out.

⚜

Running through the streets, tears running down her face, Aleni had no direction in mind. She just wanted to get away from Jacek as quickly as possible. She pushed her speed and felt the air whipping past her face. The hood fell back off her head, letting her hair stream out behind her.

Buildings flew past as she turned down streets and ran through alleys. Her subconscious mind drove her, for she soon found herself outside a very familiar house. It was the largest house in Y'ha Taesi. If not for the grime of the years it looked just like it had the last time she'd seen it.

It was the house of the royal family of the Elves.

A sudden dizziness hit her and her knees gave way as a great longing thudded through her chest. She collapsed onto the stone steps in front of the house and wept. Great sobs bubbled up from her stomach as she reached for the memory of her parents. Of all her people, why did she have to be the one to survive? Why couldn't they have just let her die with them? Did her parents really think that by saving her they were loving her?

If only they knew what had happened to her since waking up. If only they knew the loss she felt. If only they knew the guilt that hung on her shoulders like a yoke. With her face in her hands, she let out a keening wail. The sound echoed around down the street and disappeared into the shadows. She didn't know how long she sat there, but it felt like forever. Her hands became sopping with her tears. Not only was she crying over the loss of her family, but the worry of what she was going to do next terrified her. She was all alone now. She couldn't stay with Jacek. It just wasn't right. How could she call the descendant of her people's killers a friend? All the people in Selendria were now an enemy.

What was she supposed to do with her life now? She couldn't go to school, couldn't get a life partner, or have children. What were her parents thinking?

This was no life. She might be breathing, but she wasn't living. With the memories of what Krodon had done to her haunting her every waking moment, and even her sleeping moments, she wasn't sure she wanted to keep living. What was the point?

Letting her hands droop over her bent knees, she hung her head between them. A sudden heaviness fell over her and her mind numbed.

"I can't do this," she whispered in elvish. "I'm sorry mother and father. I know you sacrificed a lot for me, and want me to live, but I can't do it. There's nothing for me here."

She unsheathed the knife Jacek had given her, running her fingers over the ornate hilt. The blade glinted in the light from a nearby lantern pole. She drew her index finger over the edge of it to test its sharpness. A tiny line of blood welled on the tip. It was plenty sharp. This might be easy.

Just then she heard footsteps approaching. Her first thought was that Jacek had ignored her and was coming after her anyway. Gritting her teeth, she got to her feet and looked up, preparing to throw a verbal volley at him.

But instead of the assassin, she came face to face with her abuser, Krodon.

He stood ten feet from her with fifteen or twenty men spread out behind him. How did she not hear them approaching sooner?

Her chest constricted and she found she couldn't take a breath. For what felt like hours, but was only seconds, she was frozen to the spot. Her mind shut down all thought and her heart pounded in her ears. When time finally started again, her breaths came in short gasps. Her body trembled and broke out in a sweat despite the cool air. How did he get here? Was he actually real or had she fallen asleep?

"Hello Aleni." His voice sounded real enough. Terrifying, but real. "It's been a while since we've seen each other. Did you miss me?"

All Aleni could do was shake her head. Her voice wouldn't work. She twitched a hand, thinking that maybe she could use her magic against him. She dove inside for the radiant ball of power. There was nothing there. She couldn't find it. Just darkness and a wall. She tried to push against it mentally, but it held solid.

Feeling hands on her arms, she came back to herself and found a soldier was standing behind her, gripping her roughly. Her knife was pulled out of her hand and thrown to the side with a clatter.

"Where's the Red Hunter?" Krodon asked, looking around. His eyes hardened and his mouth turned up into a sneer.

Aleni just stared at him. Even if she could speak, she had nothing to say at that moment. Nothing that would satisfy the hatred that burned in her gut.

"No matter, I'm sure he's around here somewhere." He clicked his fingers and then swirled them in the air. Some sort of sign to his men to begin the search. They peeled off in different directions in twos and threes.

Leaving her alone with one soldier and her rapist.

☙❧

With a thickness in his throat, Jacek slumped to the floor on his knees. His stomach twisted. She was right. They had no business being friends. Or whatever they were. Jacek didn't even know how to define their relationship. Did he really think he could replace her father? It sounded pathetic now.

He was an assassin, a mercenary for hire. A violent killer. Descended from thieves, murderers and rapists. Evicted from a society of people who had committed genocide on a peaceful race of elves. He felt sick to the stomach. Letting out a heavy sigh, he stared at the white stone in his hand. It was perfectly round and as smooth as glass. Cool to the touch, it weighed about two pounds. The symbol burned onto the surface was black but there was no texture to it. If he had been blind, he wouldn't know it was there.

Aleni was his only hope of activating it. Except she had no idea how. Maybe with time she could read through documents here and learn how, but he still didn't know how long he had. He lifted his attention to Bandur, sitting patiently in front of him. The dog's tongue lolled out of his mouth casually, creating a canine smile.

Jacek rubbed his friend's ear, giving him a good scratch on the head. Bandur's eyes closed in contentment.

Maybe he should just accept his fate. He'd lived a fairly long life by Selendria standards. His parents had told him of people from the home world living for nearly a century. He couldn't imagine how old they must have looked. In his profession, dying was always a possibility. He just didn't want to die this way. With his body slowly failing and his mind still intact.

Ending it himself was not an option. He wanted to go out fighting; it was just his way.

While he wanted to respect Aleni's wishes to be left alone, he worried about her. Seeing her surrounded by the goblins still sat vividly in his mind. Goblins of course weren't the only danger in this world. Bandits, greedy people, and of course Krodon himself to name a few. She would be forever having to look over her shoulder. Even with the little he'd shown her for self-defense, she wouldn't last long. He had the skills to teach her how to stay safe, but it would take time.

Weighing up how angry she'd be, he finally decided it would be better for her if he tried to help, even if he didn't live much longer. Then at least he could leave Bandur with her.

He'd give her some time and then go find her. She had a lot to process.

Krodon stared at the young elf, taking in her beauty. Her face was a perfect ivory, smooth and flawless. Her eyes drew him in like great pools of fresh water. How could someone so young be so captivating? She didn't even fight the soldier holding her. Instead, she just stared at Krodon with wide blank eyes. There was something wrong with her. But he didn't have time to figure it out now. He had to be alert for the Red Hunter, who was bound to show up soon. He didn't know why the Hunter was interested in this girl, but she was Krodon's alone. He wasn't letting her go this time.

He had great plans, and he couldn't do it without her. All for his little Arlette.

But first, the Red Hunter had to be brought to his knees. He had to die.

Movement in the street ahead alerted Jacek to something going on. He hid with Bandur between two buildings, peering out from behind the corner to scan the surroundings. He spotted two soldiers moving cautiously further down the street, not even attempting to hide in the shadows. The magical lamps lit the streets well, leaving little room to maneuver with stealth.

He looked at Bandur and gave him a hand signal that meant go hunt. The dog bounded off down the alley behind him. He took his bow and drew an arrow from the quiver where it was strapped to his pack. These were Krodon's men. The Warlord must have followed them here. He cursed his illness yet again for his brain fog in not picking up the tail sooner. Now he had a battle on his hands. One he wasn't sure he was up for.

He had to find Aleni and warn her. But first, he had to hunt.

The bow twanged and an arrow flew with perfect accuracy toward the soldiers, lodging itself in the face of the first soldier just below his left eye. Red blossomed, and the man fell in a lifeless heap on the street. His partner gaped at his fallen comrade in horror then whipped his head around, searching the shadows, his sword held uselessly aloft. Another arrow whizzed through the air and the man fell with it protruding from his throat.

Jacek took off down the street, hugging the shadows.

At the next intersection he spotted three more soldiers creeping down another street. He took off in pursuit.

Just before he came up on them, he threw a smoke bomb on the ground at their feet, taking a mental picture of the men. A big cloud of chemical smoke wafted up from the broken ball, engulfing the three men in a clot of obscurity. Jacek drew his knife and held his breath, wading into the opaque soup. Using his ears more than his eyes, he slashed and stabbed at the soldiers.

A bark from his left alerted him to Bandur bounding in to the fray. The sound turned to a growl as leather ripped and teeth tore in. Screams erupted from the men, but they were soon silenced. Not that Jacek was too worried about them making noise. He would be gone long before anyone could investigate.

As the smoke cleared, three bodies lay in a bloody heap on the street. Jacek heaved in great lung-fulls of fresh air. The ground moved more than it should in his eyes. He gripped Bandur's scruff for balance and the two moved silently away into the gloom.

He found a small spot between two buildings where he could hide for a minute. He had to get his breath back. His legs were aching and his left hand was starting to go numb again. How much longer could he carry on like this? The last time he got into a fight he'd ended up having a fit. He'd been lucky Aleni was there to look after him. Otherwise he'd probably be rotting in Krodon's dungeon if another patrol had come across them.

Aleni wasn't here now to insist he rest. Where did she go? She better not have been caught by Krodon. Jacek didn't know what he would do if she had. He had no idea how many men Krodon had with him. Luckily for him, so far they seemed spread out in twos and threes. Easy pickings. On a good day.

Today was not a good day. Today was a desperate day.

Finally having caught his breath, Jacek got to his feet and moved off, Bandur close behind. The streets were not straight, like Amathnore, set out in a grid. These streets curved and snaked into circular intersections where they met in the middle and morphed into a graceful statue of some beautiful figure or creature. Nothing in the city was ugly or plain or rushed. It all looked carefully planned out and painstakingly built. Artisans had taken care to get every curve perfect, whether it was the gutter of a street or the edge of a breast on a statue. He liked those statues. But he didn't have time to sit and admire them now.

Near a guard tower, he heard hushed voices coming in his direction. He tried the door at the base of the tower and found it unlocked. With Bandur, he slipped inside, shutting the door firmly behind him and pushing a bolt across to lock it. Finding himself at the bottom of a spiraling stone staircase lit from somewhere above, he started climbing. Gripping his bow in his right hand, he gritted his teeth against the pain in his leg muscles as they cramped at the strain.

At the top, the stairs led out onto an open balcony with a full circle view of this part of the city. He crept to the edge which was bordered by a half wall. Crouching behind it, he peered over the top and scanned for soldiers. About fifty feet away, four men advanced down the street in his direction. Two of them had bows on their backs, while the other two had swords and wooden bucklers.

Motioning for Bandur to stay down, he nocked an arrow and took aim. He would have to take out one of the bowmen first and then hope they were disorganized enough to stand around and wait for him to kill the second one. Not likely, but one could always hope.

The arrow flew and the first bowman died with a shaft decorating the middle of his ear. Unfortunately, that was the easiest it got. The other three fled for cover in three directions. One got behind a building while the second bowman found a sturdy wooden barrel. The third man Jacek lost sight of as he ran toward the base of the tower. The soldier couldn't know yet where the arrow had come from, but he would figure it out pretty soon.

He loosed an arrow at the man behind the barrel. The soldier ducked, and it missed him by a few inches, hitting the stone building behind him and breaking in half. Swearing, Jacek ducked when the man returned fire. An arrow flew past his head by half a foot. He wasn't too bad a shot. He would definitely have to die next.

The next shot missed by an inch, nearly taking off the soldiers' ear. They traded a couple of shots each, Jacek struggling with his numb fingers. Trying to get them to work properly was distracting him which contributed to the soldier's next shot slicing through Jacek's right bicep. He flung himself to the floor of the tower, adrenaline spiking at the sudden surge in pain. He inspected the wound carefully, pulling the leather sleeve away from his skin. It was bleeding a fair bit, but it was only a flesh wound. There was pain, but he found he could still move his arm.

Just then, a banging came from the bottom of the stairs. The fourth soldier had discovered his spot and found the door. It sounded like he was trying to break the door down. Hopefully, elvish engineering would hold up long enough for him to take out the other two soldiers.

Checking his supply of arrows, he determined he only had a few shots left to get this archer before he had to try something else.

He looked in his pouch for smoke bombs. Two left. He had no idea how many more men were out there, but he wouldn't get a chance to get to them if he didn't take these shitfaces out. He hefted one of the balls and popped his head up to see what was going on. The bowman was standing, looking at his compatriot. He must think he had got Jacek in the last shot. Jacek ducked back down and put the smoke bomb away. He nocked another arrow and bobbed up again. Within a second he had the arrow sighted and let fly. The bowman dropped in a boneless heap on the ground.

Two left.

He pulled another arrow from the quiver and sighted

again. The third soldier was still huddled behind a building, popping his head out at intervals. Jacek waited until the man's head appeared and released. The wall behind him splattered with red as the man died instantly.

Now it was just the last one banging on the door. Creeping down the stairs, he listened. The soldier was whacking the door with something heavy. A rock maybe? The solid wooden door rattled against its hinges but held fast. Bandur backed up at each sound, looking uncertain. Jacek gave him a reassuring pat.

Moving to the door, he put his hand to the bolt. Between two thuds, he slid it back and stepped to the side. The door flew open on the next hit with such force, the soldier stumbled through the doorway off-balanced. He was holding a large rock which pulled him to the ground with its weight. Jacek was on him instantly, his knife sliding smoothly into the back of his neck between two vertebrae. He used his body weight to push the blade home until it exited out the front of the throat. With a gurgle the soldier breathed his last.

Jacek got to his feet, letting out a relieved sigh. He wiped his knife on the man's clothes and put it back in its sheath. He moved his arm around experimentally, which just made it bleed more. He had to bind it up or he'd lose too much blood.

Dropping his pack, he withdrew a strip of cloth. Holding one end in his teeth, he tied it tightly around his arm, covering the wound. He winced as he pulled the cloth tight. It hurt like a bitch, but it would do for now. He could deal with it more thoroughly later. If he was still alive.

Leaving his pack on the floor of the tower, Jacek and his dog set out to hunt once more.

Ten minutes later and several streets away, two more soldiers lay dead at Jacek's feet. Blood dripped from Bandur's maw.

The Hunter wiped his knife on one of the soldier's uniforms. Where was Aleni? He'd been working his way through the streets methodically, but there had been no sign of the young elf.

His legs aching and his left hand seizing up, he sheathed the knife and drew his axe. How many more soldiers were out there? And where was Krodon himself?

He took off down the street, his ears tuned for anyone else around. He kept a close eye on Bandur, as he was trained to alert when he heard a sound. He knew when to keep silent too.

At the next intersection, Bandur went still and his ears perked up. Found a mark. Jacek quickly moved into a nearby building, standing next to an open doorway. Bandur followed, staying close to his right leg.

Before long, four men stepped into the circular intersection from a building across the way. Jacek palmed a smoke bomb - his last - and waited until they were close. The men moved cautiously, with their swords out and ready, like they were expecting an ambush. It was entirely possible they'd heard the screams.

Jacek didn't want to disappoint. He threw the ceramic ball and waited for it to smash and release its contents. When it did however, only two men got caught in the smoke. The other two stepped away, their heads darting around the area. Jacek knew he had to move quickly. Man and dog burst out of the building and raced at the two men. Bandur leaped at one, using his weight to take the man to the ground. His teeth ripped into the soldier's throat with a spurt of blood.

Jacek had his hands full with the second man. He rushed in with his axe already swinging. The soldier leaned back to avoid the strike to his face just in time. He was good. His stance and balance already showed his skill. His sword came up in an attempt to slash at Jacek's chest. He danced out of the way. The two traded blows, blocking and attacking in turn. Tiring quickly, Jacek tried desperately to find an opening. Bandur let out a bark and a growl, possibly going for the other two caught in the smoke who were still coughing and spluttering. Jacek didn't have time to look. It was taking all his concentration to keep from being sliced open.

While blocking attacks and moving constantly to avoid the soldier's advancements, he waited for the man to make a mistake. Finally, the moment came. The soldier over-committed with an attack to Jacek's torso. Jacek slid to the side and let his axe come down in a quick move that left his weapon embedded in the crook of the man's neck. Blood spurted and the man screamed, dropping his sword. He fell to his knees. Jacek ripped the axe away and swung again, with more strength this time.

The soldier's head flew from his body and landed in a bloody heap several feet away. The body wavered upright for a couple of seconds before falling forwards onto the pavement.

Letting out an exhausted sigh, he turned to find Bandur standing near the dissipating smoke with a sword arm in his mouth, tugging on it furiously. The man was trying to pull away with his mouth set in a fearful grimace. There was little more terrifying than a vicious animal with his teeth sunk into a limb. The man obviously wasn't thinking straight, or he wouldn't be pulling. It was just making it worse. Bandur's teeth just tore through his flesh faster. And he wasn't letting go.

Putting his axe away, Jacek drew his knife instead. He finished the soldier off with his blade sunk in between two vertebrae. The man crumpled to the ground, his eyes blank.

The fourth soldier already lay with his throat torn out, red pooling around him like a gruesome lake. Jacek kneeled in front of his dog and rewarded him with a good scratch and a rub down his back. He wagged his tail enthusiastically, the fur around his mouth stained scarlet.

"Thanks buddy. Looks like you're doing more than your fair share today. I'm sure glad I have you here. C'mon, let's go find that girl of ours. Even if she doesn't want to be found."

❧ 24 ❧

He found her finally after ten more minutes of scouring the underground city and rooting out a few more soldiers. Jacek left them in a gruesome heap in the middle of a street. When he came upon Aleni, she was not alone. A large building that looked like a residence sat on a wide boulevard that was home to several other large residences. The one they were outside was the largest. She was being held by Krodon with a bowman next to him standing on the steps leading up to the house.

Jacek was hiding behind a low wall and watching the three when he saw Aleni look his way. She must have heard him with her well-tuned hearing. Jacek had to hold on to Bandur to make sure he didn't run over to her. He was getting excited knowing she was right there.

While he racked his brain for strategies, he noticed a slight shimmering surrounding Aleni and Krodon. Was she doing something magical? Krodon didn't appear to be worried. In fact, the warlord looked rather relaxed. Too relaxed.

He wore curved iron chest armor that gleamed in the artificial light of the street lanterns. Bear fur made up a short cloak that sat on his shoulders and flowed down his back. His legs were encased in thick black leather tucked into knee-high hardened leather boots. A large sword rode on his left hip, with a knife sheathed on his right.

He had one hand resting firmly on Aleni's right shoulder. She stood frozen in place with her face a blank mask. Jacek realized the presence and the touch of Krodon would be filling her with fear because of his past treatment of her. He clenched a fist in anger, wanting to kill Krodon even more.

Stepping out from his hiding place, he commanded Bandur to stay beside him. He raised his hands and walked towards the three on the steps. In his right hand he held the stone they'd found in the mage collegium. The bowman spotted him and drew his bow back to aim it at Jacek.

"Ah, there you are!" Krodon said, spearing Jacek with a glare. "I knew you would turn up eventually. You must really want this one." He glanced down at Aleni.

"Let her go, Krodon."

"Why would I do that? I've come all this way."

"She's no use to you."

"Ah, but that's where you're wrong. She is the key to my plan. You see, this world never used to be frozen in winter. I believe it was once a paradise, with a temperate climate. When the elves all died, the world got out of balance."

"And you think she can help get it back into balance?"

"With her I can breed the elves back into existence, restoring this world to its former glory."

Jacek's stomach turned. Aleni was a child and Krodon wanted to use her as a brood mare? Had already tried in fact. Did the man have no moral boundary? Something Aleni had told him came to mind.

"The elves don't breed as easily as us. She may not have a

child for a hundred years or more. Long after you're dead. It's pointless."

"It's worth trying. She is our only hope. And if I don't get there, others can carry on the legacy after me."

"So, what, you'll lock her up in your dungeon, just to have her as your sex slave for her entire life?"

"It's not like that." Krodon lifted his chin to look down his nose at Jacek.

"It's exactly like that!" Jacek roared.

"She will be preserving her people. Bringing them back from extinction."

"She's a child!" Jacek watched Aleni closely. She was still frozen in fear.

"She's old enough to bear children." Krodon's eyes hardened.

"Doesn't mean she should. I'm sick of your bullshit Krodon. In my hand here I have a magical artifact we found. You can have it in exchange for her."

Krodon stretched out a hand toward him. Jacek felt the stone slip from his grasp as a powerful force pulled at it. The stone hovered in the air and glided toward the warlord. Did he have magic already? Shit. They were screwed.

The stone hung in the air in front of Krodon's face. It turned as he inspected it carefully. Aleni stared up at it, her eyes only a little less blank than before.

C'mon kid, snap out of it. Jacek stared at her, trying to meet her eyes to communicate silently to her. But she continued to stare at the stone instead.

He turned his attention back to the stone and Krodon. The warlord met his gaze and gave a cold smile. The expression did not reach his eyes. With a snarl, he closed his fist and the stone broke into a hundred pieces before crumbling into sand and falling to the ground.

With it went all Jacek's hope. He watched with a sinking

heart as the last grains landed in a pile on the steps. He continued to stare at it for a few seconds before Krodon broke the silence.

"You don't look so well, Red. You've gone rather pale. What did you have the stone for? Were you hoping for something from it?"

Eyeing the archer standing to the side, Jacek threw all caution to the wind and pulled his own bow from his back. The archer didn't move. In one fluid move, he pulled an arrow from his quiver, nocked it and drew back, letting it fly right at Krodon's head. As soon as the arrow loosed, he released another one. Both stopped a few feet from Krodon, hitting an invisible barrier and dropping ineffectually to the ground. There was some sort of magical shield around him and Aleni.

His eyes dropped to Aleni. Her chest was heaving in breaths, her bright blue eyes wide. He knew if the arrows had got through, he wouldn't have hit her, but she might not have known that. He regretted scaring her, but it was worth the try.

❧

Aleni's heart pounded nearly out of her chest as she stood immobilized by Krodon's touch. Jacek had no hope against Krodon. He had a ring that appeared to hold a lot of power and was able to manipulate objects and control a shield around him. If he used it against Jacek, the assassin would die very quickly.

Then she would be taken back to the warlord's castle and thrown back into his dungeon. Back into a nightmare. Her breath quickened as the horrifying images assaulted her memory. She felt her body heat up as sweat broke out on her forehead. She couldn't go back. She couldn't. She would die first.

"Did you hope it would help you free her?" Krodon was still talking to Jacek. He squeezed her shoulder hard, making her bones creak. She let out a cry of pain that snapped her out of the memories and anchored her back in the present.

Bandur barked and charged at them. Jacek made a futile grab for the dog, but Bandur was too fast. He leaped at Krodon, but hit the magical barrier mid-flight and fell back awkwardly to the steps. The dog looked a little confused, but continued to bark at the warlord, baring teeth surrounded by crimson fur.

Time slowed then as Aleni heard the twang of the bow before she saw the arrow fly through the air in front of her. With a sickening hollow thud, the arrow pierced Bandur's chest, and the dog hit the ground with a canine yelp.

Somebody screamed. It took her a moment or two to realize it was her. She felt detached from her own body, like she was looking back on the scene like a ghost.

Jacek's mouth dropped open in horror at the sight. He made to step forward as if to go for his dog, but Krodon put out a hand towards him. Jacek seemed to push up against something and went no further. Krodon seemed to be holding him in place with magic.

Aleni struggled against Krodon's grip, trying to get to Bandur, who lay very still on the steps. His chest moved in very small breaths. Blood was pooling out of his mouth. He wasn't going to survive, she could tell. It was just like with the horse after the goblins.

Krodon pushed her towards the archer who dropped his bow and grabbed her with an arm around her chest. He pulled out a knife and held it to her throat. The point bit into her skin. She held herself still after that, focusing on the dog lying on the steps. His tail, normally wagging furiously, lay flat and limp.

Jacek breathed heavily out through his nose as his blood pounded in his ears. His best friend was dead. In an instant, his life snuffed out. His vision clouded and all he could see was the monster standing over the dog's body. The pain in his legs and hand melted away as adrenaline built and cut off all sensation. Krodon had to die now. The archer's life was also forfeit as soon as the arrow had left his bow.

All he wanted now was vengeance. Blood had to be spilled. He drew the large sword from the scabbard on his back with a smooth movement. His left hand was almost useless now, so he would have to hold the two-handed weapon with just his right. But with the single-minded purpose came a sudden strength throughout his body. He flexed his muscles as he gripped the handle of the sword.

"Ah, now you want to fight?" Krodon said.

"Fight me like a man, Krodon. Not hiding behind magic."

Krodon lowered his hand. The wall of pressure in front of Jacek fell away. "Indeed, it is time we fought." The warlord rolled his shoulders and drew his sword, stepping over Bandur's body and down the steps until he stood on the street across from Jacek. He swung his sword in a figure of eight in front of his body. Jacek stood still, one foot in front of him in a balanced fighting stance.

"My father told me I would be no match for you. Time to prove him wrong."

"Your father was wiser than I thought," Jacek replied.

"Not wise enough. I killed him with my bare hands."

"He was an old fat man. Not sure I'd be boasting about that."

"You're no spring chicken yourself. Not the legendary fighter I had heard about."

"But you have heard of me." Jacek took a step forward. "Enough chatting. Let's get on with this. The sooner you die, the sooner I can bury my dog, motherfucker."

Krodon came at him suddenly in a blur. He moved faster than Jacek had expected, but he was ready. He caught Krodon's slightly smaller blade with his own massive one, the metal ringing in his ears and the shock pulsating right up to his shoulder. With a push back, he made room for a swing at Krodon's head. The warlord blocked the huge blow with some effort and stepped to the side.

The two traded strikes and parries, pushing forward and giving ground in a careful dance to the tune of murderous intent. Sweat broke out on Jacek's body and he pulled air in through his nostrils in great heaves. Krodon didn't look anywhere near as taxed.

As Krodon slashed down on an angle from high overhead, Jacek slid inside the reach of the warlord's arm and sliced across his belly.

As it was, the long-sword cut through a layer of thick leather to only graze Krodon's skin. The warlord pulled away, creating distance between them as he felt his stomach. His hand came away with blood, but it wasn't a deep cut.

Jacek bared his teeth at his opponent, wishing he'd had the strength to cut him in half. It was true, he wasn't young any more. The strength he'd previously felt with the adrenaline was starting to flag now.

Krodon charged at him, sword straight out in front, face set in a scowl. Jacek whacked the sword to the side and stuck an elbow out as he got within range. Krodon dodged away just in time. The two circled each other, watching for the next move, waiting for an opening.

Just then, a spasm ran up Jacek's right leg, spearing pain

into the base of his spine. He grimaced and his leg collapsed underneath him. He stabbed his sword into the ground to stay upright, but the opening was there. Krodon made his move. Jacek knew he was dead.

Krodon's sword entered through his stomach and ran up on an angle, pushing out halfway up his back. Gasping at the sudden pressure in his body, his brain scrambled to catch up with what was happening. Strangely, there was no pain. His other leg collapsed then, and he struggled to hold on to his sword, the only thing keeping him up.

A high-pitched scream rang out in the vast cavern.

❧ 25 ❧

Aleni's throat felt raw after her scream died away. It hadn't even been a conscious thing. Seeing Jacek speared like a boar galvanized her into action.

She grabbed at the hand holding the knife to her throat and pushed it away with one hand while biting down on the forearm holding her. His sleeve was made of a soft leather, unlike Jacek's hardened bracers. She gave it everything she had, sinking her teeth through the leather and into flesh until blood ran freely. The soldier cried out in horror and pain. It was probably the last thing he expected her to do. Spinning out of his grasp, she shoved his knife hand toward his throat before he could react. She knew her speed was much faster than a human, and she was strong. The knife sank into the man's neck with a spurt of blood. She left him to drop to the ground and turned away toward Krodon and Jacek.

The warlord had pulled his sword out, leaving Jacek gasping for breath. She watched in dismay as he plunged it back into the assassin's body, this time higher up on his chest. Jacek's body jerked and he let out a pained breath. Krodon pulled the sword out, dripping red.

"No!" Aleni reached out her right hand in his direction. With her pain and rage, power bubbled up out of her. She didn't have to reach for it this time. It was just there at her fingertips,a vengeful dragon waiting to explode with might. The magic flew out and grabbed Krodon in a vice-like grip, lifting him up off the ground with little effort.

Krodon writhed violently in the clutches of the magic, futilely trying to escape. Aleni squeezed her fist closed, putting immense pressure on the muscular warlord. His metal breastplate crumpled inward, lines forming like folds on paper. The sound of bones cracking accompanied his screams.

Aleni let out a yell of her own, images of him on top of her branded into her brain. He had to die for what he'd done to her. For what he'd done to this world. For killing Jacek and Bandur.

Pressure built up in her head as she watched him writhe and scream in pain. Blood dripped from his ears and nose. The only sound she heard was the roaring in her head. It might have been coming from her mouth. Nothing else existed in that moment except her foe squirming in extreme pain under the force of her magic.

Her eyes dropped to Jacek on the ground, his sword lying next to him. With a tendril of power, she lifted it slowly to hover it directly over the top of Krodon, point down. The warlord's eyes widened at seeing his impending doom.

Memories of her parents flashed through her mind. Their smiling, serene faces, teaching her to be kind to all living things. Well, they weren't here now. They were long dead. This was a different world. It was kill or be killed, like Jacek said.

But as she held the blade over him, hovering just short of spearing him, she wondered how she would feel once she'd killed him. It wouldn't change what he'd done. She'd still have the memories. Her innocence would still be gone. Bandur and Jacek would still be dead. What would it do, really?

Gritting her teeth, she fought with the desire to kill him. Then another thought came into her head. He deserved to live with the pain. Death was too good for him. He currently most likely had multiple broken bones and maybe internal damage to his organs. If he had to live through that, that would be enough. Let him be crippled for life, like her.

With a drawn-out scream, she threw him down the street. He fell and rolled on the pavement in the distance and lay still. Aleni lowered the sword carefully to lie back down next to its master.

Energy flagging, she nearly fell to the ground as her knees buckled. Bracing her hands on her knees, she pushed them back into a locked position, holding herself still for a few seconds until she knew she was steady.

Rushing to Jacek's side, her hands went immediately to the two large wounds on his torso, trying to cover them. Surprised, she found him still alive. His eyes were open, but he struggled to breathe. Blood bubbled out of his mouth and his chest convulsed in a staccato rhythm.

"Jacek," she cried out. "Please don't die!" Her cheeks grew wet with tears. He was her only friend in this world. The only one who cared about her. What would she do without him?

"Ale-" he gasped out. "Remember... everything... I told... you."

"No," she sobbed, her tears falling on his chest. "No, you're going to be alright."

"You will... be alright." He coughed, a splutter of red flecking his beard. "Thank you."

"For what?" Her heart was tearing seeing him like this.

"For being the... daughter I never.... If I'd... had one... I'd want her... like you." His voice was fading.

Aleni, still sobbing, reached her arms around him and

hugged him, not caring that she was getting blood all over her face. Her tears mingled with it, streaming down her face and dripping onto his neck.

His breathing slowed and eventually stopped, his last breath long and faint. Her own breath caught in her throat as she felt him slip away. With shaking hands, she patted at his wounds, as though she could put the blood back inside. She tried to speak, but her voice only came out in a high-pitched whine. This couldn't be happening. He couldn't die on her. Her mind went numb and her vision narrowed. Her gaze tracked over to where her knife lay on the steps. Maybe she should finish what she was going to do earlier. There was nothing left for her now.

Suddenly she felt a surge of power from underneath her face. Was her power being triggered without her knowing? She stared at a light coming from a stone on a string around his neck. It was white, like the stone Krodon had crushed. Blood and tears had blended on it. White light shone out from it, blinding Aleni. She was forced to close her eyes, but she felt the power rush out. With her mind's eye she saw it envelope Jacek's body and permeate his skin, pushing through muscle and fiber to the center of his being.

Hearing a sudden sharp intake of breath, she opened her eyes to see him with his eyes wide open and his mouth slack. She tracked her gaze down his body to see the two wounds had closed, leaving only sliced, bloodstained leather.

The stone had healed him.

"Where did you get that pendant? Have you been wearing that the whole time?" she asked.

Jacek's mouth opened and closed like a fish a couple of times before he sat up, patting his body in unbelievable silence. He looked up at her, running his fingers over the stone hanging from his neck. "I got it the night I let you out of the dungeon. It was the reason I was there. I'd been hired to steal it back from Krodon. Never got a chance to give it back to the merchant who hired me. I'd almost forgotten about it."

"It was magical all this time?" Aleni was incredulous.

"Your tears must have activated it."

"So that's how it's done." Aleni pawed at her wet face, drawing her hand back to look at her wet fingertips in awe.

Jacek got to his feet, pulling Aleni up with him. "I feel great." He moved his feet experimentally. "Better than I have in a long time. My legs don't ache anymore." He opened and closed his left hand in a claw gesture. "And my hand isn't numb. My head feels clear as well. His hand went to his arm where a cloth was tied around it. He undid it, revealing a wide slice through the leather. The skin underneath looked perfect and healthy. I think..." he raised his head to look at Aleni, his eyes wide, "...I'm fully healed. My illness as well as my injuries."

Aleni's heart fluttered. She felt a grin creep across her face and leaped at him, throwing her arms around his waist. He returned the gesture with a firm embrace. She felt him kiss the top of her head and then rest his cheek on it.

⛬

They held each other for a few seconds and then Aleni released him and stepped back. Jacek took in a deep contented breath through his nose. His muscles felt relaxed and his shoulders loose. He had forgotten what it felt like to be connected to another person.

"Bandur." She turned her head to look over at the dog still lying on the steps. Together they rushed over to him.

Aleni gave Jacek a look and wordlessly he removed the pendant from around his neck. The arrow was still sticking out of Bandur's side. The dog was barely breathing, but still just alive. Jacek pulled the arrow out. Bandur didn't react at all. His eyes were closed. Were they too late?

He handed her the stone. She placed it carefully on the wound. Nothing happened.

"Why isn't it working?" Aleni asked. "Doesn't it work on animals?"

It better. "I don't know. Just wait a little longer."

The seconds dragged on for millennia, or so it seemed. Jacek held his breath. He didn't know if he could cope with the death of his best friend. Seeing his doggy grin every day was what kept him going.

Suddenly the stone lit up, spearing white light from between Aleni's fingers. Jacek squinted and held his hand up in front of his eyes to block the sight from blinding him. He felt a slight pressure coming from Bandur's body, pushing against him for a couple of seconds before dissipating.

The dog's chest rose and fell in a full breath and then he lifted his head. Jacek felt something whacking his knee and looked down to see Bandur's tail wagging profusely. A feeling of weightlessness ran through him at the sight. The dog gathered his legs under him and pushed himself to his feet.

Aleni laughed and wrapped her arms around the dog's neck. When she let him go, Bandur licked all over Jacek's face, showing his excitement in gratuitous dog saliva. Jacek found himself laughing too.

Then he noticed Aleni's face for the first time. "Do you have blood on your teeth?"

She wiped at her teeth with her finger, holding the finger in front of her to inspect. "Yes, I bit the soldier over there." She pointed at the dead archer on the ground.

He let out a booming laugh. "I'm so proud of you!"

"I'm glad I didn't kill him," Aleni said.

They were standing over Krodon, who was still unconscious on the street, blood on his face from his nose. His fingers on each hand looked twisted and broken. His legs below his knees sat at a strange angle. Jacek kneeled next to him and put a couple of fingers to his throat. A slow pulse beat against them. He was still alive.

"Why didn't you?" Jacek asked, standing back up.

"Because I didn't want to be like him. I'm not a killer. And I won't let him change me. I won't give him that power."

Jacek nodded thoughtfully. "But you killed that soldier back there." He pointed with his thumb back to the steps. He loved playing devil's advocate.

"That was self-defense. Like you taught me. What I mean is, I wouldn't kill someone if they didn't pose a direct threat to me. Once Krodon was broken, he couldn't hurt me anymore. Besides, he'll suffer more this way." She gave him a slightly evil grin.

Jacek laughed. "True. Let's just leave him here then. He can get himself out. Let's go." He put an arm out and Aleni slid under it, letting his hand rest on her shoulder. Together they walked back toward the dock, Bandur following along beside them. He retrieved his pack on the way.

When they got to the boat, they found another larger boat next to theirs. Krodon must have found one somewhere else on the lake.

He held the smaller dinghy steady and waited for Aleni to get in. "Age before beauty."

She grinned at him and stepped into the boat. Bandur bounded in after her.

They made better time going back on the water than they had going in. Jacek wasn't fighting pain and fatigue this time. He continued to marvel at the strength that had flowed back into his body. He hadn't felt this good even before he'd gotten sick. The stone had fought the result of age as well as sickness.

The pendant hung from his neck, but it had gone dormant again. Aleni said she didn't feel any power coming from it anymore. Maybe the power had drained from it. Surely it held limited magic. It was only a small stone. Perhaps it was safe to give back to the merchant now.

"I'm sorry I got angry at you." Aleni stared at her knees, sitting in the front of the boat next to Bandur. "Will you forgive me?" She looked up then, her eyes hopeful.

Jacek stopped rowing and looked her in the eye. "There's nothing to forgive. You've lost so much, and just found out how your people were killed. You had every right to be angry."

"But it wasn't your fault. You weren't even alive back then."

"Still, I realize I represent the people who killed your people."

She looked away for a second before turning back to him. "The way I see it now, you and everyone here in Selendria are outcasts from those people. So, they are probably your enemy too, right?"

"True." Jacek went back to rowing.

"I can live with that."

They exited the tunnel behind the waterfall out onto the sun dappled lake. For the first time, Jacek saw the beauty of the area. The brightness of the water reflecting the clear sky. The pure white of the snow covering the grass and trees surrounding the basin. It all seemed brighter. It was like scales had fallen off his eyes and removed a filter with it. A beauty filter. Finally, he felt content. He was no longer alone, and he didn't need to fear it. Something else inside him had healed. And he was pretty sure it wasn't the stone.

It was Aleni. He knew now connection to another person

wasn't dangerous. Through her need for protection and care, he had grown to love her without even realizing. He watched the young girl with new eyes. She had her hood down and her pure white hair flowed out down her back and shone in the sun. Her pointed ears seemed almost normal now.

She was a gift. He vowed to himself he would do everything in his power to protect her and look after her. He would do what her parents could no longer do.

"Look!" Aleni pointed at the house on the other side of the basin, near where they had borrowed the dinghy.

It was now a smoldering, blackened ruin. Krodon must have set fire to it after finding a boat to use. Jacek wondered if anyone had been inside. If there had been, Krodon would have made sure they didn't escape. The man was a blight on Selendria. Had they made the right choice in leaving him alive?

"More lives ruined by that mad man," Jacek said. "Let's hope he can no longer hurt anyone else."

"What are we going to do now?" Aleni asked.

"Well, we'll have to return this pendant to its original owner." He gestured to the stone hanging from his neck. "Might not mention its history though. I'm fairly sure the merchant just thinks of it as a keepsake from his late wife."

"Why return it at all?"

"Because I have a reputation to hold up. If word gets out that I take people's money and then don't finish the job, my future prospects won't look so good."

"Oh, right." Aleni held a finger to her chin. She looked thoughtful for a second. "Do you have a house?"

"You've seen it."

"I have?"

"The cave. Remember?"

"That's it? You don't actually live in a house?"

Jacek shrugged. "Nope. Never found a need to. I don't

want to live in towns near other people. A cave was a natural alternative."

"Let's build a house then." Aleni's eyes lit up with the idea.

Jacek lifted an eyebrow. "Where?"

"In a forest somewhere. We could have used my old house in there," she pointed towards the waterfall. "But people know about it now."

"Too enclosed for my liking anyway."

"Right. So we can live somewhere in a forest. Maybe Kamde forest? I like that one. I can help you with my magic." She held out her hands, palms out, wiggling her fingers. Bandur bent over and licked them, possibly hoping they had some sort of treat in them.

Jacek smiled. He had a family now. He may have lost everything when his parents died, but with Aleni he had a chance at something new. He couldn't believe his luck at finding her.

In trusting someone, he had found life.

❧

Thank you so much for reading Legacy of power. I hope you enjoyed it and would appreciate a review.

Check out a map of Selendria on my website http://www.jagateswrites.com/extras.

ACKNOWLEDGMENTS

Writing a book like this and getting it out to the world has been a lifelong dream. And it wouldn't have come to be without these people backing me up.

To my editor, Kimberly Hunt, thank you for your honest feedback, shaping the story into what it is today and making it readable!

To my beta readers, Rachel, Keri, Rosie, Vivienne, Jeremy and Raissa, thank you all for your feedback and encouragement. You gave me the confidence to keep going.

And to all my friends and family who encouraged me and got excited for me even when I didn't feel it. It helped more than you know!

Kia ora koutou.

ABOUT THE AUTHOR

J.A. Gates lives and works in New Zealand, where she has been working in IT for over six years, while writing novels at night. She has been studying mixed martial arts for four years, including Filipino Kali which she uses to keep fit and bring authenticity to the fight scenes in her novels. She is an active member of the Romance Writers of New Zealand.

Follow her on Twitter and check out her website www.jagateswrites.com.